THE RED THREAD
TWENTY YEARS OF NYRB CLASSICS
A Selection

Edited and with a foreword by
EDWIN FRANK

NEW YORK REVIEW BOOKS

nyrb

New York

THIS IS A NEW YORK REVIEW BOOK
PUBLISHED BY THE NEW YORK REVIEW OF BOOKS
435 Hudson Street, New York, NY 10014
www.nyrb.com

Library of Congress Cataloging-in-Publication Data
Names: Frank, Edwin, 1960– editor, writer of introduction.
Title: The red thread : 20 years of NYRB classics : a selection / edited and
    with a foreword by Edwin Frank.
Other titles: 20 years of NYRB classics : a selection | 20 years of New York
    Review Books classics : a selection | Twenty years of NYRB classics : a
    selection | Twenty years of New York Review Books classics : a selection
Description: New York : NYRB Classics, 2019. | Series: New York Review
    Books classics |
Identifiers: LCCN 2019017461 (print) | LCCN 2019021715 (ebook) | ISBN
    9781681373928 (epub) | ISBN 9781681373911 (paperback)+
Subjects: LCSH: Literature—Collections. | New York Review Books classics. |
    BISAC: FICTION / Anthologies (multiple authors). | FICTION / Classics. |
    FICTION / Literary.
Classification: LCC PN6013 (ebook) | LCC PN6013 .R38 2019 (print) | DDC
    808.8—dc23
LC record available at https://lccn.loc.gov/2019017461

ISBN 978-1-68137-391-1
Available as an electronic book; ISBN 978-1-68137-392-8

Printed in the United States of America on acid-free paper.
10 9 8 7 6 5 4 3 2 1

In Memory of
Margot Bettauer Dembo

CONTENTS

FOREWORD

IT'S CUSTOMARY to begin a piece of this sort with a shake of the head: Twenty years, all gone by just like that, a score, time enough for someone to move from youth to middle age, from middle age to old age, time enough for the mainstays of another day to have died but also, equally, for a new generation to be coming into its own, for whom what once was a new thing may now stand as a given thing, such as it is, and practically immemorial.

What was going on in the fall of 1999?

In the world of books? What comes to my mind was the surprise of Philip Roth writing a historical novel, *American Pastoral*, a reckoning with everything sadly or violently self-deceiving and self-destructive about America's pretended innocence, along with a historical novel of a very different sort, Penelope Fitzgerald's humorous and desolate *The Blue Flower*. *McSweeney's* was a nifty novelty, while *The Baffler's* dourly ironic slogan, "Commodify Your Dissent," captured the seemingly inescapable transformation of youthful rebellion into consumerism and careerism that continues apace. David Foster Wallace's *Infinite Jest* had appeared, but Dave Eggers's *A Heartbreaking Work of Staggering Genius* and Zadie Smith's *White Teeth* and Jonathan Franzen's *The Corrections* were yet to come. José Saramago, a Communist, had won the Nobel Prize in '98. Now it was Günter Grass's turn. Grass had once had the temerity to point out in a public debate that there were people in America who lacked shelter or food, and the critic James Atlas angrily demanded, "Has the Nobel become a prize with a political agenda?"

As to book publishing and bookselling: Throughout America,

independent bookstores were closing, and the superstores Barnes and Noble and the now-vanished Borders ruled, though Amazon was getting bigger all the time. In cities, local papers were still in print and respectably plump, even if many had been farmed out to chains; a few continued to feature book pages.

In the wider world? In America and Britain, it was the heyday of Bill Clinton and Tony Blair's Third Way, notwithstanding Clinton's brush with impeachment. The dot-com bubble continued to swell. Protestors were planning to descend on Seattle to shut down the latest round of international trade talks. The 2000 election loomed. Vladimir Putin was serving as the prime minister for a drunk and doddering Boris Yeltsin. China's economy was roughly the size of Italy's. The euro was not yet in circulation.

The Internet was sluggish, social media nonexistent, cell phones not yet ubiquitous and definitely not smart.

In other words, to look back to '99, that last year before the first century of a new millennium, is to look back at a world with some continuities with our own but also one that we know was about to change drastically in ways then largely unforeseeable, and there was perhaps a sense of foreboding in the air; you can certainly feel it in some of the books I mention above. On the whole, however, what strikes me most in looking back is how robustly complacent the moment was. Financial deregulation and international trade, championed by Reagan and embraced by Clinton, had "delivered growth," and that economic model was considered a model for the world. The crime rate in America's cities was rapidly dropping. With the USSR out of the way, the United States was, in the unforgettable words of Clinton's secretary of state, Madeleine Albright, not just the leader of the free world but the world's "indispensable nation." (Too bad for the dispensable rest!) It was true that in the Balkans, the Middle East, and Africa, people hadn't yet received the good news that the terrible wars of the twentieth century and centuries past were over and done with, but in any case Y2K would pass without a hitch!

*

What does any of this have to do with NYRB Classics, which in the fall of 1999 began to publish a list of what might best be described as old books and new translations?

Oddly, quite a bit, though here I have to digress into personal history for a moment. In the late '90s, I'd taken a freelance job at an outfit called the Reader's Catalog, an ambitious experiment in mail-order bookselling cooked up some years before by the veteran publisher Jason Epstein. The catalog was as big as the proverbial (which is all it is now) phone book, where you could easily browse among and find out a little about and, if you chose, order one or two or all of "the 40,000 best books in print." The idea was that readers lost in America without a bookstore would find it, well, indispensable. Like Amazon, you could say, just missing the Internet.

Working on the catalog, I soon discovered that a lot of what I at least took to be the best books weren't in fact in print. How come?

Well, the obvious answer was that they didn't sell, and yet obvious as that was it wasn't quite right. It's not that these books didn't sell, so much as they didn't sell enough for the market as it had been reshaped —and here we come back to the historical moment—by years of mergers among corporate publishers and the imperative to look after share prices. Books that had done well enough over the years were cast aside in favor of new books that, such was the hope, would do much better, especially with the help of the marketing muscle of the superstores.

Simultaneously, complementarily, the new, now-unrivaled ascendancy of the United States meant that all sorts of old bothersome problems, essentially the rest of the world, could be conveniently forgotten—or at least rigorously compartmentalized—and the already pronounced tendency to pay no attention to books from outside of the Anglosphere, happily indulged. "We Are the World" was at last proved true! If during the Cold War writers from the Soviet Union and Eastern Europe had been given a hearing as dissidents, well, we had won that fight, and why bother with them now? W. S. Merwin and Clarence Brown's pioneering translation of the great poet Osip Mandelstam went out of print; Vasily Grossman's *Life and Fate*, just as it could finally appear in Russia, likewise.

Economism, triumphalism, provincialism, and presentism were the order of the day, when what was deemed to make a book interesting was, in the critical parlance then current, being "smart and sexy." (This was before our own *fierce* and *sharp* and *gorgeous* and, God help us, *crafted* took the floor.)

The literature of the world out there, where there were all sorts of extraordinary books that had never even been translated into English, and the literature hidden away in publishers' backlists would become our resource. To those of us at what was then the Reader's Catalog but would soon branch out into New York Review Books—supported, attentively, unstintingly, and wonderfully, by Angela and Rea Hederman, as ever since—it seemed impossible that there could not be a distinct and devoted audience for such books. There was, for example, the audience, both sophisticated and inquiring, commanded by *The New York Review of Books*, our relative with its offices down the hall. That said, none of us, I think, realized quite how cross-grained, withershins, backward-looking, haplessly wishful, and finally hopeless our new project must have seemed to more experienced hands.

A list of lost books, but of course countless books have been lost, for all sorts of reasons, good and bad. A gathering of ghosts, okay, but who gets an invitation and on what grounds, and in what sense would their coming together be said to constitute a list? This because one of my earliest convictions was that the idea and character of the list was just as important to the endeavor as the books on it; or rather, if the endeavor was to find readers for those books, the best way to do it was through a list. *List* is etymologically related to *love* (and *lust*), and, when I first began to read voraciously and omnivorously, the sort of paperback series that then existed, lists that had for the most part sprung up during World War II because of paper shortages and to serve soldiers and had proliferated in the decades after, among them Anchor Books, Meridian Books, Mentor Books, New Directions Books, Penguin Modern Classics (for many years only available as exotic imports), each with an editorial and graphic character of its own, and, in many cases, in the back a list of other books on the list, a small virtual library to pore over—these had been my nourishment, and indeed one list led to another, gradually compiled inside the back cover of my loose-leaf binder for school, of books to look out for when I got to the bookstore at last. It struck me as strange, in '99, that these lists had, like many of the books on them, disappeared.

So, NYRB Classics, a list, and so—what? Obviously the list had to include good books, books to delight and enlighten and surprise readers, but it also had to be surprising in its own right, making connections with a spark, and, of course, it had to be recognizable as a series. It needed a look, which, following an early design about which the less said the better, Katy Homans stepped in and beautifully provided. Equally, however, there were things it couldn't be. Notwithstanding the moniker "classics," it couldn't primarily be a list of classics, ancient or modern, for the simple reason that these books weren't lost. No one needed to be sold on *The Scarlet Letter* or *The Yellow Wallpaper*, especially not a rising generation of readers who had endured endless schooling and testing and training in symbolic analysis and whatnot, so much that one could only imagine that if they retained any yen to read at all it would be for something seriously extracurricular. Then again it shouldn't be a list of weird cult books or books of studied smallness that get deemed lost treasures or of books important or popular in their day and quaint and curious now or of great one-offs or of books that stand out because they are absolutely like nothing else. It couldn't be any of those things, because it had in a sense to be all of them, displaying a life of its own comparable to any real reader's reading life, moving in and among different books and kinds of books with an explorer's spirit.

"This is the city and I am one of the citizens, / Whatever interests the rest interests me, politics, wars, markets, newspapers, schools, / The mayor and councils, banks, tariffs, steamships...." Walt Whitman writes in "Song of Myself" (the list goes on). "You must know everything" is how the Soviet writer Isaac Babel put it, no less imperative for being impossible. The series had to mix everything up, and so the first fourteen books that came out in the fall of 1999 sought to do. There is Edmund Wilson's selection of Anton Chekhov's late, long stories, among them "Three Years," about the exhaustion of love and the exhaustion of language and ending, with perfect and devastating poise, on the blankest of clichés: "Time flies." The story is certainly a classic, as is Robert Walser's mysterious *Jakob von Gunten*, written not long after the Chekhov, whose curious hero is a disconcerting model of rock-ribbed meekness. Charles Duff's *Handbook on Hanging* is a Swiftian polemic against the death penalty, and *Prison Memoirs of an Anarchist*, by Alexander Berkman, who tried to assassinate Henry Frick in 1892, is a record of how a fanatical young revolutionary discovers the distance between theory and life. Both books are remarkable page by page—Berkman's should be part of the American canon—and both books also spoke to the moment, opening perspectives on America's appallingly swollen prison population and its ongoing affair with the death penalty. That too was a reason to publish them. Analogously, we would publish C. V. Wedgwood's *The Thirty Years War* not long after the American invasion of Iraq in 2003.

Also on that first list (and you will, by the way, find a chronological list of every book so far in the series toward the end of this book) were two memoirs by J. R. Ackerley, *My Dog Tulip* and *My Father and Myself*, which slyly upend standard understandings of what life and love and memoirs are or should be, as well as two wonderful novels from the 1920s, *A High Wind in Jamaica* and *Lolly Willowes*, which had largely fallen off the literary map, perhaps because while being utterly modern in sensibility—both are post–World War I parables about the impossibility of innocence—they were not in the least modernist. There is nothing programmatic at all about either book, nothing tendentious. Each is the author's first book—they are works of pure, upwelling, realized invention—and both are somewhat teasingly, or deceptively, fantastical and satirical. Both, above all, are scarily alive to the inescapably lonely and scary core of life.

That was the beginning. The challenge for me and for my colleagues over the years—Stephanie Smith, Kerry Fried, Amy Grace Lloyd, Stephen Twilley, Jeffrey Yang, Susan Barba, and, throughout, Sara Kramer, and abetted in more ways than I can say by suggestions from writers, translators, friends, family, fellow publishers, booksellers, and, above all, readers—has been to go on adding to the mix without succumbing to an empty eclecticism. I've described the series in the past as having various strands. You could also say it has a variety of logics. Translation is certainly central to it—from Russian, Chinese, Italian, French, German, and Hungarian, among other languages— each responsive to its particular, complicated history and complex sense of literary possibility. There are also a number of writers we publish extensively: Victor Serge, Andrey Platonov, Vasily Grossman, Eileen Chang, Henry Green, Tove Jansson, Mavis Gallant, Elizabeth Hardwick, and Eve Babitz are some of them. The power of genre literature—noir and crime and horror fiction, nature and travel writing—is another thing we've sought to bring out. The essay, ranging from the great spreading girth of Richard Burton's *The Anatomy of Melancholy* to the concentrated fury of Simone Weil's "The *Iliad*, or the Poem of Force" in *War and the Iliad*, is prominently featured, while I myself am taken by a certain kind of old-fashioned memoir, one that doesn't novelize a life, or epically aggrandize it (see Chateaubriand's *Memoirs from Beyond the Grave*), but seeks to account for it amusingly, anecdotally, forthcomingly, the better to draw up its moral balance. S. Josephine Baker's *Fighting for Life*, about setting up the New York public health system, is like that. So is Ben Sonnenberg's *Lost Property: Memoirs and Confessions of a Bad Boy*, about spending years running away from a huge fortune before finding fulfillment in running a little magazine—that we will publish next year.

The whole, then, has to be considered a work in progress, changing as it goes. My own larger sense of literature, as must have become clear by now, does tend to locate the work of the imagination in relation to history, which it both responds to and seeks to reshape. A book endures as long as it has a recognizable authority, originality, individuality, and truth to experience, one that attests to the circumstances, personal, historical, literary historical, out of which it arises, while also rising above them enough to suggest something else, beyond or within. *Transcend* is the old word for that, and I don't think we should be embarrassed to use it, presuming it means being left hanging as much as reaching some higher plane. Transcending its own origins, the good book also affords readers a measure of transcendence over their own particular circumstances, momentarily freeing them from them, allowing them to feel and reflect on things good, bad, ugly, and beautiful that they might otherwise have never known (and in certain cases can only hope they will never know). It is to that extent just as much an experience of critical awareness as it is of imaginative enlargement. The good book is alive, independently of the interests of the person, place, or time that gave rise to it, and we take life from it, and it lives through us. Reading, like writing, is an exercise in *not* knowing—what will happen next, to begin with—and, you might say, of *un*knowing. Art that is something more than distraction or propaganda engages us in such a way that we suspend not only disbelief but our preconceptions and pay full attention. And in the end, and most especially, I'd say, if the end is happy, we are still left in a state of suspense.

Twenty years now flash by in which, I don't need to say, there have been many changes, among them something of an improvement in the fortunes of independent bookstores and the readership for foreign literature, and in which the complacency of 1999 that I mentioned has been succeeded by a state of comprehensive alarm—not necessarily an improvement—to bring you the little book you have in hand. The red thread: In China this is said to be a metaphor for a binding tie that exists between people unknown to each other, and I suppose we can say that that is one thing literature may be. In Greek mythology, it was thanks to the ball of red thread given him by a besotted Ariadne that Theseus, having tracked down and killed the Minotaur at the heart of the labyrinth, was able to find his way back out—and abandon the girl. Literature is also a kind of labyrinth in which heroes and monsters and plain people do battle; sometimes they fall in love. Who is what is not always clear, and perhaps it is no less unclear what is lost or found there, much less who has lost or won.

But enough. The little book in your hand is an anthology that I have put together to reflect something of the consistency and variety of the NYRB Classics series as a whole. A sampler. It isn't a greatest hits, by any means, though it does contain a fair amount of work by writers who have several books in the series. Putting it together, I found it taking, as by a will of its own, the form of an itinerary or road book, and that is one way of looking at the series, I suppose. The order here is perhaps best described as intuitive, if not whimsical, based on links between the pieces, ways they speak back and forth and agree and disagree with each other, that pleased me as I shuffled them together, but I don't know that there is a real red thread to *The Red Thread* (the poor astronaut on the cover appears to have gotten lost indeed while looking for it). Each piece is also in any case capable of standing on its own—at least I hope so—and now I am reminded of Mavis Gallant's strangely moving remark in the afterword to her collected stories (included in *Paris Stories*): "Stories are not chapters of novels. They should not be read one after another, as if they were meant to follow along. Read one. Shut the book. Read something else. Come back later. Stories can wait." There are a lot of animals, I don't know why. James Crossley, of Madison Books, in Seattle, suggested the section of Patrick Leigh Fermor's *Mani* that's included, and I am grateful to him for that. There is one novelty: Elizabeth Hardwick's portrait of Billie Holiday appears as it appeared when it first came out in *The New York Review of Books* and not as in her novel *Sleepless Nights*. I did start this book with one particular thought in mind, however, which was to begin with Platonov and to end (or, as you'll see, almost) with Serge. Once I'd put everything in place, I discovered that the two pieces both conclude with the same word: *astonishment*. It surprised me. It wasn't something I had planned, but it seems right.

—EDWIN FRANK

THE RED THREAD

THE CAMEL

Andrey Platonov

FOUR BOATS were getting ready to sail from Chardzhou to Nukus with supplies for the cooperatives there. Chagataev did not try to make use of his official status, since this was something only faintly recognized; instead he got himself taken on as an untrained sailor. It was agreed that he would travel as far as the Khiva oasis, and would then go ashore.

Long days of sailing began. In the mornings and evenings the river was transformed into a flood of gold, thanks to the sun's oblique light penetrating the water through its living, drifting silt. This yellow earth traveling in the river already looked like the corn it would become, like flowers or cotton, or even like the body of a human being. Sometimes a small, strange, many-colored bird would be sitting on top of a rush, fidgeting from inner excitement, its feathers shining under the living sun as it sang something in a radiant, delicate voice, as if bliss had already dawned for all creatures. The bird reminded Chagataev of Ksenya, the small woman with different-colored eyes who was now thinking something or other about him.

After fourteen days and nights Chagataev went ashore at the Khiva oasis, receiving his pay and the thanks of the captain.

Chagataev stayed for a few days in Khiva and then set off down the road of childhood towards his birthplace, Sary-Kamysh. He remembered this road from landmarks that were no longer so impressive: the sand dunes seemed lower, the canal less deep, and the path to the nearest well had grown shorter. The sun shone the same as ever, but it was not as high as when Chagataev was small. The burial mounds and yurts, the donkeys and camels he met on the way, the trees along

3

the irrigation channels, the flying insects—everything was unchanged, but indifferent to Chagataev now, as if it had gone blind without him. Feeling hurt, he walked as if through a foreign world, staring at everything around him and recognizing things he had forgotten, though still going unrecognized himself. It seemed as though every little creature, object or plant was prouder, more independent of former attachment, than a human being.

As he came to the dried-up bed of the Kunya-Darya, Nazar Chagataev saw a camel sitting like a human being, propped up on his front legs in a drift of sand. He was thin, his humps had sagged, and he was looking shyly out of black eyes, like a sad and intelligent human being. Chagataev walked up to the camel, but the camel paid no attention to this man coming up to him. He was watching the motion of some dead stems of grass being blown about by a current of wind: would they come close or would they pass by out of reach? One blade moved along the sand right up to his mouth; then the camel chewed the grass with his lips and swallowed it. In the distance a ball of tumbleweed was drifting along the ground; the camel watched this large, living plant with eyes made kind by hope, but the tumbleweed passed by to one side. The camel then closed his eyes, because he did not know how he was meant to cry. Chagataev inspected the camel. The animal had grown thin long ago, from illness and hungry need, and almost all his hair had fallen out, leaving only a few clumps, and so he was shivering from an unaccustomed chill. He had probably been part of some passing caravan, abandoned here because weakness of strength made him unable to carry his load—or else his master had died and, until he had expended his own reserve of life, the animal was going to wait for him. After losing the capacity for movement, the camel had used what remained of his strength to raise himself up on his front legs, so he could see blades of grass being driven towards him by the wind and consume them. When there was no wind, he closed his eyes, not wanting to expend vision to no purpose, and was in a doze. He didn't want to sink back and lie down, because then he would never be able to get up again, and so he remained sitting all the time—now vigilant, now half-asleep—waiting for death to bring him down or for some insignificant desert beast to finish him off with a single blow of a small paw.

For a long time Chagataev sat beside the camel, watching him and understanding. Then he fetched several armfuls of tumbleweed from some way away and gave them to the camel to eat. He couldn't give the camel water because he only had two flasks for himself, though he knew that farther along the bed of the Kunya-Darya there were shallow wells and ponds with fresh water. But it would be difficult to carry a camel across the sands on his shoulders.

Evening set in. Chagataev went on feeding the camel, fetching grass for him from round about, until the camel put his head down on the ground and fell into the meek sleep of new life. Because of night, it began to turn cold. After eating some nan breads from his bag, Chagataev pressed himself against the camel's body for warmth and dozed off. He was smiling. Everything in the existing world seemed strange to him; it was as if the world had been created for some brief, mocking game. But this game of make-believe had dragged on for a long time, for eternity, and nobody felt like laughing any more. The desert's deserted emptiness, the camel, even the pitiful wandering grass—all this ought to be serious, grand and triumphant. Inside every poor creature was a sense of some other happy destiny, a destiny that was necessary and inevitable—why, then, did they find their lives such a burden and why were they always waiting for something? Chagataev curled up against the camel's stomach and fell asleep, full of astonishment at strange reality.

Excerpted from "Soul"; translated from the Russian by
Robert and Elizabeth Chandler and Olga Meerson,
with Jane Chamberlain and Eric Naiman

THE LONG CROSSING

Leonardo Sciascia

THE NIGHT seemed made to order, the darkness so thick that its weight could almost be felt when one moved. And the sound of the sea, like the wild-animal breath of the world itself, frightened them as it gasped and died at their feet.

They were huddled with their cardboard suitcases and their bundles on a stretch of pebbly beach sheltered by hills, between Gela and Licata. They had arrived at dusk, having set out at dawn from their own villages, inland villages far from the sea, clustered on barren stretches of feudal land. For some of them this was their first sight of the sea, and the thought of having to cross the whole of that vast expanse, leaving one deserted beach in Sicily by night and landing on another deserted beach, in America and again by night, filled them with misgivings. But these were the terms to which they had agreed. The man, some sort of traveling salesman to judge from his speech, but with an honest face that made you trust him, had said: "I will take you aboard at night and I will put you off at night, on a beach in New Jersey only a stone's throw from New York. Those of you who have relatives in America can write to them and suggest that they meet you at the station in Trenton twelve days after your departure... Work it out for yourselves... Of course, I can't guarantee a precise date...We may be held up by rough seas or coastguard patrols... One day more or less won't make any difference: the important thing is to get to America."

To get to America was certainly the important thing; how and when were minor details. If the letters they sent to their relatives arrived, despite the ink-blotched, misspelled addresses scrawled so laboriously on the envelopes, then they would arrive, too. The old saying, "With a tongue in your head you can travel the world," was right. And travel they would, over that great dark ocean to the land of the *stori* (stores) and the *farme* (farms), to the loving brothers, sisters, uncles, aunts, nephews, nieces, cousins, to the opulent, warm, spacious houses, to the motor cars as big as houses, to America.

It was costing them two hundred and fifty thousand lira each, half on departure and the balance on arrival. They kept the money strapped to their bodies under their shirts like a priest's scapular. They had sold all their saleable possessions in order to scrape the sum together: the squat house, the mule, the ass, the year's store of provender, the chest of drawers, the counterpanes. The cunning ones among them had borrowed from the money-lenders with the secret intention of defrauding them, just this once, in return for the hardship they had been made to endure over the years by the usurers' greed, and drew immense satisfaction from imagining the expression on their faces when they heard the news. "Come and see me in America, bloodsucker: I just may return your money—without interest—if you manage to find me." Their dreams of America were awash with dollars. They would no longer keep their money in battered wallets or hidden under their shirts; it would be casually stuffed into trouser pockets to be drawn out in fistfuls as they had seen their relatives do; relatives who had left home as pitiable, half-starved creatures, shriveled by the sun, to return after twenty or thirty years—for a brief holiday—with round, rosy faces that contrasted handsomely with their white hair.

Eleven o'clock came. Someone switched on an electric torch, the signal to those aboard the steamship to come and collect them. When the torch was switched off again, the darkness seemed thicker and more frightening than ever. But only a few minutes later, the obsessively regular breathing of the sea was overlaid with a more human, more domestic sound, almost like buckets being rhythmically filled and emptied. Next came a low murmur of voices, then, before they realized that the boat had touched the shore, the man they knew as Signor Melfa, the organizer of their journey, was standing in front of them.

"Are we all here?" asked Signor Melfa. He counted them by the light of a torch. There were two missing. "They may have changed their minds, or they may be arriving late ... Either way, it's their tough luck. Should we risk our necks by waiting for them?"

They were all agreed that this was unnecessary.

"If anyone's not got his money ready," warned Signor Melfa, "he'd better skip out now and go back home. He'd be making a big mistake if he thought he could spring that one on me when we're aboard; God's truth, I'd put the whole lot of you ashore again. And, as it's hardly fair that everyone should suffer for the sake of one man, the guilty party would get what's coming to him from me and from all of us; he'd be taught a lesson that he'd remember for the rest of his life—if he's that lucky."

They all assured him, with the most solemn oaths, that they had their money ready, down to the last lira.

"All aboard," said Signor Melfa. Immediately each individual became a shapeless mass, a heaving cluster of baggage.

"Jesus Christ! Have you brought the whole house with you?" A torrent of oaths poured out, only ceasing when the entire load, men and baggage, was piled on board—a task accomplished not without considerable risk to life and property. And for Melfa the only difference between the man and the bundle lay in the fact that the man carried on his person the two hundred and fifty thousand lira, sewn into his jacket or strapped to his chest. He knew these men well, did Signor Melfa, these insignificant peasants with their rustic mentality.

The voyage took less time than they expected, lasting eleven nights including that of the departure. They counted the nights rather than the days because it was at night that they suffered so appallingly in the overcrowded, suffocating quarters. The stench of fish, diesel oil and vomit enveloped them as if they had been immersed in a tub of hot, liquid black tar. At dawn they streamed up on deck, exhausted, hungry for light and air. But if their image of the sea had been a vast expanse of green corn rippling in the wind, the reality terrified them:

their stomachs heaved and their eyes watered and smarted if they so much as tried to look at it.

But on the eleventh night they were summoned on deck by Signor Melfa. At first they had the impression that dense constellations had descended like flocks onto the sea; then it dawned upon them that these were in fact towns, the towns of America, the land of plenty, shining like jewels in the night. And the night itself was of an enchanting beauty, clear and sweet, with a crescent moon slipping through transparent wisps of cloud and a breeze that was elixir to the lungs.

"That is America," said Signor Melfa.

"Are you sure it isn't some other place?" asked a man who, throughout the voyage, had been musing over the fact that there were neither roads nor even tracks across the sea, and that it was left to the Almighty to steer a ship without error between sky and water to its destination.

Signor Melfa gave the man a pitying look before turning to the others. "Have you ever," he asked, "seen a skyline like this in your part of the world? Can't you feel that the air is different? Can't you see the brilliance of these cities?"

They all agreed with him and shot looks full of pity and scorn at their companion for having ventured such a stupid question.

"Time to settle up," said Signor Melfa.

Fumbling beneath their shirts, they pulled out the money.

"Get your things together," ordered Signor Melfa when he had put the money away.

This took only a few minutes. The provisions that, by agreement, they had brought with them, were all eaten and all that they now had left were a few items of clothing and the presents intended for their relatives in America: a few rounds of goat-cheese, a few bottles of well-aged wine, some embroidered table-centers and antimacassars. They climbed down merrily into the boat, laughing and humming snatches of song. One man even began to sing at the top of his voice as soon as the boat began to move off.

"Don't you ever understand a word I say?" asked Melfa angrily. "Do you want to see me arrested? ... As soon as I've left you on the shore you can run up to the first copper you see and ask to be repatriated on the spot; I don't give a damn: everyone's free to bump himself off any way he likes . . . But I've kept my side of the bargain; I said I'd dump you in America, and there it is in front of you . . . But give me time to get back on board, for Crissake!"

They gave him time and enough to spare, for they remained sitting on the cool sand, not knowing what to do next, both blessing and cursing the night whose darkness provided a welcome mantle while they remained huddled on the shore, but seemed so full of menace when they thought of venturing further afield.

Signor Melfa had advised them to disperse, but no one liked the idea of separation from the others. They had no idea how far they were from Trenton nor how long it would take them to reach it.

They heard a distant sound of singing, very far away and unreal. "It could almost be one of our own carters," they thought, and mused upon the way that men the world over expressed the same longings and the same griefs in their songs. But they were in America now, and the lights that twinkled beyond the immediate horizon of sand-dunes and trees were the lights of American cities.

Two of them decided to reconnoiter. They walked in the direction of the nearest town whose lights they could see reflected in the sky. Almost immediately they came to a road. They remarked that it had a good surface, well maintained, so different from the roads back home, but to tell the truth they found it neither as wide nor as straight as they had expected. In order to avoid being seen, they walked beside the road, a few yards away from it, keeping in the trees.

A car passed them. One of them said: "That looked just like a Fiat 600." Another passed that looked like a Fiat 1100, and yet another. "They use our cars for fun, they buy them for their kids like we buy bicycles for ours." Two motorcycles passed with a deafening roar. Police, without a doubt. The two congratulated themselves on having taken the precaution of staying clear of the road.

At last they came to a roadsign. Having checked carefully in both directions, they emerged to read the lettering: SANTA CROCE CA-MARINA—SCOGLITTI.

"Santa Croce Camarina ... I seem to have heard that name before."

"Right; and I've heard of Scoglitti, too."

"Perhaps one of my family used to live there, it might have been my uncle before he moved to Philadelphia. I seem to remember that he spent some time in another town before going to Philadelphia."

"My brother, too, lived in some other place before he settled in Brooklyn ... I can't remember exactly what it was called. And, of course, although we may read the name as Santa Croce Camarina or Scoglitti, we don't know how the Americans read it, because they always pronounce words in a different way from how they're spelled."

"You're right; that's why Italian's so easy, you read it exactly how it's written ... But we can't stay here all night, we'll have to take a chance ... I shall stop the next car that comes along; all I've got to say is 'Trenton?' ... The people are more polite here ... Even if we don't understand what they say, they'll point or make some kind of sign and at least we'll know in what direction we have to go to find this blasted Trenton."

The Fiat 500 came round the bend in the road about twenty yards from where they stood, the driver braking when he saw them with their hands out to stop him. He drew up with an imprecation. There was little danger of a hold-up, he knew, because this was one of the quietest parts of the country, so, expecting to be asked for a lift, he opened the passenger door.

"Trenton?" the man asked.

"*Che?*" said the driver.

"Trenton?"

"*Che trenton della madonna,*" the driver exclaimed, cursing.

The two men looked at each other, seeking the answer to the same unspoken question: Seeing that he speaks Italian, wouldn't it be best to tell him the whole story?

The driver slammed the car door and began to draw away. As he put his foot on the accelerator he shouted at the two men who were standing like statues: "*Ubriaconi, cornuti ubriaconi, cornuti e figli di ...*" The last words were drowned by the noise of the engine.

Silence descended once more.

After a moment or two, the man to whom the name of Santa Croce had seemed familiar, said: "I've just remembered something. One year when the crops failed around our parts, my father went to Santa Croce Camarina to work during the harvest."

As if they had had a rug jerked out from beneath their feet, they collapsed onto the grass beside the ditch. There was, after all, no need to hurry back to the others with the news that they had landed in Sicily.

Translated from the Italian by Avril Bardoni

NEW YORK CONFIDENTIAL
Eve Babitz

I WENT to New York on March 6th, 1966, and left on March 5th, 1967. One year.

Because what I was supposed to be doing was being the "office manager" of the *East Village Other* (an underground newspaper), I had the advantage of knowing everyone and everything at once. It wasn't like I came from Kansas and went to work at Woolworth's. John Wilcock (one of the founders of *EVO*) talked about me so much that some girl who got around started calling me "Wondercunt" before I'd even shown up, I was so famous. John had some idea that I was going to stage this party, the *East Village Other* April Fools Ball (or something), and he convinced Walter Bowart, the Editor, that I was just the one for the job. I have never considered having a party a job.

When I arrived in New York, John it turns out is in Chicago, so Walter Bowart, whom I'd never met before and who didn't believe there was such a place as California and who was suspicious of John anyway because John liked Andy Warhol and Walter thought Andy Warhol was the Death of Art, Walter put me up my first night in New York in the apartment of a friend. The friend had written speeches for Senator McCarthy and spent 5 years in jail for changing his mind. In New York, everybody was a story.

Walter and I were born on consecutive days. We always understood each other perfectly and had a wonderful time pulling the wool over everyone's eyes until he saw the dove of peace on acid, which was a drag. But anyway, we are friends. He's an orphan, it was part of his story.

The second morning he took me to Carol's and it was love at first sight to this very day, only she's up in San Francisco with children and I can't stand children. Carol was perfect. She looked exactly like me, only she was black. She was from the Bronx and was a proofreader and she'd once been one of Walter's girl friends when he tended bar at Stanley's, a Lower East Side Bar. Carol and I took acid every chance we got.

While I was in New York Donovan's *Sunshine Superman* album came out and so did *Revolver*. The poet Frank O'Hara got run over on Fire Island and died.

The party I had was one of those things where everyone who wasn't there wishes they'd been, but actually at the time it was like a Bruegel, too sweaty and people hanging from the rafters. I invited seven bands, and since it was held in the Village Gate or whatever that place is called on Bleecker, there was only a tiny dressing room. There were seven drum sets, never mind amps. Right before the thing was to start Buzzy Linhart, who is my friend, handed me a piece of colored paper and told me to eat it, and 20 minutes later things started to get real shiny and then I was completely on acid and couldn't handle a thing for the entire rest of the party. Carol did everything.

LSD was not illegal in those days.

It was all right that I was out of control because the party was completely homogeneous. Everyone knew what to do, I was pleased to observe. The seven bands played, Timothy Leary stood on that stage and gave a speech about levels of consciousness (I snickered behind my hand as he turned into Billy Graham and the rest of the room started pulsing), television cameras interfered beautifully with everything and Flexus, a group who staged happenings and from whence we have Yoko Ono and the husband who's skipped with the kid, Tony Cox, Flexus were all dressed in overalls and had tall ladders and throughout the night they put up crepe-paper streamers in that den of iniquity like a high-school gym. Nobody saw them, it was like they were invisible. There were about 700 people there. The room fit about 500. And all those amps, TV cameras and sweaty bodies.

"How could Bruegel stand it?" I demanded of a girl standing next to me. "How could he live?"

"Like this," she said and pushed her blouse ruffle away from the inside of her wrist, where I saw a sun tattooed in every color. But just then we were dragged onto the stage under all those TV lights, and the businessmen decided there had to be a fake Slum goddess crowned. The word "Slum goddess" was Ed Sanders' from the Fugs (he played their band), and these fat men with mustaches and cigars had decided the gimmick would be to crown a Slum goddess, so there I was holding Carol's hand and trying to hide behind the girl with the tattooed wrist on the stage with all these lights. Buzzy Linhart, Gentleman Buzzy, strode manfully out and took the crown from the man and put it on his own head. Buzzy was shirtless and his hair stuck out a foot in every direction and it was just the right touch to give the men with cigars the slip.

"You can ask me anything you want," Buzzy whispered to me, "except what's happening."

Buzzy played in a band called the Seventh Son or Sun and he was a vibe player and guitar player of astounding genius who, in those days, abused drugs so much that I'm surprised he's still alive, but he is. He doesn't even drink any more. He has a face of beauty and a soul of Olympian goodness and, boy, could he play the guitar. Everyone stole from him.

Buzzy's story now is that he wrote Bette Midler's theme song.

The girl with the tattoo turned out to be my friend. She used to have cats that would leap right through the glass of her ninth-story apartment window and live. She once told me, "Marianne Faithfull has 36 pairs of shoes and goes around barefoot. She's the kind of a girl who is always carrying books about witchcraft, only they're *new*." This girl with the tattoo, Suzanna, wore kohl and dressed like Bip by Marcel Marceau.

I wanted to be Slum goddess. That was the sort of Playmate of the Month the *East Village Other* came up with using Ed Sanders' name. There was a girl who was supposed to be it that issue, but since I was right there in the office, I aced her out. We have been in a stage of ambivalence toward each other since that moment, and when she tried to take my boy friend away from me at a party, I was not surprised.

I paid her back later. I am sure she'll get me again someday. It's the fortunes of war that Robin, who is a girl of enormous deadpan talent (she's an actress, but not an L.A. kind of one), should forever be out to get me, but somehow simultaneously we have maintained what would pass as a friendship to an observer. She was more beautiful than me and should have been the Slum goddess.

The Fugs used to rehearse every day at the Astor Theater up in Cooper Union and I used to go watch them. Ed Sanders, Tuli Kupferberg, Ken Weaver and this kid named John Anderson were in that weird thing together. The only one who knew how to play really was John Anderson, and then he allowed himself to be drafted (Weaver never got over it and neither did I). Everyone said that Ed Sanders was a poet.

I met tons of poets in New York. There are none whatsoever in L.A.

If anyone in L.A. said they were a poet, everyone would get mildly embarrassed and go look for someone else to talk to.

I ran into Ed Sanders when he was doing the Manson book later in L.A., and I don't know about poetry, but prose he can write.

When summer came, I found myself a boy friend who had air-conditioning. He was one of my favorite kinds of men—German. Is it because I'm Jewish that German accents do it to me? He was the third name. There were three names on all the material, and his was always the third—Leary, Alpert and Metzner. I cannot believe that either Timothy Leary or Richard Alpert ever got in the way of Ralph Metzner doing the hard part. They all grew to loathe each other, it seemed to me, as time went by, but they were stuck in it together because their three names were on all the papers and books. And they had to have Ralph there. The German accent gave the thing an air of authenticity you couldn't get otherwise.

One Friday, Ralph suggested we leave the City and go to the Country. The Country was Millbrook, the Castalia Foundation where Tim had settled into this rich-kids mansion that had about 40 rooms in it and a place called the bungalow. Somehow a Victorian mansion with Buddhas everywhere wasn't really the Country, but it was different. Timothy Leary's Rosemary used to cook or supervise breakfast, lunch and dinner for 35 people a day. They got crates of Velveeta cheese. Everyone smoked Pall Mall Menthols.

The life in the Country was slow, so Ralph and I went to bed at about 10:30. At 1:00 there was a knock at the door. We were in the attic, so it was unlikely that anyone would be knocking on the door, but they were.

"Who's there?" Ralph asked.

"Police."

The man came in with a flashlight, and I sat innocently up in bed, letting the sheet slide from my naked body and pretending I was 10.

"Oh," he stammered, shining the light away. He was a gentleman from Poughkeepsie who had been deputized for the raid, not a real cop. "Oh... I'll be back in half an hour to search the room."

Which was good.

Marya Mannes was there doing a story for *McCall's*, and she had to strip for the matron. She held my hand and we got along fine. There were about 40 adults there and 4 of them got busted. The phone was suddenly out of order and no one was allowed to leave the house, so no lawyer could be telephoned until the morning from a phone booth at a gas station, though when Ralph came back the phone was working again. They were looking, those gentlemen from Poughkeepsie, for the only thing that seemed worthwhile to them—pornography. They were positive that young girls were forced to make stag movies, and when they came upon Tim Leary's son's darkroom, they went into completely "we were right" police seriousness. They took *The Agony and the Ecstasy* as part of their evidence. Nothing pornographic ever went on around that ex-Harvard professor. He wasn't the type. What he used to do in secret was read the sports page and drink Scotch. Timothy Leary is innocent.

Well, that was the Country. We went a few more times to testify, but the charges were dropped against the four. They busted a kid who was sleeping outside in the forest because he had about enough grass to roll half a joint. They busted a married couple who were unable to dispose of the evidence because the evidence was an attache case neatly fitted out to hold bottles in which every psychedelic known to the civilized world was contained in labeled jars. They also busted Timothy Leary and actually handcuffed him. He wore white and no shoes and looked divine. Even Marya Mannes succumbed at the moment, though later she wrote this piece in *McCall's* which made me fly into a rage. They busted Tim because it was his house.

They tried to get Rosemary to testify before a grand jury about Tim, and when she wouldn't answer they put her in jail for a month. They were going to keep her longer, but at the end of the month Tim just kind of came and got her, smiling, and they figured . . . Rosemary was innocent.

Because they questioned us without lawyers (which couldn't be reached on account of the phone), they had to let everyone go. Which was lucky. That whole weekend was not very Country.

I never liked Millbrook.

The kid who got busted with half a joint became my dearest friend in the world and now I can't find him and no one knows where he is and no one has even heard anything about him for about 4 years. He is the only person I know like that.

I didn't know him until later, months after I'd moved away from Ralph and back to my own wretched 40-dollar-a-month slanting-floor Polish–Puerto Rican home. While I was at Ralph's they used my apartment as the headquarters of the Timothy Leary Defense Fund, and a girl, a secretary, put her cigarette out in my antique papier-mâché bird box from Persia. She was much more guilty than most people. The whole time I lived in New York I knew I was going back to L.A. so I never believed I was actually living there and never furnished my apartment with more than a bed and a chair. Once I started making collages, the magazines took over and then the place was really really ungodly, scraps all over the slanting floor, glue.

One day Barry came down to the *East Village Other* because he was a photographer and thought they paid for pictures. They paid for almost nothing there, but I went back to the Chelsea with him. He lived in the Chelsea Hotel on the 4th floor, so you had to take the elevator with all the old women with turquoise jewelry. The elevator was the slowest in the city of New York.

Barry was extremely young; he was only about 21. He was from Detroit and wanted to be Avedon. He was one of my obvious inclinations; all women simply adored him. He would have adored me if I'd weighed 109 and was two inches taller. As it was, I weighed 145 and was 5' 7". I was way too fat. But I had to do something in New York, and eating seemed less evil than the other alternatives, like Bellevue or the needle.

On Friday, I would call Barry (by this time I was working uptown as a secretary) and tell him to get up, I was coming over. Oh, he'd say, what time is it? Four, I'd say. He sometimes slept for weeks and wouldn't go out of his room unless someone called him. Why doesn't anyone call me or come over? he asked me once after three weeks of total divorce from the world, which had only been broken into because I thought he might like me even though I was fat. Barry, I told him, everyone loves you. It's just that you never have any beer.

The next time I came over five people were sitting on the floor drinking beer.

"Do you think I should get Fritos?" he asked, worried. The young host.

"Not unless you want them to hang around forever."

"I do."

"Well, I'll go down and get some for you."

The beer was outside on the window ledge, freezing.

On Friday I would call him and after work I'd take the subway down to the Chelsea and go and wake Barry up again. He was one of the most darling men I ever knew. His looks were all tawny and nice. He used to wear polo coats and could have worn spats. He had tawny thick hair which he didn't wear too long and he grew a mustache so that when he smiled and you saw one front tooth was missing. It was really funny. He used to write LSD in Magic Marker on the walls of uptown elevators very neatly in small capital letters.

He used to make me kiss him on 22nd Street and 7th Avenue when he was eating a banana.

For Christmas I gave him a cane with an ivory wolf head on top, and he developed a limp without further ado.

On Friday I would knock on his door and he'd come groggily to let me in before going back to bed. I'd turn on the television and get things going until finally he'd feel it was safe to get up. There were proof sheets everywhere. He shot fashion.

By about 7, we'd be downstairs trying to get a taxi. Either I'd blow all my money or he'd blow all his money. It was the only sensible thing to do. Once when I was mortally depressed and thought about dying, Barry got a check for a thousand dollars and we spent the entire thing in one weekend on champagne cocktails. It seemed the only sensible thing to do.

I'd run up to my horrid apartment and dump food out for the cat and run back down again and the world was our oyster. We usually went to the Koh-i-noor, an Indian restaurant on like Second Avenue and 4th Street or around there.

"Andy Warhol's having a party," I'd turn over delicately. The evening lay naked before us. We could go anywhere or do anything. It was New York City.

"Yeah?"

"Yeah, and they're having one at the Dakota too."

"Oh, boy!"

"And *Un Chien Andalou* is playing." (It was Barry's favorite movie.)

"Oh, well let's go see that."

"O.K."

We'd get let out at the restaurant and go across the street and get beer to drink with the food. Ale. Ballantine. No Ranier in New York City. By the time we were halfway finished with dinner an almost unearthly sense of well-being would lift us both to the highest planes of food-gladness.

"Ahhhhh . . ." Barry would say, leaning back and smiling.

We never went anywhere. We'd think when we were done that we might go to Max's, but in the end we just went back to the Chelsea and watched TV. Barry had fantastic drugs and sometimes we'd go onto the roof of the Chelsea and smoke DMT, but mostly we'd just smoke hash and watch TV for the entire weekend. Every now and then I'd go home and feed the cat.

We were not lovers.

Barry's friends were mostly tied up in this agency that took fantastically New York City color photographs of things like Gleem Toothpaste. I could never be friends with them and that's why I can't find out where he is. I asked Tim Leary and he doesn't know. He hasn't heard anything about any of those people, though even the straight photographers once lived at Millbrook.

Salvador Dalí loved Barry. Maybe he knows where he is. Anyway, Salvador Dalí speaks wretched English and Barry speaks no French or Spanish, but somehow Dalí telephoned Barry the first day he arrived in New York at the St. Regis and they managed to communicate into complete madness.

It was Barry who made it possible for me to introduce Frank Zappa to Salvador Dalí, one of my favorite things I ever did. Frank Zappa had been there always in Los Angeles and I have known him since I was about 17. He came to New York to do a record and we were walking down Madison Avenue one evening handing out "We Will Bury You" buttons that Frank had had made up of himself glowering over the top of his glasses, sitting behind a desk. The time was right.

"Meet us at the King Cole Bar," Barry said.

Frank wore a monkeyskin coat that came down to his feet. Underneath that he wore pink and yellow striped pants, shoes (it was cold) and a silken jersey basketball T-shirt in neon yellow-orange. His hair curled sweetly around his narrow, pointy face. The guy at the door said he had to wear a tie.

Frank tied it in a bow. It was silver satin and not a bow tie, and handed him one.

Dalí took one look at Frank from across the room and rose to his feet in immediate approbation. If Frank was not for Dalí, Dalí didn't care; he was for Frank.

So I really had very little trouble introducing them.

We drank chartreuse.

Dalí said he would like to see the Mothers rehearse, which Frank was doing later on. They planned to meet at the Dom on St. Mark's Place, which was where Frank was playing. Dalí was very anxious to see that act, as you can imagine.

The management of the Dom was having trouble with the management of Frank Zappa and locked Frank Zappa out so that we sat on the steps, locked out, as Dalí and Gala, his wife, pulled up and got out of a taxi into the dangers of the Lower East Side.

It was a shame.

When it turned out positively that they weren't going to let us in, Dalí and Gala dejectedly got another cab and went back to the St. Regis. I went to the Chelsea to find Barry and Frank went back to the Hotel Albert or wherever he was staying to argue with the fucking management who had ruined something that was very delicate and could only happen once. Dalí and Zappa alone together in a big empty room with musical instruments.

Barry and I went drinking.

Max's was where everyone went to drink.

Barry got a girl friend, one of those thin ones who looked like Holyoke or Vassar and horses. She didn't know what I was and Barry couldn't figure out how to explain, so we saw less of each other.

Also, I moved in with an anarchist dealer who taught art and had red hair. He had aliases. He's the only person I ever knew with an alias. I called him by it. I didn't even know it was made up.

He had red hair and a German shepherd and we talked for hours and hours and drank Wild Turkey. He had a chair which was made out of leather, an easy chair that you could lean back in, and every so often it fell over and you wound up looking at the ceiling. He thought this was a good anarchistic chair. His alias was Mike.

I met him one morning as he was walking by with a day-old pumpkin pie he'd bought for 15 cents. He insisted I come with him and eat it, so I did in spite of the fact that he had a dog and I hate dogs. The next day I moved in. I kept my apartment for Rosie, my cat, who hated dogs even more than I did.

Mike was a thief and a gourmet.

I lost about 15 pounds living with him because we only ate the finest, and being around Mike got you involved in a lot of physical exercise that didn't just come from fucking. I used to run off because he was such a shoplifter. Wine and stuff, he'd steal.

I worked on Madison Avenue as a secretary, though I could neither type nor acquiesce to my circumstances. I hated being a secretary on Madison Avenue. I hated being put on hold and I hated waiting for elevators. My boss acted like he'd just shot meth. Always.

He'd come in in the morning, his trench coat flapping, the door slamming open and him in mid-sentence in a voice too anxious and too loud, "Any messages, any messages? What do I have to do today? Where's the mail? What are my appointments like? Did you do the expense account?" Shit.

He was an ad salesman for magazines. I told him Barry was my fiancé and got a ring at the dime store. The only good thing that happened was when it snowed so hard no traffic could go up and down Madison Avenue and my boss was stuck, there was nowhere to turn. He was fat and had blue eyes like a baby and I think he thought he was crafty and maybe he was, but shit!, that "Any messages?" thing made me want to kill him.

In February on Valentine's Day Mike and I put a sticker heart on the German shepherd's forehead and went to our favorite restaurant, John's, on 12th Street between 1st and 2nd Avenues, I think. I realized that it was almost March, and in March I could go.

I wondered how I was going to get all those magazines back to L.A., the main part of my life being centered around collages. It was like the white corpuscles, it staved off disaster. So I sent 90 pounds of *Life*s to L.A. in a duffel bag by Greyhound Bus. It wasn't too expensive.

I took a cab to the airport without telling anyone but Carol and Mike that I was leaving. I didn't want to call Barry in front of Mike. I called Barry from the airport.

"Where've you been?" he asked. He was working. You could hear rock-and-roll shooting music in back of him; photographers play rock and roll to shoot. Barry usually played the Stones.

"I'm leaving, I am done, the year's over," I said.

"Where're you going."

"L.A."

"You didn't say goodbye to me. Tomorrow's my birthday."

"I'm at the airport."

"Oh . . . well, maybe I'll come see you."

"You won't. Anyway, I love you."

"I love you."

I sent him a singing telegram for his birthday. He sent me two postcards from London. And that was the end of him.

But I just couldn't stay in New York, though confidentially, it might be fun to go back and try and look for him. He must be around there somewhere. I should have stayed for his birthday.

The cat, I took.

I didn't put in about how I testified about LSD to Teddy Kennedy in the room the McCarthy hearings were held in or about the time I woke up to someone telling me not to scream with their hand over my mouth or about how Walter Bowart had to find me an uptown job because the amount of money I was embezzling nearly floored him, but they were just stories. Everything about New York was a story.

My friend Annie told me that when she was in New York last time she'd been doing so many things that when she finally found herself alone she decided to just take a kind of a here-and-there ramble "just to think," she said, "you know." Rounding the corner, she was confronted with a wino wielding a broken glass bottle, so she threw five dollars at him and ran. That always seemed like the whole thing; they'll let you have stories, but you can't ever think in a certain way. There are no spaces between the words, it's one of the charms of the place. Certain things don't have to be thought about carefully because you're always being pushed from behind. It's like a tunnel where there's no sky.

A PASSION IN THE DESERT

Honoré de Balzac

"THAT PERFORMANCE was terrifying!" she cried out as she left Monsieur Martin's menagerie.

She was there to contemplate the dashing performer *working* with his hyena, as the advertising poster put it.

"How did he manage," she went on, "to tame his animals to the point where he is so certain of their affection that—"

"That accomplishment, which seems so strange to you," I interrupted her, "is in fact something very natural."

"Oh!" she cried, allowing an incredulous smile to play over her lips.

"So you think that animals have no passions?" I asked her. "Here's proof that we can give them all the vices belonging to our stage of civilization."

She looked at me in astonishment.

"But," I continued, "seeing Monsieur Martin for the first time, I confess that, like you, I could not contain my surprise. At that time I found myself seated next to an old veteran with a missing right leg. He struck me as an impressive figure. He had one of those intrepid heads marked by war and inscribed by Napoleonic battles. That old soldier had an aura of frankness and cheer about him that always makes me favorably disposed. No doubt he was one of those unflappable troopers who laugh at a comrade's final rictus, cheerfully strip or enshroud him, command cannonballs to be fired with dispatch, deliberate swiftly, and deal with the devil without a qualm. After paying close attention to the menagerie's owner as he was leaving the loge, my companion pursed his lips in a gesture of mocking disdain, with the sort of pout that allows superior men to single out the gullible. And when I exclaimed at Monsieur Martin's courage, he smiled and said to me with a knowing look, shaking his head: 'Same old story.'

"'Same old story? What do you mean?' I asked him. 'I would be much obliged if you would explain this mystery to me.'

"After spending several moments exchanging introductions, we went to dine at the first restaurant we came across. Over dessert, a bottle of champagne coaxed this curious old soldier to refresh his memories in all their clarity. He told me his tale and I saw that he was right to cry out, 'Same old story!'"

As I was seeing my companion home, she begged and pleaded with me until I agreed to write up the soldier's confidences for her. The following day she received this episode from a saga that could be entitled "The French in Egypt."

During the expedition undertaken in Upper Egypt by General Desaix, a soldier from Provence fell into the hands of the Maghrebis and was taken by those Arabs into the desert situated beyond the cataracts of the Nile. In order to put sufficient distance between themselves and the French army and so ensure their peace of mind, the Maghrebis undertook a forced march, stopping only at night. They made camp around a water source hidden by palm trees where they had buried provisions some time before. Having no idea that their prisoner might take it into his head to flee, they were content to bind his hands, and all went to sleep after eating a few dates and feeding their horses. When the bold man from Provence saw his enemies incapable of keeping watch over him, he used his teeth to steal a scimitar, then, employing his knees to steady the blade, he cut the cords that bound his hands and freed himself. He instantly grabbed a rifle and a dagger, provisions of dried dates, a small sack of barley, some powder and bullets, strapped on a scimitar, hopped on a horse, and headed quickly in the direction he thought the French army must have taken. Impatient to join his bivouac, he rode his already tired mount so hard that the poor animal expired, its flanks torn to shreds, leaving the Frenchman in the middle of the desert.

After walking for some time in the sand with all the courage of an escaped convict, the soldier was forced to stop at nightfall. Despite the beauty of the sky during the Oriental night, he hadn't the strength to continue on his way. Fortunately, he was able to climb a promontory crowned by several palm trees, whose long visible fronds had awakened the sweetest hopes in his heart. His fatigue was so great that he stretched out on a piece of granite whimsically shaped like a camp bed and slept without a thought to defend himself. He had made the sacrifice of his life. His last thought was even a regret. He repented having left the Maghrebis, whose nomadic life was beginning to please him, now that he was far from them and quite helpless.

He woke with the sun, whose pitiless rays were falling directly on the granite and generating an unbearable heat. Now, our man from Provence had had the poor judgment to place himself on the other side from the shade projected by the verdant and majestic tops of the palm trees... He looked at those solitary trees and shivered! They reminded him of the elegant capitals, crowned with the long leaves, that distinguish the Saracen columns of the Arles cathedral. But after counting the palms, he cast his glance around him and felt the most terrifying despair sink deep into his soul. He saw a limitless ocean. The blackened sand of the desert extended unbroken in every direction, and it glittered like a steel blade struck by harsh light. He did not know whether this was a sea of ice or of lakes smooth as a mirror. Borne on waves, a mist of fire whirled above this moving earth. The sky was an Oriental burst of desolate purity, for it left nothing to the imagination. Sky and earth were on fire. The silence was frightening in its savage and terrible majesty. The immensity of the infinite pressed on the soul from all sides: not a cloud in the sky, not a breath of air, no undulation in the depths of the sand that shifted in small, skittering waves on the surface. Finally, the horizon ended like a sea in good weather, at a line of light as slender as the edge of a sword. The man from Provence squeezed the trunk of one of the palm trees as if it were the body of a friend; then, in the shelter of the straight, spindly shade that the tree inscribed on the granite, he wept, sitting and resting there, deeply sad as he contemplated the implacable scene that lay before him. He cried out to test his solitude. His voice, lost in the crevices of the heights, projected a thin sound into the distance that found no echo; the echo was in his heart: He was twenty-two years old, he loaded his rifle.

"There'll always be time enough!" he said to himself, laying the weapon of his liberation on the ground.

Looking in turn at the black and the blue spaces around him, the soldier dreamed of France. He caught the delightful scent of Parisian rivulets, he remembered the cities he had passed through, the faces of his comrades, and the most trivial circumstances of his life. And his southern imagination soon conjured the stones of his dear Provence in the play of heat that undulated above the extended sheet of the desert. Fearing all the dangers of this cruel mirage, he went down the other side of the hill he had climbed the day before. He felt great joy in discovering a kind of grotto naturally carved into the gigantic crags of granite that formed the base of this small peak. The remains of a mat told him that this refuge had already been inhabited. Then, several feet farther on, he saw palm trees laden with dates. The instinct that attaches us to life awoke in his heart. He hoped to live long enough for the passage of some Maghrebis, or perhaps indeed he would soon hear the noise of cannon; for just now Bonaparte was marching through Egypt.

Revived by this thought, the Frenchman whacked down several clusters of ripe dates whose weight seemed to bend the date palm's branches, and as he sampled this unanticipated manna he was certain that the grotto's inhabitant had cultivated the palm trees. The delicious, cool flesh of the date provided clear evidence of his predecessor's labors. The man from Provence shifted unthinkingly from dark despair to an almost mad joy. He climbed back up to the top of the hill and busied himself for the rest of the day cutting down one of the infertile palm trees that had provided him with a roof the previous night. A vague memory made him think of the animals of the desert, and foreseeing that they might come to drink at the watering hole lost in the sands that appeared at the base of the rocky outcropping, he resolved to guard against their visits by putting a barrier at the door of his hermitage. Despite his enthusiasm, despite the strength he drew from his fear of being devoured as he slept, he found it impossible to cut the palm tree into several pieces in the course of the day, but he succeeded in felling it.

When toward evening this king of the desert finally fell, the noise of its collapse echoed in the distance, like a groan uttered by the solitude. The soldier shivered as if he had heard some voice announcing disaster. But like an heir who does not grieve for long at a parent's death, he stripped the fine tree of the long, broad green leaves that define its poetic decoration and used them to repair the mat on which he would sleep. Worn out by the heat and his labors, he slept under the red walls of his damp grotto.

In the middle of the night his sleep was disturbed by an extraordinary noise. He sat up, and in the deep silence he recognized the sound of something breathing with a savage energy that could not belong to a human creature. A deep fear made even greater by the darkness, by the silence, and by the fancies of his sudden awakening chilled his heart. He barely even felt his scalp crawl when his dilated pupils glimpsed in the darkness two faint yellow beams. At first he attributed these lights to some reflection of his own eyes, but soon the vivid brightness of the night helped him by degrees to distinguish objects within the grotto, and he perceived an enormous animal lying two steps away from him. Was it a lion, a tiger, or a crocodile? The man from Provence did not have enough education to know in what subspecies to place his enemy, but his fright was all the more violent since his ignorance caused him to assume all these disasters at once. He endured the cruel torture of hearing, of grasping the irregularities of this breathing without losing any of its nuances, and without daring to make the slightest movement. An odor as strong as a fox's breath but more penetrating, more serious, we might say, filled the grotto, and when the man from Provence had taken it in with his nose, his terror was at its height, but he could no longer doubt the existence of the terrifying companion whose royal lair served as his bivouac.

Soon the rays of the moon sailing toward the horizon lit up the den and the subtly gleaming skin of a spotted panther. This royal Egyptian beast was sleeping rolled over like a large dog, peaceful possessor of a sumptuous nook at the door of a grand house. Its eyes opened for a moment, then closed again. It had its face turned toward the Frenchman. A thousand jumbled thoughts passed through the soul of the panther's prisoner. At first he wanted to kill it with a rifle shot, but he saw that there was not enough space between them to aim properly—the barrel would have extended beyond the animal. And what if he were to wake it up? This hypothesis stopped him in his tracks. Listening to the beating of his heart in the silence, he cursed the pounding pulsations of his blood, dreading to disturb the sleep that allowed him to find a solution to his advantage. He put his hand twice on his scimitar, planning to cut off his enemy's head, but the difficulty of cutting through such a tough hide forced him to give up his bold project. "Fail to kill it? Surely that would be a death sentence," he thought. He preferred the odds of combat and resolved to wait for daylight. And daylight was not long in coming. The Frenchman then was able to examine the panther; its muzzle was tinged with blood. "She's had a good meal!" he thought, without worrying whether the feast had been one of human flesh. "She won't be hungry when she wakes up."

It was a female. The fur of the white belly and thighs glimmered. Several little velvety spots formed pretty bracelets around the paws. The muscular tail was also white but tipped with black rings. The upper part of the coat, yellow as matte gold but very smooth and soft, bore those characteristic spots shaped like roses that distinguished panthers from other kinds of *Felis*. This calm and formidable hostess purred in a pose as graceful as that of a cat reclining on the cushion of an ottoman. Her bloody paws, twitching and well armed, lay beneath her head, whose sparse, straight whiskers protruded like silver wires. If she had been in a cage, the man from Provence would surely have admired the grace of this beast and the vigorous contrasts of strong colors that gave her simarre an imperial splendor, but just now he felt his viewing disturbed by its ominous aspect.

The panther's presence, even asleep, made him experience the effect produced by the hypnotic eyes of a snake on, they say, a nightingale. The soldier's courage failed for a moment before this danger, although he would surely have been exalted facing cannon spewing a hail of shot. However, an intrepid thought blossomed in his soul and halted at its source the cold sweat running down his forehead. Acting like men whom misfortune has pushed to the end of their rope, challenging death to do its worst, he saw a tragedy in this adventure without being conscious of it, and resolved to play his role with honor, even to the final scene.

"The day before yesterday, perhaps the Arabs would have killed me," he said to himself. Considering himself a dead man already, he bravely waited with restless curiosity for his enemy to awake. When the sun appeared, the panther silently opened her eyes; then she violently extended her paws, as if to loosen them up and dissipate any cramps. At last she yawned, displaying the fearsome array of her teeth and her grooved tongue, as hard as a grater. "She's like a little mistress!" thought the Frenchman, seeing her rolling around and making the gentlest, most flirtatious movements. She licked the blood that stained her paws, wiped her muzzle, and scratched her head with repeated gestures full of delicacy. "Good! Make your toilette," the Frenchman thought to himself, recovering his cheer by summoning courage. "We'll wish each other good morning." And he grabbed the short dagger he had taken from the Maghrebis.

Just then the panther turned her head toward the Frenchman and stared at him without moving. The rigidity of those metallic eyes and their unbearable clarity made the man from Provence shiver, especially when the beast walked toward him. But he gazed at her caressingly and steadily, as if attempting to exert his own animal magnetism, and let her come near him; then, with a movement as gentle, as amorous as if he had wanted to caress the prettiest woman, he passed his hand over her entire body, from head to tail, using his nails to scratch the flexible vertebrae that ran the length of the panther's yellow back. The beast voluptuously raised her tail, her eyes softened, and when the Frenchman completed this self-interested petting for the third time, she made one of those purring noises by which our cats express their pleasure. But this murmur came from a gullet so powerful and so deep that it sounded in the grotto like the last drones of a church organ. The man from Provence, understanding the importance of his caresses, redoubled his efforts to stun and stupefy this imperious courtesan. When he felt certain of extinguishing his capricious companion's ferocity, remembering that her hunger had been so fortunately satisfied the evening before, he rose to leave the grotto. The panther let him go, but when he had climbed the hill, she leaped with the lightness of monkeys jumping from branch to branch and came to rub herself against the soldier's legs, curving her back like a cat. Then, looking at her guest with an eye whose brightness had become less rigid, she uttered a wild call, which naturalists compare to the noise of a saw.

"How demanding she is!" cried the Frenchman, smiling. He tried to play with her ears, caress her belly, and scratch her head hard with his nails. And seeing his success, he tickled her skull with the point of his dagger, looking for the moment to kill her. But the hardness of the bones made him tremble at the possibility of failure.

The sultana of the desert noted with approval her slave's talents by raising her head, stretching out her neck, marking her intoxication by her repose. The Frenchman suddenly thought that in order to kill this savage princess in one blow, he would have to stab her in the throat, and he raised his blade just as the panther, no doubt sated with this play, lay down graciously at his feet, giving him looks now and then which, despite an inborn rigidity, displayed something like benevolence. The poor man from Provence ate his dates, leaning against one of the palm trees, but he glanced inquiringly at the surrounding desert in every direction, searching for liberators, and at his terrifying mate, keeping an eye on her uncertain clemency. The panther looked at the place where the date pits were falling every time he threw one of them, and then her eyes expressed a skeptic's suspicion. She examined the Frenchman with a calculating caution that concluded in his favor, for when he had finished his meager meal she licked the soles of his shoes, and with her rough, strong tongue miraculously cleaned the encrusted dust from their creases.

"But when she gets hungry?" thought the Provençal soldier. Although this idea caused him a shiver of fear, he began out of curiosity to measure the proportions of the panther, certainly one of the most beautiful examples of the species, for she was three feet high and four feet long, not counting her tail. This powerful weapon, thick around as a gourd, was nearly three feet long. Her head, as large as the head of a lioness, was distinguished by a rare expression of refinement; a tiger's cold cruelty was dominant, of course, but there was also a vague resemblance to the facial features of a cunning woman. Just now the face of this solitary queen revealed something like Nero's drunken gaiety: She had quenched her thirst for blood and wanted to play. The soldier tried to come and go, and the panther let him move freely, content to follow him with her eyes, less like a faithful dog than like a large angora cat made restless by everything, even her master's movements. When he returned, he noticed the remains of his horse next to the fountain, where the panther had dragged the cadaver. Around two-thirds of it had been devoured. This spectacle reassured the Frenchman. It was easy to explain the panther's absence and the respect she had shown him while he slept.

This first happiness emboldened him to attempt the future: He conceived the mad hope of getting on well with the panther all that day, engaging every means to win her over and ingratiate himself. He came near her once more and had the inexpressible happiness of seeing her wave her tail with a subtle movement. So he sat near her without fear and they began to play together. He took her paws, her muzzle, he twisted her ears, rolled her onto her back, and scratched her warm, silky flanks hard. She participated willingly, and when the soldier tried to smooth the fur of her paws, she carefully retracted her claws, curved like steel blades. The Frenchman, who kept one hand on his dagger, was still of a mind to plunge it into the overly trusting belly of the panther, but he was afraid of being instantly strangled in her last wild convulsion. And besides, his heart filled with a kind of remorse that begged him to respect a harmless creature. He felt he had found a friend in this boundless desert. Unbidden thoughts came to him of his first mistress, whom he had called ironically by the nickname "Mignonne" because she was so violently jealous that as long as their passion lasted, he was afraid of the knife with which she used to threaten him. This memory of his youth prompted him to try and impose the name on the young pantheress, whose agility, grace, and softness he now admired less fearfully.

Toward the end of the day, he had become used to his perilous situation, and he almost enjoyed its anguish. His companion had become used to looking at him when he called in a falsetto voice: "Mignonne." By sunset, Mignonne uttered a deep and melancholy cry several times.

"She is well brought up!" thought the cheerful soldier. "She is saying her prayers!" But this unspoken pleasantry came to him only when he had noticed his companion's peaceful attitude. "Go on, my little blonde, I will let you go to bed first," he said to her, counting heavily on escaping by foot as quickly as possible while she slept and finding another shelter for the night. The soldier waited impatiently for the moment of his getaway, and when it came, he walked vigorously in the direction of the Nile, but scarcely had he gone a quarter of a league in the sands than he heard the panther leaping behind him, periodically uttering a harsh cry, still more terrifying than the heavy sound of her leaps.

"Come now!" he said to himself. "She's taken a shine to me… Perhaps this young panther never met anyone before, it is flattering to have won her first love!" At this moment the Frenchman fell into one of those quicksand traps travelers so dread and from which it is impossible to extricate yourself. Feeling caught, he let out a cry of alarm, and the panther grabbed him by the collar with her teeth. And jumping powerfully backward, she pulled him from the abyss, as if by magic. "Ah, Mignonne," cried the soldier, caressing her enthusiastically. "We're bound to each other now in life and death. But no practical jokes, all right?" And he retraced his steps.

From then on the desert seemed populated. It held one being to whom the Frenchman could talk and whose ferocity was softened for him, although he could not grasp the reason for this unbelievable friendship. However powerful the soldier's desire to remain standing and on the alert, he slept. Upon waking, he could not see Mignonne; he climbed the hill, and in the distance he glimpsed her moving by leaps and bounds according to the habit of those animals for whom running is out of the question because of the extreme flexibility of their spinal column. Mignonne arrived with her chops bloodied and received the necessary caresses from her companion, testifying by several deep purrs how happy she was with him. Her eyes turned with even more sweetness than the evening before on the man from Provence, who spoke to her as to a domestic animal.

"Ah, ah, mademoiselle, such a respectable girl you are, aren't you? Do you see that? We love to be cuddled. Aren't you ashamed? Perhaps you've eaten some Maghrebi? Well, well! They're animals like you! But at least don't go deceiving a Frenchman . . . or I will not love you anymore!"

She played the way a young dog plays with his master, rolling, sparring, patting each other by turns, and sometimes she aroused the soldier by putting her paw on him with a solicitous gesture.

Several days passed this way. Her company allowed the man from Provence to admire the sublime beauties of the desert. From the moment he found there alternating hours of fear and tranquillity, provisions, and a creature who occupied his thoughts, his soul was buffeted by contrasts . . . It was a life full of opposites. Solitude revealed all its secrets to him, wrapped him in its charms. In the sunrise and sunset he discovered unfamiliar dramas. A shiver went down his spine when he heard the soft whistling of a bird's wings above his head—a rare passing creature—and saw the clouds merge together, multihued, ever-changing travelers! During the night he studied the effects of the moon on the oceans of sands where the simoon produced waves, undulations, and rapid changes. He lived the Orient's day, he admired its marvelous pomp, and often, after enjoying the terrifying spectacle of a hurricane on that plain where the rising sands produced dry, red mists, fatal clouds, he saw the night come on with delight, followed by the life-giving coolness of the stars. He listened to the imaginary music of the spheres.

Then solitude taught him to savor the treasure of daydreams. He spent whole hours remembering trivia, comparing his past life to his life in the present. Finally, he was fascinated by his panther, for he had a need for love. Whether his will, powerfully projected, had modified his companion's character, or she found abundant nourishment thanks to the combat unleashed in these deserts, she respected the life of the Frenchman, who no longer mistrusted her, seeing her so well tamed. He spent the greater part of his time sleeping, but he was forced to keep watch, like a spider in the middle of his web, so as not to miss the moment of his deliverance if someone should pass in the sphere bounded by the horizon. He had sacrificed his shirt to make a flag, hung on the top of a palm tree stripped of its foliage. Instructed by necessity, he knew how to find the means of keeping it flying by holding it out with sticks, for the wind might not have moved it at the very moment when the anticipated traveler would be looking in the desert.

It was during the long hours when hope abandoned him that he amused himself with the panther. He had come to know the different inflections of her voice, the expression in her eyes, had studied the caprices of all the spots that moderated the gold of her robe. Mignonne no longer growled even when he took her by the tuft at the end of her formidable tail in order to count the graceful decoration of black and white rings that shone in the sun like precious stones. He took pleasure in contemplating the supple, delicate lines of her contours, the whiteness of her belly, the grace of her head. But it was especially when she frisked about that he took such pleasure in watching her, and the agility, the youth of her movements always surprised him. He admired her suppleness when she began to leap, crawl, glide, burrow, cling, roll over, flatten herself, dash forward in every direction. She was lightning fast in passion, a block of granite slipping forward, and she froze at the word "Mignonne."

One day under a fiery sun, a huge bird was gliding in the sky. The man from Provence left his panther to examine this new guest, but after a moment's pause, the sultana let out a low growl. "God help me, I think she is jealous," he cried to himself, seeing her eyes harden. "Virginie's soul must surely have passed into this body!"

The eagle disappeared in the sky while the soldier admired the panther's crouching haunches. There was such grace and youth in her shape! She was as pretty as a woman. The blond fur of her coat was matched by the delicate tint of matte white tones that colored her thighs. The profuse light from the sun made that vivid gold and those brown spots shine with ineffable allure. The man from Provence and the panther looked at each other with an intelligent understanding, the coquette trembled when she felt her friend's nails scratch her skull, her eyes shone like two beams, then she closed them firmly.

"She has a soul," he said, studying the calmness of this queen of the sands, gold and white like them, like them solitary and burning…

"Ah well," my companion said to me, "I have read your plea in favor of animals. But how did it end between two beings so well suited to understand each other?"

"Ah, that's it … They ended the way all grand passions end, through a misunderstanding! One or the other believes he has been betrayed, pride prevents understanding, stubbornness prompts a falling out."

"And sometimes in the most exquisite moments," she said. "One look, one exclamation is enough. Now will you finish this story?"

"It's terribly difficult, but you understand what the old fellow had already confided in me when, finishing his bottle of champagne, he cried: 'I don't know how I'd hurt her, but she turned on me as if enraged, and with her sharp teeth she bit me in the thigh, weakly no doubt. As for me, believing that she wanted to devour me, I plunged my dagger into her throat. She rolled over letting out a cry that froze my heart, I saw her struggling while looking at me without anger. I would have given anything in the world, even the Legion of Honor that I didn't yet have, to bring her back to life. It was as if I'd murdered a real person. And the soldiers who had seen my flag and who ran to my rescue, found me in tears . . . Well, monsieur,' he continued after a moment of silence, 'since then I've gone to war in Germany, Spain, Russia, and France. I've faithfully dragged my carcass all over and I've seen nothing equal to the desert . . . ah, how beautiful it is!'

"'What do you feel there?' I asked him.

"'Oh, it can't be put into words, young man. Besides, I don't always regret my stand of palm trees and my panther . . . it's only when I feel sad. In the desert, you see, there is everything and there is nothing.'

"'Still, can you explain it to me?'

"'Well,' he went on, letting a gesture of impatience escape him, 'it is God without men.'"

Paris, 1832
Translated by Carol Cosman

THE SHORT DAYS OF WINTER
Henry David Thoreau

FEB. 29. For the past month there has been more sea-room in the day, without so great danger of running aground on one of those two promontories that make it arduous to navigate the winter day, the morning or the evening. It is a narrow pass, and you must go through with the tide. Might not some of my pages be called "The Short Days of Winter"?

March 1. Linnæus, speaking of the necessity of precise and adequate terms in any science, after naming some which he invented for botany, says, "Termini praeservarunt Anatomiam, Mathesin, Chemiam, ab idiotis; Medicinam autem eorum defectus conculcavit." (Terms (well defined) have preserved anatomy, mathematics, and chemistry from idiots; but the want of them has ruined medicine.) But I should say that men generally were not enough interested in the first-mentioned sciences to meddle with and degrade them. There is no interested motive to induce them to listen to the quack in mathematics, as they have to attend to the quack in medicine; yet chemistry has been converted into alchemy, and astronomy into astrology.

However, I can see that there is a certain advantage in these hard and precise terms, such as the lichenist uses, for instance. No one masters them so as to use them in writing on the subject without being far better informed than the rabble about it. New books are not written on chemistry or cryptogamia of as little worth comparatively as are written on the *spiritual* phenomena of the day. No man writes on lichens, using the terms of the science intelligibly, without having something to say, but every one thinks himself competent to write on the relation of the soul to the body, as if that were a *phæno-gamous* subject.

After having read various books on various subjects for some months, I take up a report on Farms by a committee of Middlesex Husbandmen, and read of the number of acres of bog that some farmer has redeemed, and the number of rods of stone wall that he has built, and the number of tons of hay he now cuts, or of bushels of corn or potatoes he raises there, and I feel as if I had got my foot down on to the solid and sunny earth, the basis of all philosophy, and poetry, and religion even. I have faith that the man who redeemed some acres of land the past summer redeemed also some parts of his character. I shall not expect to find him ever in the almshouse or the prison. He is, in fact, so far on his way to heaven. When he took the farm there was not a grafted tree on it, and now he realizes something handsome from the sale of fruit. These, in the absence of other facts, are evidence of a certain moral worth.

March 4. It is discouraging to talk with men who will recognize no principles. How little use is made of reason in this world! You argue with a man for an hour, he agrees with you step by step, you are approaching a triumphant conclusion, you think that you have converted him; but ah, no, he has a habit, he takes a pinch of snuff, he remembers that he entertained a different opinion at the commencement of the controversy, and his reverence for the past compels him to reiterate it now. You began at the butt of the pole to curve it, you gradually bent it round according to rule, and planted the other end in the ground, and already in imagination saw the vine curling round this segment of an arbor, under which a new generation was to re-create itself; but when you had done, just when the twig was bent, it sprang back to its former stubborn and unhandsome position like a bit of whalebone.

If I were to paint the short days of winter, I should represent two towering icebergs, approaching each other like promontories, for morning and evening, with cavernous recesses, and a solitary travel-ler, wrapping his cloak about him and bent forward against a driving storm, just entering the narrow pass. I would paint the light of a taper at midday, seen through a cottage window half buried in snow and frost, and some pale stars in the sky, and the sound of the woodcutter's axe. The icebergs with cavernous recesses. In the foreground should appear the harvest, and far in the background, through the pass, should be seen the sowers in the fields and other evidences of spring. The icebergs should gradually approach, and on the right and left the heavens should be shaded off from the light of midday to midnight with its stars. The sun low in the sky.

March 9. A warm spring rain in the night.

3 P.M.—Down the railroad.

Cloudy but springlike. When the frost comes out of the ground, there is a corresponding thawing of the man.

Again it rains, and I turn about.

The sound of water falling on rocks and of air falling on trees are very much alike.

Though cloudy, the air excites me. Yesterday all was tight as a stricture on my breast; to-day all is loosened. It is a different element from what it was.

March 10. I see flocks of a dozen bluebirds together. The warble of this bird is innocent and celestial, like its color. A woodchopper tells me he heard a robin this morning. What is the little chick-weed-like plant already springing up on the top of the Cliffs? There are some other plants with bright-green leaves which have either started somewhat or have never suffered from the cold under the snow.

March 14. Sunday. Rain, rain, rain; but even this is fair weather after so much snow.

March 15. This afternoon I throw off my outside coat. A mild spring day. I must hie to the Great Meadows. The air is full of bluebirds. The ground almost entirely bare. The villagers are out in the sun, and every man is happy whose work takes him outdoors. My life partakes of infinity. The air is as deep as our natures. I go forth to make new demands on life. I wish to begin this summer well; to do something in it worthy of it and of me; to transcend my daily routine and that of my townsmen; to have my immortality now, that it be in the *quality* of my daily life; to pay the greatest price, the greatest tax, of any man in Concord, and enjoy the most!! I will give all I am for *my* nobility. I will pay all my days for *my* success. I pray that the life of this spring and summer may ever lie fair in my memory. May I dare as I have never done! May I persevere as I have never done! I am eager to report the glory of the universe; may I be worthy to do it; to have got through with regarding human values, so as not to be distracted from regarding divine values. It is reasonable that a man should be something worthier at the end of the year than he was at the beginning.

March 16. Before sunrise.

Spent the day in Cambridge Library.

The Library a wilderness of books. The volumes of the Fifteenth, Sixteenth, and Seventeenth Centuries, which lie so near on the shelf, are rarely opened, are effectually forgotten and not implied by our literature and newspapers. When I looked into Purchas's Pilgrims, it affected me like looking into an impassable swamp, ten feet deep with sphagnum, where the monarchs of the forest, covered with mosses and stretched along the ground, were making haste to become peat. Those old books suggested a certain fertility, an Ohio soil, as if they were making a humus for new literatures to spring in. I heard the bellowing of bullfrogs and the hum of mosquitoes reverberating through the thick embossed covers when I had closed the book. Decayed literature makes the richest of all soils.

March 18. This afternoon the woods and walls and the whole face of the country wear once more a wintry aspect, though there is more moisture in the snow and the trunks of the trees are whitened now on a more southerly or southeast side. These slight falls of snow which come and go again so soon when the ground is partly open in the spring, perhaps helping to open and crumble and prepare it for the seed, are called "the poor man's manure." They are, no doubt, more serviceable still to those who are rich enough to have some manure spread on their grass ground, which the melting snow helps dissolve and soak in and carry to the roots of the grass. At any rate, it is all the poor man has got, whether it is good or bad. There is more rain than snow now falling.

March 30. Having occasion to-day to put up a long ladder against the house, I found, from the trembling of my nerves with the exertion, that I had not exercised that part of my system this winter. How much I may have lost! It would do me good to go forth and work hard and sweat. Though the frost is nearly out of the ground, the winter has not broken up in me. It is a backward season with me. Perhaps we grow older and older till we no longer sympathize with the revolution of the seasons, and our winters never break up.

March 31. Intended to get up early this morning and commence a series of spring walks, but clouds and drowsiness prevented.

Perhaps after the thawing of the trees their buds universally swell before they can be said to spring.

Perchance as we grow old we cease to spring with the spring, and we are indifferent to the succession of years, and they go by without epoch as months. Woe be to us when we cease to form new resolutions on the opening of a new year!

A cold, raw day with alternating hail-like snow and rain.

It would be worth the while to tell why a swamp pleases us, what kinds please us, also what weather, etc., etc.,—analyze our impressions. Why the moaning of the storm gives me pleasure. I sometimes feel that I need to sit in a far-away cave through a three weeks' storm, cold and wet, to give a tone to my system. The spring has its windy March to usher it in, with many soaking rains reaching into April. Methinks I would share every creature's suffering for the sake of its experience and joy. The song sparrow and the transient fox-colored sparrow,—have they brought me no message this year? Have I heard what this tiny passenger has to say, while it flits thus from tree to tree? I love the birds and beasts because they are mythologically in earnest. I reproach myself because I have regarded with indifference the passage of the birds; I have thought them no better than I.

April 1. Saw the first bee of the season on the railroad causeway, also a small red butterfly and, later, a large dark one with buff-edged wings.

Walden is all white ice, but little melted about the shores. The very sight of it carries my thoughts back at once some weeks toward winter, and a chill comes over them.

We have had a good solid winter, which has put the previous summer far behind us; intense cold, deep and lasting snows, and clear, tense winter sky. It is a good experience to have gone through with.

April 2. 6 A.M.—The sun is up. The air is full of the notes of birds,— song sparrows, red-wings, robins (singing a strain), bluebirds,—and I hear also a lark,—as if all the earth had burst forth into song. A few weeks ago, before the birds had come, there came to my mind in the night the twittering sound of birds in the early dawn of a spring morning, a semiprophecy of it, and last night I attended mentally as if I heard the spray-like dreaming sound of the midsummer frog and realized how glorious and full of revelations it was. Expectation may amount to prophecy. The clouds are *white* watery, not such as we had in the winter.

It appears to me that man is altogether too much insisted on. The poet says the proper study of mankind is man. I say, study to forget all that; take wider views of the universe. That is the egotism of the race. What is this our childish, gossiping, social literature, mainly in the hands of the publishers? Look at our literature. What a poor, puny, social thing, seeking sympathy! The author troubles himself about his readers,—would fain have one before he dies. He stands too near his printer; he corrects the proofs. Not satisfied with defiling one another in this world, we would all go to heaven together.

I do not value any view of the universe into which man and the institutions of man enter very largely and absorb much of the attention. Man is but the place where I stand, and the prospect hence is infinite. It is not a chamber of mirrors which reflect me. When I reflect, I find that there is other than me. The universe is larger than enough for man's abode.

Landed on Tall's Island. On the rocky point, where the wind is felt, the waves are breaking merrily, and now for half an hour our dog has been standing in the water under the small swamp white oaks, and ceaselessly snapping at each wave as it broke, as if it were a living creature. He, regardless of cold and wet, thrusts his head into each wave to gripe it. A dog snapping at the waves as they break on a rocky shore. He then rolls himself in the leaves for a napkin. We hardly set out to return, when the water looked sober and rainy. There was more appearance of rain in the water than in the sky,—April weather look. And soon we saw the dimples of drops on the surface. I forgot to mention before the cranberries seen on the bottom, as we pushed over the meadows, and the red beds of pitcher-plants.

April 3. It is a clear day with a cold westerly wind, the snow of yesterday being melted. When the sun shines unobstructedly the landscape is full of light, for it is reflected from the withered fawn-colored grass, as it cannot be from the green grass of summer. (On the back of the hill behind Gourgas's.)

The bluebird carries the sky on his back.

Edited by Damion Searls

THE WEDDING RING

Mavis Gallant

ON MY WINDOWSILL is a pack of cards, a bell, a dog's brush, a book about a girl named Jewel who is a Christian Scientist and won't let anyone take her temperature, and a white jug holding field flowers. The water in the jug has evaporated; the sand-and-amber flowers seem made of paper. The weather bulletin for the day can be one of several: No sun. A high arched yellow sky. Or, creamy clouds, stillness. Long motionless grass. The earth soaks up the sun. Or, the sky is higher than it ever will seem again, and the sun far away and small.

From the window, a field full of goldenrod, then woods; to the left as you stand at the front door of the cottage, the mountains of Vermont.

The screen door slams and shakes my bed. That was my cousin. The couch with the India print spread in the next room has been made up for him. He is the only boy cousin I have, and the only American relation my age. We expected him to be homesick for Boston. When he disappeared the first day, we thought we would find him crying with his head in the wild cucumber vine; but all he was doing was making the outhouse tidy, dragging out of it last year's magazines. He discovers a towel abandoned under his bed by another guest, and shows it to each of us. He has unpacked a trumpet, a hatchet, a pistol, and a water bottle. He is ready for anything except my mother, who scares him to death.

My mother is a vixen. Everyone who sees her that summer will remember, later, the gold of her eyes and the lovely movement of her head. Her hair is true russet. She has the bloom women have some-times when they are pregnant or when they have fallen in love. She can be wild, bitter, complaining, and ugly as a witch, but that summer is her peak. She has fallen in love.

My father is—I suppose—in Montreal. The guest who seems to have replaced him except in authority over me (he is still careful, still courts my favor) drives us to a movie. It is a musical full of monstrously large people. My cousin sits intent, bites his nails, chews a slingshot during the love scenes. He suddenly dives down in the dark to look for lost, mysterious objects. He has seen so many movies that this one is nearly over before he can be certain he has seen it before. He always knows what is going to happen and what they are going to say next.

At night we hear the radio—disembodied voices in a competition, identifying tunes. My mother, in the living room, seen from my bed, plays solitaire and says from time to time, "That's an old song I like," and "When you play solitaire, do you turn out two cards or three?" My cousin is not asleep either; he stirs on his couch. He shares his room with the guest. Years later we will be astonished to realize how young the guest must have been—twenty-three, perhaps twenty-four. My cousin, in his memories, shared a room with a middle-aged man. My mother and I, for the first and last time, ever, sleep in the same bed. I see her turning out the cards, smoking, drinking cold coffee from a breakfast cup. The single light on the table throws the room against the black window. My cousin and I each have an extra blanket. We forget how the evening sun blinded us at suppertime—how we gasped for breath.

My mother remarks on my hair, my height, my teeth, my French, and what I like to eat, as if she had never seen me before. Together, we wash our hair in the stream. The stones at the bottom are the color of trout. There is a smell of fish and wildness as I kneel on a rock, as she does, and plunge my head in the water. Bubbles of soap dance in place, as if rooted, then the roots stretch and break. In a delirium of happiness I memorize ferns, moss, grass, seedpods. We sunbathe on camp cots dragged out in the long grass. The strands of wet hair on my neck are like melting icicles. Her "Never look straight at the sun" seems extravagantly concerned with my welfare. Through eyelashes I peep at the milky-blue sky. The sounds of this blissful moment are the radio from the house; my cousin opening a ginger-ale bottle; the stream, persistent as machinery. My mother, still taking extraordinary notice of me, says that while the sun bleaches her hair and makes it light and fine, dark hair (mine) turns ugly—"like a rusty old stove lid"—and should be covered up. I dart into the cottage and find a hat: a wide straw hat, belonging to an unknown summer. It is so large I have to hold it with a hand flat upon the crown. I may look funny with this hat on, but at least I shall never be like a rusty old stove lid. The cots are empty; my mother has gone. By mistake, she is walking away through the goldenrod with the guest, turned up from God knows where. They are walking as if they wish they were invisible, of course, but to me it is only a mistake, and I call and run and push my way between them. He would like to take my hand, or pretends he would like to, but I need my hand for the hat.

My mother is developing one of her favorite themes—her lack of roots. To give the story greater power, or because she really believes what she is saying at that moment, she gets rid of an extra parent: "I never felt I had any stake anywhere until my parents died and I had their graves. The graves were my only property. I felt I belonged somewhere."

Graves? What does she mean? My grandmother is still alive.

"That's so sad," he says.

"Don't you ever feel that way?"

He tries to match her tone. "Oh, I wouldn't care. I think everything was meant to be given away. Even a grave would be a tie. I'd pretend not to know where it was."

"My father and mother didn't get along, and that prevented me feeling close to any country," says my mother. This may be new to him, but, like my cousin at a musical comedy, I know it by heart, or something near it. "I was divorced from the landscape, as they were from each other. I was too taken up wondering what was going to happen next. The first country I loved was somewhere in the north of Germany. I went there with my mother. My father was dead and my mother was less tense and I was free of their troubles. That is the truth," she says, with some astonishment.

The sun drops, the surface of the leaves turns deep blue. My father lets a parcel fall on the kitchen table, for at the end of one of her long, shattering, analytical letters she has put "P.S. Please bring a four-pound roast and some sausages." Did the guest depart? He must have dissolved; he is no longer visible. To show that she is loyal, has no secrets, she will repeat every word that was said. But my father, now endlessly insomniac and vigilant, looks as if it were he who had secrets, who is keeping something back.

The children—hostages released—are no longer required. In any case, their beds are needed for Labor Day weekend. I am to spend six days with my cousin in Boston—a stay that will, in fact, be prolonged many months. My mother stands at the door of the cottage in nightgown and sweater, brown-faced, smiling. The tall field grass is gray with cold dew. The windows of the car are frosted with it. My father will put us on a train, in care of a conductor. Both my cousin and I are used to this.

"He and Jane are like sister and brother," she says—this of my cousin and me, who do not care for each other.

Uncut grass. I saw the ring fall into it, but I am told I did not —I was already in Boston. The weekend party, her chosen audience, watched her rise, without warning, from the wicker chair on the porch. An admirer of Russian novels, she would love to make an immediate, Russian gesture, but cannot. The porch is screened, so, to throw her wedding ring away, she must have walked a few steps to the door and *then* made her speech, and flung the ring into the twilight, in a great spinning arc. The others looked for it next day, discreetly, but it had disappeared. First it slipped under one of those sharp bluish stones, then a beetle moved it. It left its print on a cushion of moss after the first winter. No one else could have worn it. My mother's hands were small, like mine.

1969

AN UNUSUAL YOUNG LADY AND
HER UNUSUAL BEAUX
Gyula Krúdy

MASZKERÁDI—were he asked in the great beyond to speak truth-fully about his earthly doings—would confess that he had especially feared those women who remembered his lies the day after; otherwise, he had preferred to pass his days at weddings.

Maszkerádi had lived in Pest back in the days when one could see on Chamois Street in the evening the white-stockinged daughters of the bourgeoisie sitting on benches under fragrant trees in the court-yards of single-storied townhouses, listening to the music of distant accordions, their hearts overflowing with love, like a stone trough whose water drips from a little-used faucet. In winter this part of town gave off the smells of the grab bags of itinerant vendors; in summer the predominant scent was that of freshly starched petticoats. Had he the inclination, Maszkerádi could have seduced and abducted the entire female population of Chamois Street. He was a stray soul, French or German in origin, variously prince in exile or cardsharp, refined gentleman or midnight serenader, fencing master or freeloader, as the occasion demanded. Married middle-class ladies cast down their eyes when he flashed a glance at them, while their husbands loathed the sight of his lithe limbs; in her book of hours every girl had a certain prayer picked out for her by Maszkerádi. Sometimes there were as many as four or five young misses bent piously over the supplication of a fallen soul at Sunday Mass in the Franciscans' Church. At night the occasional report of a firearm disturbed the tranquility of the quarter: a father or husband taking a shot at Masz-kerádi who had been glimpsed lurking around the sleeping household. He sported a black beard and there was animal magnetism in his voice. He must have retained in his possession intimate letters from some extremely prominent Inner City ladies (for a while he had resided in that quarter)—to have avoided incarceration in the darkest prison of Pest.

One day this disreputable adventurer was found dead in mysterious circumstances in his apartment at Number Ten, where irate husbands had so often waited, posted by the front entrance, expecting to see their dear little errant wives. (Although the road to Maszkerádi was fraught with peril, women still ran off to his place on snowy afternoons before a ball, on spring mornings before an outing to the Buda hills, or after a funeral, aroused by the tears shed at the last rites. On rainy nights there were barefoot women lowering themselves on the drainspout—in short, no other man in town could lay claim to such traffic.) The coroner readily agreed to inter this dangerous individual without a thorough inquest; he didn't even insist on dripping hot candle wax on the fingertips of the deceased. Although the knitting needle stuck in the victim's heart and the nail protruding from the crown of his head were duly noted, the reprobate was not deemed worthy of much fuss. The sooner the meat wagon transported this carrion out of town, the better.

Not two weeks after Maszkerádi's demise the thunder of a gun was again heard late at night in Autumn Street. The newlywed Libinyei had discharged his blunderbuss; he must have seen a ghost, although he swore up and down that he awoke from a nightmare to glimpse Maszkerádi jumping up from his bride's side and escaping through the window. Lotti was pallid, trembled from top to toe, and later confessed to her mother, in strictest confidence, a most peculiar dream that had surprised her like a warm breeze. "If I become pregnant I'll throw myself in the Danube!" the young bride swore, but later reconsidered the matter.

Less than two weeks later, Lotti's sister-in-law, the other Mrs. Libinyei, Helen of the springtime blue eyes, white shoulders like a Madonna, and the sweetness of walnuts, had to wake up her husband in the middle of the night.

"There's someone in the room," she whispered.

The husband, a dyer in blue, pulled the quilt over his face but even so he could hear the door quietly open as someone exited through the front entrance. His trembling hands groped for Helen's shoulder.

"Phew, you have such a cemetery-smell. Just like Lotti," blurted the surprised dyer.

Although this scene had transpired in the innermost family sanctum, the townsfolk still learned about the affair and began to give the two Mrs. Libinyeis the strangest looks. After all, it was most irregular that sisters-in-law should share a dead man of ill repute as their lover.

At the civic rifle club meeting, over a glass of wine, one tipsy citizen, possibly a kinsman, brought up this evil rumor in front of the two husbands. By then the story had it that it was the two Mrs. Libinyeis who had done away with the adventurer: one hammered the nail into his skull, the other plunged the knitting needle into his heart, for being unfaithful to them. Apparently he had gone serenading elsewhere in the night, attended the latest weddings and whispered his depraved lies into the ears of the newest brides. So now the dead man was taking his revenge by leaving the cold sepulchral domain of his cemetery ditch to haunt the two murderous women.

Did the Libinyei brothers give credence to the words of their bibulous companion? A nasty row ensued, in the course of which the Libinyei boys, befitting their noble Hungarian origins, and in homage to their warlike kuruc freedom-fighter forebears, broke the skulls of several fellow citizens. Swinging chair legs, rifle butts and their fists, they defended the honor of their women. For this reason the rifle association's get-together ended well before midnight, the precious ecstasy of the local Sashegy wines evaporated from under the citizens' hats, and the ragtag band of Gypsy musicians quit playing their discordant tunes among the early spring lilac trees of the municipal park. The grim and much booed Libinyeis hung their heads and trudged homeward on Király Street—the abode, in those days, of midnight-eyed Jewesses and dealers smelling of horsehides.

Reaching their house in Autumn Street at this unusually early, pre-midnight and sober hour, they stopped short, astonished hearts a-thumping, in front of the ground-floor windows. They saw, behind the white lace curtains, the rooms lit up by festive lamplight, while the sounds of music filtered out into the night, just like at certain Inner City townhouses marked by red lanterns where even a stranger from distant parts could count on the warmest reception. The screech of the violin resembled a serenade of tomcats on moonlit rooftops.

The elder Libinyei clambered up on the quoin that was decorated by a carving. (It must have come under the scrutiny of every Josephstadt dog by late February.)

Having climbed up, Libinyei the elder peeked through the window into his own home.

Whereupon, without a sound, he tumbled from the wall and fell headlong on the pavement, stretched out very much like one who has concluded his business here on earth.

In a furor Pál Libinyei, the younger brother, sprang up on the cornerstone. His eyes immediately narrowed, as if he had received a terrible blow in the face. The wealthy blue-dyer glimpsed a sight he would not have thought conceivable. The two women, Lotti and Helen, in a state of shameless undress, were treating Maszkerádi to the pleasures of a fully laid groaning board. The ham loomed like a bulls-eye and the wine from Gellért Hill glowed as if a volcano had deposited lava in it. Slices of white bread shone like a bed inviting the tired traveler. In the corner an itinerant musician's calloused fingers twanged the strings, with enough energy for a whole orchestra, while he witnessed the hoopla with the pious expression of a medieval monk.

Libinyei's murderous fist smashed the window.

In the last flicker of the guttering candles he could see the pilgrim-faced musician leap to his feet in the corner, raise his gleaming instrument and deal Maszkerádi's skull a deadly blow, fully meaning to dispatch him to the other world, this time once and for all. Indeed, the libertine collapsed like a whirling mass of dry leaves, when the autumn wind suddenly withdraws behind a tombstone in the municipal park to overhear the conversation of two lovers. The reveler with the bushy, overgrown eyebrows and black evening wear vanished into the flagstones of the floor. For years, the inhabitants of the house would search for him in the cellar, whenever they heard a wine cask creak, but it was only the new wine fermenting in the silence of the night.

By the time Libinyei made his way into the house he had grabbed an iron bar and was savoring glorious visions of murder as his sole road to salvation. However, both women (each in her own bedchamber) appeared to be as sound asleep as if there were no tomorrow. The itinerant musician had slipped away like a mendicant friar. Libinyei spent the night in his brother's wife's room, and attempted to convince Lotti that her dead husband lying under the window would arise and presently enter the house bleeding and gasping, to hold ordeal by fire over her. In a whisper Lotti confessed her mortal sins to her brother-in-law: she alone had laid Maszkerádi to waste, by means of the iron nail and the knitting needle, thereby earning the gratitude of every Josephstadt mother. Above all, Lotti had been outraged by the balding libertine's latest schemes to seduce the youngest girls awaiting confirmation.

"Oh, you witch," the blue-dyer stammered, sobbing and in love, "I'm going to take care of you from now on. And I'll skin you alive if you ever conjure up Maszkerádi from the beyond to come for dinner again."

Lotti solemnly swore, and at dawn they brought the corpse in from the sidewalk, where the itinerant musician had been guarding it as tenaciously as a ratter.

Such were the circumstances surrounding Malvina's birth.

Lotti died in childbirth; the attending doctors delivered the child of a mother who was more dead than alive. For the first fifteen years of her life she never heard a word spoken about her parents. She was raised by a black-clad, thin-lipped, dagger-tongued woman (Helen) to whom Libinyei, the girl's stepfather, never said a word. This woman spent her nights in a separate apartment of the house, with the taciturn itinerant musician on her doorstep, performing all sorts of hocus-pocus to keep the ghosts away. Libinyei, at times, addressed the girlchild as Miss Maszkerádi. (Later, after she had left her boarding school, Malvina used the pen name "Countess Maszkerádi" in her correspondence with classmates.) One day the monkish itinerant reported that Helen was in her last hour, whereupon his mysterious presence vanished forever from the household. By that time Libinyei had amassed such a fortune that he barely grieved over the death of his neglected wife. His possessions included mansions, land in the country, and real estate in Buda.

Good fortune and wealth did their best to console him. After Helen's death all kinds of relatives came to stay at the townhouse, but none of them won Libinyei's approval. Springtime visits to spas, quack remedies, barbers and doctors all failed to rejuvenate him. Soon enough he followed Helen, Lotti, and Maszkerádi into the great beyond. Malvina became the wealthiest heiress in Budapest: somber, frosty, intrepid, and miserable.

Malvina Maszkerádi was Eveline's best and only friend, entrusted with all of the girl's secrets, like a private diary.

A few days after the Tarot reading Miss Maszkerádi arrived at Bujdos-Hideaway.

"I sensed that you are in some kind of danger," said the solemn girl, her eyes downcast. "I wanted to be by your side."

Miss Maszkerádi had stayed at Bujdos before. She knew by name each dog, each horse and rooster. The migrating swallow and the stork nesting on the chimney of the servants' quarters both greeted the melancholy maiden. The servants dared not look her in the eye, but stared after her as they would at a creature from another world.

Eveline both loved and worried about her strange friend. But her vernal insomnia immediately passed as soon as Miss Maszkerádi joined the Hideaway household. Like one preparing for the grave, Eveline related her recent experiences in the minutest detail, including Andor Álmos-Dreamer's enigmatic demise and resurrection.

"He's crazy, but honest. This village Don Juan's going to be your downfall yet," observed Miss Maszkerádi. "And what about your gambler?" she inquired. "Show me the gambler's letters."

Eveline shook her head.

"He's afraid to write me. Sometimes in the morning I stand by the window and watch the mailman trudging along on the road far away. That gray old man always comes the same way, sad as autumn

and just as hopeless. If he were to deliver a letter from Pest one day...
But I don't even know if I'd like to receive a letter..."

"Your gambler's crazy, too... He thinks you're some otherwordly
creature," Miss Maszkerádi replied scornfully. "I assume every man
to be insane, and usually the events prove me right. Oh, there's the
ass who believes you are a demon, an angel of death, and who wants
to escape into death when he feels he's lost his freedom. Meanwhile
another inane male will worship you like a saint or a holy icon, and
expect you to perform miracles. Only I know you exactly as you really
are: a scatterbrained, bored, orphaned young miss. Why, by now you
should have married a first lieutenant or some young gent with a
duck's ass haircut. But you believe life is more interesting this way.
Well, one fine day some maniac will snag you by the throat like a fox
taking a goose."

"Please calm down," implored Eveline. "Haven't you ever been in
love?"

"Oh yes, with a dog... or a horse... or a wooden cross at the old
Buda military cemetery over the grave of a young officer whose fiancée'd
run off to work the cash register at a nightclub. Men stink. If I were
to find one guy whose mouth had a pleasing aroma, maybe I'd let
him kiss me. Or rather I wouldn't wait but kiss him myself. If, God
forbid, I should find a man I like, I'd pick him like a roadside poppy.
If I could only live... If it were really worthwhile to be alive, I'd show
you how to live life. But I'm not in good health, and I'm not old
enough to enjoy being in poor health."

"Just simmer down," Eveline repeated. "Can't you hear someone
lurking around the house? Every night I hear him and my heart almost
bursts..."

It was a spring night.

"Nah, it's just the unusual weather we're having," Miss Maszkerádi
replied, unmoved. "It's all that meteoric crap—ashes and dust from
burnt-out stars—the winds sweep into the atmosphere... It's only
the night, plucking an old mandolin string in the attic that's been
lying silent for years. No need to go mushroom-crazy, like some
fungus that suddenly pops up, so glad to be among us."

"But I tell you, someone goes past my window every night. I tell myself, perhaps it's Kálmán, and my heart nearly screams out like a bird that's caught. Perhaps it's Álmos-Dreamer, and my tears soak the pillow...Or it's the night watchman, so I just sigh—but the candle still burns till dawn, I simply can't get resigned to living this way. But how else should I live?"

Sitting on the edge of the bed, listening to her friend, Miss Maszkerádi folded her arms.

"In old Russian novels people asked such questions, behaving like cardboard characters...But today it's totally different. Novels only show you how to die. I don't even know who my father was. One thing for sure, he never thought of me. My mother had no way of knowing, either, that I would be here some day. I came into being and grew like an icicle under the eaves. This is why I'll never have a child. I just can't recommend this lifestyle for you, Eveline, although I know you want me to. Well, each to her own...suit on suit, heart to heart," mocked Miss Maszkerádi.

"Malvina, you'll never be happy," prophesied Eveline, speaking as if from the pages of some novel.

"I must always look within myself, for everything. I believe only in myself, and myself alone, and don't give a damn about others' opinions. I view each of my acts as if I were reading about it fifty years from now, in a newly found diary. Did I do something ridiculous and dumb? I ask myself each night when I close my eyes. I think over each word, each act: will I regret it, come tomorrow? I am my own judge and I judge myself as harshly as if I'd been lying in my grave these hundred years, my life a yellowed parchment diary, its end known in advance. I will not tolerate being laughed at or cheated. I want to know this very minute what I will think ten years from now about today, about today's weather and about this night...Will I have to be ashamed of some weakness or tenderness? Is there one circumstance worth disrupting my life for, rising an hour earlier, or using more words than usual? I try to modulate my decisions and my emotions by looking ahead and seeing whether I'd regret it tomorrow. And I'm never nervous, it's simply not worth it.

"Had I been born a man, I would have been a Talmudist, an Oriental sage, a scholar who delves into decaying millennial mysteries. Too bad, I was not admitted at the university. But if possible, I would still marry a great, gray-bearded, immensely wise rabbi or Oriental scholar. Possibly Schopenhauer... or my first teacher, Gyula Sámuel Spiegler, if that little old Jew were still alive... Oh, you won't catch me crying on account of rival women, actresses, danseuses! The hell with the strumpets! What do I care if my husband sometimes sees them? As long as they stay away from me with their dirt."

Eveline heard out these words of wisdom with eyes closed. All her life repelled by women of easy virtue, she still envisioned them to be like the first one she had ever seen, in her childhood in the Inner City, near her convent school. A fat, ungainly, wide-mouthed, coarsely painted towering idol of flesh that passed by with petticoats lifted, like a killer of men, cruelly smiling. The little schoolgirls had nightmares about this otherworldly monster who probably roamed the town to entice inexperienced men to her cave in the mountains where she would devour them like a dragon. Ever after, the educated, curious and clairvoyant young woman still imagined fallen women to be like that. (She was most amazed at the Pest racing turf one summer Sunday when she attended the St. Stephen's Cup races with her lady companion, and Kálmán pointed out from afar a gentle, unimpeachably clean-cut angel, all blonde English-style curls, as one of the city's most depraved creatures who spent her days in the company of elderly counts.)

Miss Maszkerádi, all her Talmudic wisdom notwithstanding, loved to refer to women of easy virtue as wondrous creatures who lived off their bodies. She preferred French novels that described life in brothels, and would have given much to clandestinely observe the goings-on at some sordid club one night. She was convinced that the best way to get to know a man was by witnessing his coarsest words and acts.

"Had I a father or brother, I would send them to accompany my would-be fiancé on a visit to the *filles de joie*. I'd want to know how my future life-companion acted, how he behaved there..." Miss

Maszkerádi insisted. "But I don't want to get married. Because then I'd have long ago become an expert in midwifery, and in all the seductive practices of loose women."

And on this childish note the wise Miss Maszkerádi closed the evening's proceedings. She went to bed in her room, smiling in quiet scorn at Eveline, who would listen all night long for the sound of footsteps coming and going around the house. She knew it was nothing but the spring wind fidgeting out there.

Translated from the Hungarian by John Bátki

SHUI LING
Qiu Miaojin

SHUI LING. Wenzhou Street. The white bench in front of the French bakery. The number 74 bus.

We sit at the back of the bus. Shui Ling and I occupy opposite window seats, the aisle between us. The December fog is sealed off behind glass. Dusk starts to set in around six, enshrouding Taipei. The traffic is creeping along Heping East Road. At the outer edge of the Taipei Basin, where the sky meets the horizon, is the last visible wedge of a bright orange sun whose radiance floods through the windows and spills onto the vehicles behind us, like the blessing of some mysterious force.

Silent, exhausted passengers pack the aisle, heads hung, bodies propped against the seats, oblivious. Through a gap in the curtain of their winter coats, I catch Shui Ling's eye, trying to contain the enthusiasm in my voice.

"Did you look outside?" I ask, ingratiatingly.

"Mmm," comes her barely audible reply.

Then silence. For a still moment, Shui Ling and I are sitting together in the hermetically sealed bus. Out the windows, dim silhouettes of human figures wind through the streets. It's a magnificent night scene, gorgeous and restrained. The two of us are content. We look happy. But underneath, there is already a strain of something dark, malignant. Just how bitter it would become, we didn't know.

In 1987, I broke free from the draconian university entrance-exam system and enrolled in college. People in this city are manufactured and canned, raised for the sole purpose of taking tests and making money. The eighteen-year-old me went through the high-grade production line and was processed in three years, despite the fact that I was pure carrion inside.

That fall, in October, I moved into a second-floor apartment on Wenzhou Street. The leaseholders were a married couple who had graduated a few years earlier. They gave me a room with a huge window overlooking an alley. The two rooms across from mine were rented by two sisters. The young married couple was always in the living room watching TV. They spent a fair amount of time on the coffee-colored sofa. "We got married our senior year," they told me, smiling. But most of the time, they didn't say a word. The sisters would spend all night in one of their rooms watching a different channel. Passing the door, you'd hear bits of lively conversation. I never saw my housemates unless I had to. Just came and went on my own. Everyone kept to themselves.

So despite the five of us living together under one roof, it might as well have been a home for the deaf.

I lived in solitude. Lived at night. I'd wake up at midnight and ride my bike—a red Giant—to a nearby store where I'd buy dried noodles, thick pork soup, and spring rolls. Then I'd come home and read while I ate. Take a shower, do laundry. In my room, there was neither the sound of another human being nor light. I'd write in my journal all night, or just read. I became obsessed with Kierkegaard and Schopenhauer. I devoured all kinds of books for tortured souls. Started collecting issues of the independence movement's weekly. Studied up on political game theory, an antidote to my spiritual reading. It made me feel like an outsider, which became my way of recharging. At the break of dawn, around six or seven, like a nocturnal creature afraid of the light, I'd finally lay my head—which by then was spilling over with thoughts—down onto the comforter.

That's how it went when things were good. Most of the time, however, I didn't eat a single thing all night. Didn't shower. Couldn't get out of bed. Didn't write in my journal or talk. Didn't read a single page or register the sound of another human being. All day long, I'd cry myself sick into my pillow. Sleep was just another luxury.

Didn't want anyone around. People were useless to me. Didn't need anyone. I started hurting myself and getting into all sorts of trouble.

Home was a credit-card bill footed by Nationalist Party voters. I didn't need to go back. Being in college gave me a sense of vocation. It exempted me from an oppressive system of social and personal responsibility—from going through the motions like a cog, from being whipped and beaten by everyone for not having worked hard enough and then having to put on a repentant face afterward. That system had already molded me into a flimsy, worthless shell. It drove my body to retreat into a self-loathing soul, and what's even scarier is that nobody knew or seemed to recognize it. My social identity was comprised of these two distinct, co-existing constructs. Each writhed toward me with its incessant demands—though when it came down to it, I spent more time getting to know my way around the super-market next door than I did getting comfortable in my own skin.

Didn't read the paper. Didn't watch TV. Didn't go to class—except for gym, because the teacher took attendance. Didn't go out and didn't talk to my roommates. The only time I ever spoke at all was in the evenings or afternoons at the Debate Society, where I would go to preen my feathers and practice social intercourse. All too soon I realized that I was an innately beautiful peacock and decided that I shouldn't let myself go. However lazy, a peacock still ought to give its feathers a regular preening, and having been bestowed with such a magnificent set, I couldn't help but seek the mainstream of society as a mirror. With that peacock swagger, I found it hard to resist in-dulging in a little strutting, but that's how it went, and it was a fundamentally bad habit.

The fact is, most people go through life without ever living. They say you have to learn how to construct a self who remains free in spite of the system. And you have to get used to the idea that it's every man for himself in this world. It requires a strange self-awareness, whereby everything down to the finest detail must be performed before the eyes of the world.

Since there's time to kill, you have to use boredom to get you to the other side. In English, you'd say: *Break on through.* That's more like it.

———

So she did me wrong. If my old motto was *I'm sentencing her to the guillotine*, my new motto contained a revelation: *The power to construct oneself is destiny.* If only it weren't for you, Shui Ling. In spite of everything, the truth is I still can't take it. I can't take it. Really, I can't. No matter how far I've come, it's never far enough. The pattern was already in place.

It must have been around October 1987. I was biking down Royal Palm Boulevard and passed somebody. I remembered it was their birthday. It was at that precise moment that all of my pent-up grief and fear hit me at once. I knew more or less that I'd been rejected and that was the bottom line. But somehow, I was convinced I had to get even.

She'd just turned twenty. I'd turned eighteen five months earlier. She and some friends from high school walked past me, and I managed to glance at her. But as for what significance that glance held, it was as if my whole life had flashed before my eyes. Though they were off in the distance, I could still feel the glow of her smile. It left me with the acute sense that she never failed to elicit the adoration and affection of others, that she was someone who radiated a pure, child-like contentment.

Even now I'm still in awe of her innate power to command such devotion—not only her charms but how it felt to be deprived of them. She maintained only a handful of friendships. In the past, the people around her had clung dearly to her, giving her their entire attention. She didn't need any more of that, but she didn't have much of a choice. She was trapped and suffocating. Whenever I was around her, I'd become clingy, too. If I wasn't by her side, I felt distant from other people, when in fact she was the one who was distant. That's how it worked. It was her natural gift.

I didn't see her my entire senior year of high school. I was careful to avoid her. Didn't dare take the initiative, though I longed for her to notice me in the crowd. An upperclassman and my senior, she was an ominous character, a black spade. To shuffle and draw the same card again would be even more ominous.

The lecture hall for Introduction to Chinese Literature was packed. I got there late and had to sheepishly lift my chair up higher than the rostrum and carry it all the way to the front row. The professor stopped lecturing, and all the other sheep turned and gawked at me and my antics.

Toward the end of class, someone passed a note from behind:

Hey, can I talk to you after class?

Shui Ling

She had sought me out. I knew it would happen. Even if I had switched to a different section, she would have sought me out all the same. She who hid in the crowd, who didn't want anyone to see her with her aloofness and averted eyes. When I stepped forward, she stepped out, too. And she had pointed with a child's wanton smile and said, "I want that one." There was no way I could refuse. And like a potted sunflower that had just been sold to a customer, I was taken away.

This, from a beautiful girl whom I was already deeply, viscerally attracted to. Things were getting good. There she was, standing right in front of me. She brushed the waves of hair away from her face with a seductiveness that painfully seared my heart like a tattoo. Her feminine radiance was overpowering. I was about to get knocked out of the ring. It was clear from that moment on, we'd never be equals. How could we, with me under the table, scrambling to summon a different me, the one she would worship and put on a pedestal? No way was I coming out.

"What are you doing here?" I was so anxious that I had to blurt something out. She didn't say a word or seem the least bit embarrassed.

"Did you switch to this section to make up a class?" She didn't look up at me. She just stood there, dragging one foot behind her in the hallway, and didn't say a thing, as if this one-sided conversation had nothing to do with her.

"How'd you know I switched?" Abruptly, she broke her silence. Her eyes were shimmering with amazement, and I could finally meet them. She was now looking right at me, wide-eyed.

"Well, of course I'd know!" I didn't want her to think I'd been noticing her. "You finally said something!" I said, heaving an exaggerated sigh of relief. She smiled at me shyly, even teasingly, and I let out a huge laugh, relieved that I'd made her smile. The glow on her face was like rays of sunshine along a golden beach.

She told me that she'd started to feel nervous as soon as I walked into the room. She wanted to talk to me, but didn't know what to say. I pointed to her shoelaces. She gingerly leaned forward to tie them. She said when she saw me, she couldn't bring herself to speak, and then she didn't want to say anything, so then she just stood there. She threw her purple canvas backpack over her shoulder and crouched on the floor. As she started talking, I felt the sudden urge to reach over and touch her long hair, which looked so soft and supple. You don't know a thing, but I figured it all out in an instant, I told her silently in my heart. I reached over and held her backpack instead, and feeling mildly contented by the closeness of its weight, wished that she would go on tying her shoes.

It was already six when class ended. Shadows had lengthened across the campus, and the evening breeze lilted in the air. We grabbed our bikes and headed off together. We took the main thoroughfare on campus, keeping with the leisurely pace of the traffic on the wide open road. I didn't know if I was following her, or if she was following me. Within a year, the two of us would come to cherish our ambiguous rapport, at once intimate and unfamiliar, and tempered by moments of silent confrontation.

"Why'd you come over and talk to me?" In my heart I already knew too much but pretended to know nothing.

"Why wouldn't I talk to you?" She sounded slightly irritated. The dusk obscured her face, so I couldn't read her expression. But as soon as she spoke, I could tell she'd had a tough freshman year. There was a curious note of dejection in her answer. I already knew her all too well.

"I'm just an underclassman you've seen, like, three times!" I nearly exploded.

"Not even," she said coolly to herself.

My eyes were fixed on her long skirt as it wafted in the breeze. "Weren't you worried that I wouldn't remember you, or wouldn't want to talk to you?"

"I knew you weren't like that." Her reaction was perfectly composed, as if everything to do with me was already set in stone.

We reached the school gates, not quite sure what to do next. She seemed to want to see where I lived. The way she suggested it conveyed a touch of familial kindness, like a tough but pliable cloth whose inner softness made my heart ache. Besides, as they say, if the flood-waters are rushing straight toward you, what are you going to do to stop them? This was how she treated me, for no apparent reason. I took her toward Xinsheng South Road, back to Wenzhou Street.

"How's this year going?" I tried to break through her gloom.

"I don't want to talk about it." She squeezed her eyes shut and grimaced slightly, lifting her chin in a hopeless look.

"You don't want to tell me?" I was practically edging her onto the road. I was sure she was going to get hit by a car.

She shook her head. "I don't want to tell anyone."

"How did you get this way?" It pained my heart to hear her speak such nonsense.

"Yeah, well, I've changed." Her eyes flickered with haughtiness, underscoring the boldness of her statement.

Her answer was so immature that I felt tempted to tease her. "Into what?"

"I've just changed, that's all. I'm not the same person I was in high school." I could detect a note of self-hatred in the viciousness of her tone.

Hearing those words, "I've changed," made me truly sad. The traffic had illuminated Xinsheng South Road in an opulent yellow. We followed the red brick wall that enclosed the school grounds, pausing to lean against a railing. To our left were the city streets, whose bright lights seemed to be calling. To our right was the dimly lit campus, teeming with the splendors of solitude. There's nothing that won't change, do you understand? I said in my heart. "Can you count the number of lights that are on in that building over there?" I pointed to a brand-new high-rise at the intersection.

"Uh, I see lights in five windows, so maybe, like, five?" she said brightly.

Just wait and see how many there are later on. Will you still remember? I asked myself, answering with a nod.

The first semester she was my lifeline. It was a clandestine form of dating—the kind where the person you're going out with doesn't know it's a date. I denied myself, and I denied the fact that she was part of my life, so much so that I denied the dotted line that connected the two of us and our entire relationship to a crime. But the eye of suspicion had been cast upon me from the very beginning, and this extraordinary eye reached all the way back to my adolescence. My hair started to go gray early. Life ahead was soon supplanted by a miserable prison sentence. It was as if I never really had a youth. Nonetheless, I was determined at all costs to become a person who would love without boundaries. And so I locked myself and that eye together in a dark closet.

Every Sunday night, however, I was forced to think about her. It was like a chore I dreaded. I'd resolve not to go to Intro to Chinese

Lit, and every Monday I would sleep in until almost three, waking up just in time to rush to class on my bike. Every Monday after class, Shui Ling would follow me matter-of-factly back to Wenzhou Street, as if she were merely passing by on her way home. Afterward, I'd wait with her for the number 74 bus. There was a bench in front of the French bakery. Our secret little rendezvous were tidy and simple. They were executed with the casual deftness of a high-class burglary: bribing the guards with one hand, feeding a criminal appetite with the other.

The rest of the week, we barely spoke. She was an apparition seen only on Mondays. On Mondays, she would appear like the answer to a dying man's prayers—roses in hand, draped in white muslin, barefoot and floating, come to grant me a reprieve. In a primal mating dance, eyes closed in rapture, she scattered rose petals into the wilderness. Roses every week and she didn't even know it, and it was amid roses that it seemed I might live after all. I reached for those roses, and for a new life, only to discover a glass wall. When I extended my hand, so did my reflection. When Monday ended, the glass that stood between me and my reflection thickened.

The room on Wenzhou Street. Elegant maroon wallpaper and yellow curtains. What did I even talk to her about in there? She sat on the floor, in the gap between the foot of the wooden bed frame and the wardrobe, with her back to me, almost silent. I talked nonstop. Most of the time it was just me talking. Talking about whatever. Talking about my horrible, painful life experiences. Talking about every person I'd ever gotten entangled with and couldn't let go of. Talking about my own complexities, my own eccentricities. She was always playing with something in her hands. She would look up at me in disbelief and ask what was so hard to understand about this or what was so strange about that. She accepted me, which amounted to negating my negation of myself. Those sincere eyes, like a mirror, hurt me. But she accepted me. In my anguish, about every third sentence out of my mouth was: *You don't understand.* Her eyes were suffused with a profound and translucent light, like the ocean gazing at me in silence, as if it were not necessary to speak at all. *You don't understand.* She thought she understood. And she accepted me. Years later, I realized that had been the whole point.

Those wrenching eyes, which could lift up the entire skeleton of my being. How I longed for myself to be subsumed into the ocean of her eyes. How the desire, once awakened, would come to scald me at every turn. The strength in those eyes offered a bridge to the outside world. The scarlet mark of sin and my deep-seated fear of abandonment had given way to the ocean's yearning.

———

I am a woman who loves women. The tears I cry, they spring from a river and drain across my face like yolk.

My time was gradually consumed by tears. The whole world loves me, but what does it matter since I hate myself? Humanity stabs a bayonet into a baby's chest, fathers produce daughters that they pull into the bathroom to rape, handicapped midgets drag themselves onto highway overpasses to announce that they're about to end it all just to collect a little spare change, and mental patients have irrepressible hallucinations and suicidal urges. How can the world be this cruel? A human being has only so much in them, and yet you must learn through experience, until you finally reach the maddening conclusion that the world wrote you off a long time ago, or accept the prison sentence that your crime is your existence. And the world keeps turning as if nothing had happened. The forced smiles on the faces of the lucky ones say it all: It's either this, or getting stabbed in the chest with a bayonet, getting raped, dragging yourself onto the highway overpass, or checking into a mental institution. No one will ever know about your tragedy, and the world eluded its responsibility ages ago. All that you know is that you've been crucified for something, and you're going to spend the rest of your life feeling like no one and nothing will help you, that you're in it alone. Your individual circumstances, which separate you from everyone else, will keep you behind bars for life. On top of it all, humanity tells me I'm lucky. Privilege after privilege has been conferred upon me, and if I don't seem content with my lot, they'll be devastated.

Shui Ling, please don't knock on my door anymore. You don't know how dark it is here in my heart. I don't know who I am at all. What's ahead of me is unclear, yet I must move forward. I don't want to become myself. I know the answer to the riddle, but I can't stand to have it revealed. The first time I saw you, I knew I would fall in love with you. That my love would be wild, raging, and passionate, but also illicit. That it could never develop into anything, and instead, it would split apart like pieces of a landslide. As flesh and blood, I was not distinct. You turned me into my own key, and when you did, my fears seized me in a flood of tears that soon abated. I stopped hating myself and discovered the corporeal me.

She didn't understand. Didn't understand she could love me, maybe that she already did love me. Didn't understand that beneath the hide of a lamb was a demonic beast that had to suppress the urge to rip her to shreds. Didn't understand that love, every little bit of it, was about exchange. Didn't understand that she caused me suffering. Didn't understand that love was like that.

She gave me a puzzle in a box. She put the pieces together patiently, one by one, and completed the picture of me.

Translated from the Chinese by Bonnie Huie

CHORAL ODE FROM *HIPPOLYTOS*

Euripides

CHORUS (*first stasimon*)
   Eros, Eros, deep down the eyes
   you distill longing,
      sliding
   sweet pleasure
         into the soul where you make war:
   I pray you never come at me with evil,
         break my measure.
   No weapon,
     not fire,
       not stars,
         has more power
         than Aphrodite's
     shot from the hands
   of Eros, child of Zeus.

   In vain, in vain, beside Apollo's river
   and his shrine
     do Greeks
   slaughter oxen.
         Yet that tyrant god who has the key
   to Aphrodite's chambers of love,
         that god Eros
   we do not worship,
     though he plunders

mortal men
and sends them
through all
manner of misfortune
when he comes.

Wild little horse of Oichalia
unbroken in bed,
never yoked to a man,
never yoked to marriage,
from her father's house,
like a running naiad,
like a girl gone mad,
in blood,
in smoke,
in a wedding of murder,
to Herakles
Aphrodite yoked her,
Aphrodite gave her,
O
bride of sorrow!

O holy wall of Thebes,
O river mouth of Dirke,
you too could bear witness
how Aphrodite comes on.
To flaming thunder
she gave Semele
as a bride
and laid
the girl to bed
in bloody death.
Aphrodite's breath is felt
on everything there is.

Then like a bee
she
flicks away.

Translated from the Ancient Greek by Anne Carson

CHARLOTTE
François-René de Chateaubriand

ABOUT four leagues from Beccles, in a small village called Bungay, there lived an English clergyman, the reverend Mr. Ives, a great Hellenist and mathematician. He had a still young wife, charming in her person, her mind, and her manner, and an only daughter, who was fifteen.* Having been introduced into this household, I was more warmly welcomed there than anywhere else. We drank together in the old English fashion, Mr. Ives and I, staying at table for two hours after the women had withdrawn. This man, who had seen America, loved telling tales of his travels, hearing the story of mine, and talking about Newton and Homer. His daughter, who had studied hard to please him, was an excellent musician, and she sang as well as Madame Pasta sings today.† She would reappear at teatime and charm away the old parson's infectious drowsiness. Leaning on the end of the piano, I would listen to Miss Ives in silence.

When the music was over, the young lady questioned me about France and literature; she asked me to draw up courses of study. She especially wanted to acquaint herself with the Italian authors, and begged me to give her some notes on the *Divina Commedia* and the *Gerusalemme*. Little by little, I began to feel the timid charm of an affection that springs from the soul. I had bedecked the Floridians with flowers, but I would not have dared to pick up Miss Ives's glove.

---

*Charlotte, born March 9, 1781, was sixteen or seventeen years old at the time.
†Madame (Giuditta) Pasta (1797–1865) was an Italian opera singer.

I felt embarrassed when I tried to translate a few passages of Tasso: I was more at ease when I turned my hand to Dante, a genius more masculine and chaste.

Charlotte Ives's age and mine were in concord. Something melancholy enters into relationships not formed until the middle of our lives. If two people do not meet in the prime of youth, the memories of the beloved are not mixed in the portion of days when we breathed without knowing her, and these days, which belong to other companions, are painful to recall and, as it were, severed from our present existence. Is there a disproportion of age? Then the drawbacks increase. The older one began his life before the younger one was born, and the younger one, in turn, is destined to live on alone; the one walked in solitude on the far side of the cradle, and the other shall walk in solitude on the near side of the grave. The past was a desert for the first, and the future shall be a desert for the second. It is difficult to love with all the conditions of happiness, youth, beauty, and opportunity, and with a harmony of heart, taste, character, graces, and years.

Having taken a fall from my horse, I stayed some time in Mr. Ives's house. It was winter, and the dreams of my life began to flee in the face of reality. Miss Ives became more reserved. She stopped bringing me flowers, and she no longer wanted to sing.

If someone had told me that I would spend the rest of my life in obscurity at the hearth of this isolated family, I would have died of joy. Love needs nothing but continuance to be at once Eden before the Fall and a Hosanna without end. Make beauty stay, youth last, and the heart never grow weary, and you shall re-create heaven on earth. Love is so much the supreme happiness, it is haunted always by the illusion of infinitude. It wishes to make only irrevocable promises. In the absence of its joys, it attempts to eternalize its sorrows. A fallen angel, it still speaks the language it spoke in the incorruptible abode, and its hope is never to die. In its double nature and its double illusion here below, it aspires to perpetuate itself by immortal thoughts and unending generations.

I foresaw with some dismay the moment when I would be obliged to leave. On the eve of my departure, dinner was a gloomy affair. To my great surprise, Mr. Ives withdrew after dessert, taking his daughter with him, and I remained alone with Mrs. Ives. She was extremely embarrassed. I suspected she was going to reproach me for an inclination that she must have long since guessed, but of which I had never spoken a word. She looked at me, lowered her eyes, and blushed. She herself was, in her discomfort, quite seductive: there was no feeling she could have failed to inspire in me. At long last, making an effort to overcome the obstacle that prevented her from speech, she said to me, in English: "Sir, you have seen my confusion: I do not know if Charlotte pleases you, but it is impossible to deceive a mother. My daughter has certainly become attached to you. Mr. Ives and I have discussed the matter. You suit us in every respect and we believe you would make our daughter happy. You no longer have a native country, you have just lost your family, and your property has been sold. What could possibly take you back to France? Until you inherit from us, you can live with us, here."

Of all the painful things that I had endured, this was the greatest and most wounding. I threw myself on my knees at Mrs. Ives's feet and covered her hands with kisses and tears. She thought I was weeping with happiness and started sobbing with joy. She stretched out her arm to pull the bell-rope and called out to her husband and her daughter.

"Stop!" I cried. "I am married!"

Mrs. Ives fell back in a faint.

I left and set out on foot without returning to my room. When I reached Beccles, I caught the mail coach for London, after having written a letter to Mrs. Ives. I regret I did not keep a copy.

I have retained the sweetest, most tender, and most grateful recollection of these events. Before my name was known far and wide, Mr. Ives's family were the only people to take an interest in me and the only ones to welcome me with sincere affection. When I was poor, unknown, outcast, without beauty or allure, they offered me a definite future, a country, an enchanting wife to draw me out of my shell, a mother almost equal to her daughter in beauty to take the place of my own aged mother, and a well-educated father who loved and cultivated literature to replace the father whom Heaven had taken from me. What did I have to offer in recompense for all that? No illusions could have entered into their choice of me; I had a right to believe myself loved. Since that time, I have met with only one attachment lofty enough to inspire me with the same confidence.* As for the interest which was shown in me later, I have never been able to sort out whether external causes—the fracas of fame and the prestige of parties, the glamour of high literary and political status—were not a cloak that drew such eagerness around me.

I see now that, had I married Charlotte Ives, my role on earth would have changed. Buried in a county of Great Britain, I would have become a gentleman *chasseur* and not a single line would have issued from my pen. I might even have forgotten my language, for I could write in English and even the thoughts in my head were beginning to take form in English. Would my country have lost so much by my disappearance? If I could set aside what has consoled me, I would say that I might already have counted up many days of calm, instead of the many troubled days fallen to my lot. What would the Empire, the Restoration, and all the other divisions and quarrels of France have meant to me? I wouldn't have had to palliate failings and combat errors every morning of my life. Is it even certain that I have real talent: a talent worth all the sacrifices of my life? Will I survive my tomb? And if I do live beyond the grave, given the transformations that are even now taking place, in a world changed and occupied by entirely different things, will there be a public there to hear me? Will I not be a man of another time, unintelligible to the new generations? Will my ideas, my feelings, my very style not seem boring and old-fashioned to a sneering posterity? Will my shade be able to say, as Virgil's did to Dante: *Poeta fui e cantai*? "I was a poet and I sang."†

Translated from the French by Alex Andriesse

*Madame Récamier.
†Dante's *Inferno*, Canto 1, line 74.

ETHICS AND AESTHETICS

THE CHINESE LESSON

Simon Leys

IN THE catalogue of an individual retrospective held a year and a half ago at the Stedelijk Museum in Amsterdam, there is a striking statement by the painter to whose memory the exhibition was devoted. At a crucial turning point in his career, the artist in question sent a batch of recent paintings to a friend and explained to him: "The next lot has to be better and I just don't feel capable of being better yet . . . I have the awful problem now of being a better person before I can paint better."

No, it wasn't a Chinese scholar-painter from another century who wrote these lines. It was in fact Colin McCahon (1919–87), an important New Zealand painter of our age. The author of the catalogue, Murray Bail—a true connoisseur of Western art—in quoting this statement could not hide his puzzlement: can one imagine Michelangelo or Rubens, Ingres or Delacroix, Matisse or Picasso making such an extraordinary statement?

For traditional Chinese aesthetes, on the other hand, such a notion goes without saying, and McCahon was doing little more than repeating a truth which, in their eyes, should be obvious to any serious artist. How the self-taught New Zealand painter, locked away in the isolation of his far-off land, had come to develop, without realising it, such a "Chinese" view remains an enigma which we will not try to elucidate here. We will simply note that he read a great deal and that since the middle of the twentieth century, numerous philosophical and aesthetic elements of Chinese and Japanese thought have been filtering into Western consciousness via countless works of vulgarisation, indeed even best-selling novels. Remember, for example, Robert

Pirsig and his famous *Zen and the Art of Motorcycle Maintenance* (an astonishing best-seller in the '70s, the book, even today, retains its freshness and originality; it bears re-reading): "You want to know how to paint a perfect painting? It's easy. Make yourself perfect, and then just paint naturally."

As they are the products of our common human nature, it is quite normal that all the great civilisations should cultivate values that are basically similar, but they go about it in different ways and without necessarily attaching to them the same importance. What one may consider a basic axiom, regard as fundamental and embrace as a tenet may appear in the other only as a brilliant intuition, grasped by a few exceptional individuals.

This idea that the aesthetic quality of the work of art reflects the ethical quality of its author is so essential to Chinese thought that it sometimes runs the risk of becoming an oft-repeated cliché whose meaning can end up being distorted through mechanical and simplistic application. In the West, on the other hand, though not entirely unheard of, this same notion rarely undergoes methodical development. Thus Vasari, for example, can quite naturally point to a link between the spiritual beauty of Fra Angelico's painting and the saintliness that characterised his monastic existence, but, by the same token, it would hardly occur to him to attribute the artistic shortcomings of other works to the moral failings of their authors.

China's four major arts—poetry, calligraphy, painting (in ink, by means of a calligraphic brush) and music for *qin* (seven-stringed zither)—are practised not by professionals but by amateurs belonging to the scholarly class. Traditionally, these various disciplines could not be performed as a profession: an artist who would accept payment for his art would disqualify himself and see himself immediately reduced to the inferior condition of artisan. Although the poet, musician, calligrapher and painter (and quite often the same man is all of these at once) may let connoisseurs or a few chosen friends enjoy gratis the products of their art (sometimes, also, it is this limited but talented public that fires their inspiration), the fact remains that the prime aim of their activity is the cultivation and development of their own inner life. One writes, one paints, one plays the zither in order to perfect one's character, to attain moral fulfilment by ensuring that one's individual humanity is in harmony with the rhythms of universal creation.

The Chinese aesthetic, which, in the field of literary, calligraphic, pictorial and musical theories has produced a wealth of philosophical, critical and technical literature, developed without making any reference to the concept of "beauty" (*mei*; the term *meixue*, "study of beauty," is a modern one, especially coined to translate the Western notion of aesthetics). When this concept crops up it is often in a pejorative sense, since to strive for beauty is, for an artist, a vulgar temptation, a trap, a dishonest attempt at seduction. Aesthetic criteria are functional: does the work do what it does efficiently, does it nourish the vital energy of the artist, does it succeed in capturing the spirit that informs mountains and rivers, does it establish harmony between the metamorphoses of forms and the metamorphoses of the world?

But even as he is creating his work, it is always and essentially on himself that the artist is working. If one realises this, one can understand the meaning and *raison d'être* behind the numerous statements and precepts which, through the ages, constantly associate the artistic quality of the painting with the moral quality of the painter. One could give any number of examples: "If the man is of high moral quality, this will inevitably be reflected in the rhythm and spirit of his painting"; "the qualities and flaws of the painting reflect the moral superiority or mediocrity of the man"; "he who is of inferior moral worth would not be able to paint"; "those who learn painting put the development of their moral self above all else"; "the painting of those who have succeeded in building this moral self breathes with a deep and dazzling sense of rectitude, transcending all formal aspects. But if the painter lacks this quality, his paintings, charming as they may superficially appear, will give out a kind of unwholesome breath which will be obvious in the merest brushstroke. The work reflects the man: it is true in literature and it is just as true in painting."

But some critics have gone even further and have tried to identify in the works of famous artists either the expression of particular virtues they have shown in their lives or a reflection of their moral failings. For instance, the eighteenth-century scholar-poet Zhang Geng wrote:

> What a man writes presents a reflection of his heart, allowing one to perceive his vices and virtues. Painting, which comes from the same source as writing, also holds up a mirror to the heart. In the beginning, whenever I looked at the paintings of the Ancients, I still doubted the soundness of this opinion, but after studying the lives of the painters, I venture to say that it is correct. Indeed, if we look at the different artists of the Yuan period (that is to say a period of national humiliation, under the Mongol occupation) we see Ni Zan had broken all ties with the ordinary, everyday world, and his painting is also characterised by a severe austerity and a detached elegance stripped of all ornamentation. Zhao Mengfu, on the other hand, could not resist temptation (he collaborated with the invaders) and his calligraphy, like his painting, is tainted with prettiness and a vulgar desire to please . . .

This last passage, contrasting two emblematic figures—Ni Zan and Zhao Mengfu—opens a dangerous trend in criticism: the deep meaning of an ethical reading of the work of art is lost only to be replaced by a sort of narrow and dogmatic "political correctness." There is no doubt that the art of Ni Zan is sublime—a limpid and distant vision of pale, empty landscapes, cleansed of all worldly blemishes—but very little is known about the historical person Ni Zan himself, and the anecdotes attesting to his purity and his detachment could well be no more, on the whole, than an imaginary projection of the virtues suggested by his paintings. The case of Zhao Mengfu is even more curious: an aristocrat who agreed to put himself at the service of the Mongol invaders, he was traditionally regarded by posterity as a vile traitor, but the problem is that, in his painting and especially in his calligraphy, he also proves himself a prodigiously talented artist. In order to resolve this embarrassing contradiction, it is conventional for critics generally to choose to condemn, despite the evidence before their eyes, the "vulgarity" of his overly splendid calligraphy (a judgement that tends to bring to mind the famous condemnation pronounced by the Surrealists against Paul Claudel: "One cannot be French ambassador and poet"—as if Claudel hadn't been both one and the other!).

But even such naïve and simplistic rantings have failed to affect the deep understanding the great Chinese artists have always retained regarding this ethical dimension of their work. And the calligraphers, in particular, are all the more conscious of it, since the practice of their art constitutes for them a daily asceticism, a genuine hygiene of their whole physical, psychic and moral being, whose efficacy they themselves can measure in an immediate and concrete fashion. Moreover, in this sense calligraphy is not just the product of their character—their character itself becomes a product of their calligraphy. This reversal of the "graphological causality" has been noted by Jean-François Billeter in his *Art chinois de l'écriture*, and he has supported his observation with aptly chosen quotations. The supreme beauty of a piece of calligraphy indeed does not depend on beauty. It results from its natural appropriateness to the "truth" that the calligrapher nurtures within himself—authenticity, original purity, absolute naturalness (what the Germans call *Echtheit*): "In calligraphy, it is not pleasing that is difficult; what is difficult is not seeking to please. The desire to please makes the writing trite, its absence renders it ingenuous and true," wrote the calligrapher Liu Xizai, quoted by Billeter, who further illustrates these words with a statement by Stendhal: "I believe that to be great in anything at all, you must be yourself."

In fact to invoke Stendhal in this context strikes me as particularly interesting. The perfection of the work of art depends entirely on the true human worth of the artist; this moral notion at the basis of all Chinese aesthetics is found also in the West, but here it is more the mark of a few exceptional minds, of which Stendhal is a perfect example. His whole aesthetic sense is passionately and furiously moral—

remember for example his condemnation of Chateaubriand: "I have never been able to read twenty pages of Chateaubriand . . . At seventeen I almost had a duel because I made fun of *la cime indéterminée des forêts* which had many admirers in the 6th Dragoons . . . M. de Chateaubriand's fine style seems to me to tell a lot of little fibs. My whole belief in style lies in this word." In this same spiritual family of geniuses both sublime and "eccentric" (in the Chinese sense of the word), we must also include Simone Weil (a whole aesthetic could be constructed from the rich mine of her *Cahiers*)—or again Wittgenstein, one of whose statements seems to me particularly appropriate as a conclusion to this little article, for indeed it proposes a criterion for literary criticism that is as original as it is effective (speaking of Tolstoy): "There is a real man, who has a *right* to write."

2004

A TALK WITH GEORGE JACKSON

Jessica Mitford

THE IDEA of interviewing George Jackson about his writing occurred to me last autumn when I read *Soledad Brother*, his remarkable
and moving collection of prison letters. Although I had never done
an author interview, I have read many and know roughly how they
go: "When do you do your best work?" "At dusk, in a Paris bistro,
over a glass of Pernod." "What childhood influences shaped your
literary tastes?" "My parents' home was a gathering place for the
foremost writers of the day...."

But authors are sometimes elusive and this one, through no wish
of his own, proved exceptionally so. Prison walls, I soon discovered,
are not only to keep convicts in but to keep reporters out. After
months of frustrating and fruitless negotiations with prison officials,
who refused to permit the interview, Jackson's lawyer, at his request,
secured a court order for my visit.

George Jackson, now aged twenty-nine, has been in prison almost
continuously since he was fifteen. Seven of those years were spent in
solitary confinement. In his introduction to *Soledad Brother*, Jean
Genêt calls it "a striking poem of love and combat," and says the letters "perfectly articulate the road traveled by their author—first the
rather clumsy letters to his mother and his brother, then letters to his
lawyer which become something extraordinary, half-poem, half-essay,
and then the last letters, of an extreme delicacy...." What was that
road, and what kind of person is the author?

As to the latter question, the San Quentin guard in charge of
visitors undertook to enlighten me. "We have to set up this interview
for you," he said. "You'll be seeing Jackson in the attorney's room.

Now we suggest posting a guard in the room for your protection. He's an extremely dangerous, desperate man, liable to try *anything*." I replied, a trifle stiffly, that I preferred a private interview as specified in the court order. "Then we can post a guard by the window—he won't hear the conversation, but he'll be able to look through and see everything that goes on." No thanks. "We can erect a heavy wire screen between you and the prisoner?" No wire screen, thank you. Thus my interlocutor unwittingly acted out for my benefit the most pervasive cliché in all prisondom: "They treat the convicts like caged animals."

Jackson's appearance surprised me in two respects: unlike other prisoners I have met, whose stooped, impoverished physique attests to their long years of confinement, he has the bearing of an athlete. Nor does he affect the stony, ungiving glare of so many of his black revolutionary contemporaries on the outside; on the contrary, he came forward with both hands outstretched, face wreathed in smiles, and exclaimed, "How wonderful to see you!"

I had been warned by no less an authority than Alex Haley, author of *The Autobiography of Malcolm X*, that it is extremely difficult to get political, revolutionary people to talk about themselves. This proved true in Jackson's case. From a long discussion, ranging across the globe and over the centuries, I distilled the following "author interview":

Q. What time of day do you do your writing?
A. I don't stick to any regimen. I generally get two or three hours of sleep a day, six hours of exercise, and the rest reading and writing.

[In the letters, Jackson describes the exercises possible in his tiny solitary cell: "One thousand fingertip push-ups a day. I probably have the world's record on push-ups completed. . . ."]

Q. Do you get a certain number of hours of writing in each day?
A. Of course. After my six and three, I write. At present I'm engaged

in a study of the working-class movement here in the United States and an in-depth investigation of history of the last fifty years, when Fascism swept the Western world. I split my writing time between that and correspondence with people I love.

Q. Do you revise much?

A. I write strictly off the top of my head. I don't go over it because I haven't time.

Q. What about writing equipment? I noticed that the letter you sent me was written with a very stubby pencil.

A. That's all they allow you. I have thirty pencils in my cell right now. But keeping them sharp—the complication is I have to ask the pigs to sharpen them.

Q. Yes, I see. But do they sharpen them?

A. Sometimes yes, sometimes no, depending on whim.

Q. Typewriters are not allowed?

A. No, of course not. There's metal in typewriters.

Q. Your book has been hailed here and in Europe as a superb piece of writing. How did you become such a good writer?

A. You've got to understand that I'm from the lumpen, that every part came real hard. I spend a lot of time with the dictionary. I spend forty-five minutes a day learning new words. I'll read, and I'll come across words that I'm not familiar with. I record them on a piece of paper, in a notebook I have laying beside me. I look them up in a dictionary and familiarize myself with the entire meaning.

Q. Were there any problems about sending out the original letters to your family that make up the bulk of *Soledad Brother*?

A. The letters that went to the family had to go through the censor, of course, and they were all watered down. Three-fourths of the letters were returned. There's a rule here stipulating one cannot make criticisms of the institution or society in general.*

Q. What's the mechanism for censorship of letters? It starts with the guard, right?

A. They go through about three censorships. The first one is the unit officer who picks the mail up. He reads them. Then they go to the mail room and a couple of people over there read them. And in special cases—when it was a question of whether I was attacking the institution or the social system—they go from the mail room to the Warden or the Assistant Warden, and he reads them. Every one of my letters has been photostated or Xeroxed, and placed in my central file folder.

Q. If the warden decides he doesn't want a letter to go out, does it come back to you with notations, or what?

A. Either that or they'll just put it in my file and I'll never hear anything else about it.

Q. In other words, you eventually find out from the person you wrote it to that it was never received?

A. That's all.

Q. In *Soledad Brother* you describe your grandfather, the stories and allegories he made up to tell you. Did anyone else stimulate your imagination as a child?

A. Well, my mother. She had bourgeois ideas, but she did help me. I can't give all the credit to my grandfather, Papa Davis. My mother had a slightly different motivation than my grandfather. Her idea, you know, was to assimilate me through the general training of a

*In January 1970, Jackson's lawyers secured an injunction prohibiting the authorities from tampering with prisoners' letters to them, which explains those letters in *Soledad Brother* described by Genêt as "a call to rebellion."

black bourgeois. Consequently, her whole presentation to me was read, read, read. "Don't be like those niggers." We had a terrible conflict, she and I. Of course I wanted a life on the street with guys on the block and she wanted me to sit on the couch and read. We lived in a three-story duplex and the only way out was through the kitchen. It was well guarded by Big Mama. I'd throw my coat out the window and volunteer to carry out the garbage and she wouldn't see me any more for a couple of days. But while I was home, Mom made me read.

Q. What books did she give you?
A. *Black Boy*, by Richard Wright, was one. All of her life she had the contradictions of black people living in this country. She favored W. E. B. Du Bois. She tried to get me interested in black intellectualism with overtones of integration. When I was twelve or thirteen, I'd read maybe two books a week, also newspapers and periodicals.

Q. Can you think back and remember a favorite book you read as a child?
A. Strangely enough, *The Red and the Black*. I read that when I was about thirteen. I got a deep, let's say, understanding of some of the degenerate, contradictory elements of Western culture from reading *The Red and the Black*.

Q. What about reading in prison? In your book you mention reading Sabatini and Jack London.
A. I was about fifteen in Paso Robles [Youth Authority facility] when I read those light things. I like Sabatini. Sabatini is fabulous. I read Shakespeare, Sabatini, Jack London with my bathrobe on. I played dummy. Went along with what they told me to do; pretended I was hard of hearing, an absent-minded bookworm, an idiot. And I got by with it. I've read *thousands* of books. Of course years ago I read Dostoevski's *Crime and Punishment*, but mainly my interests are economics and political economy.

Q. What are the books that you'd say impressed you most of all?

A. A brother gave me a copy of Engels' *Anti-Dühring*.

Q. About what year—how old would you have been then?

A. It was in '61. I struggled with that, it took me three months. The same brother gave me a copy of the *Communist Manifesto*. Then I went deep into such things as William J. Pomeroy—*The Forest*, *On Resistance*. And then Nkrumah. And do you know who I was really impressed with, although he isn't a Socialist or a Communist? I was impressed with Henry George's stuff. I've read all his stuff.

Q. Oh, really? His theories of economics?

A. Yes. His single-tax idea is not correct. But I like his presentation— I like the explanation he advanced explaining how the ruling class over the years managed through machinations to rob and despoil the people.

Q. What particular books are you reading for your historical study?

A. *The Nature of Fascism*, edited by Woolf; and then Wilhelm Reich's *Mass Psychology of Fascism*. That's a beautiful book. I think it should be required reading for all of us, and there's one statement in there that appeals to me in a very, very, very significant way. It goes like this: "Man is biologically sick."

Q. What about black poetry, fiction, biography?

A. Poetry is not my bag. Not my medium. I have no sense of poetry at all. You know, the formalistic meter-type poetry. But I like some of the Langston Hughes stuff. Nice old guy. I like some of his stuff. Of course, I read the outstanding poems—and I've quoted them, such as the one that arose out of the riot written by Claude McKay. I like such things as "Invictus." But as a student of poetry—no.

Q. What black biographies have you read?

A. Malcolm's, of course. And let me think. Several. I've had Wright's stuff. And—what's his name?—Little skinny guy. James Baldwin.

Q. Now, since the book has been published, who do you feel you have reached with this book; what do you think the effect has been on readers?

A. Well, I have mixed opinions, mixed emotions about the whole thing. But one strange thing has evolved out of the whole incident: it seems that parts of the book appeal to the right-wing blacks and parts appeal to the left. I've had letters of commendation from a hundred different sects that represent the whole black political spectrum from right to left. So there's parts in there that the progressive left, black left, can relate to. I've gotten letters from black people eight feet tall, celebrities, entertainers, et cetera.

Q. What were the prisoners' reactions?

A. Well, the prisoners accepted it, of course. They loved it, especially the sections near the end. Well, you know we're all considered trapped in here, without voice, and they seem to be gratified that one of us had the opportunity to express himself. For one, you understand we're an oppressed people. And that events like that, you know, a prisoner getting a book published, getting ideas across, speaking for them, speaking for us—all that's appreciated.

Q. Did the guards ever say anything to you about the book?

A. Well, you have a difference of character, a character difference. Some laughed and said, "I'm reading, I'm learning about myself," and then there are others that look at me with daggers in their eyes. And it's pretty clear that what they're saying is that "First chance I get, nigger, I'm going to kill you." They're saying, "Look, we have a mutual understanding." When I use the word "pig," one officer will take it as a terrible, terrible attack on him, whereas another will laugh.

Q. When Greg Armstrong [senior editor at Bantam Books] presented you with the first copy of your book on the day it was published, it was immediately confiscated by a guard, is that true?

A. True. Later on my lawyers raised a fuss and they finally let me have a hardback and softback copy. But without the fuss, I'd never have gotten them.

Q. Is your book available in the prison library at the present time?
A. No. The publisher sent a hundred copies to the prison library. The librarian distributed the books, but one month later, after the officials had read the book, they started confiscating it, so now it's underground. It's being picked up by the search-and-destroy squad. They invade the cells and look for contraband. It's considered contraband, but there's copies circulating around, underground. Now I'm locked up, but that's the way I heard it.

[I checked with Officer McHenry, librarian at San Quentin. He told me the prison had received thirty-five copies of *Soledad Brother*, they were checked out immediately to inmates who wanted to read them, there was never any censorship of the book so far as he knew. The mystery was further compounded by Jackson's lawyer, John Thorne, who told me his copy of *Soledad Brother* was taken from his briefcase by a guard and held as contraband when he went to visit his client— what is the truth of the matter? With Jackson locked up, and me locked out, we can each but report what we are told.]

Q. Now, at the time of publication Greg Armstrong flew out here for the customary publisher's champagne party—which, in this case, was held at the gates of San Quentin. What did the prisoners think about that?
A. They love that sort of thing. You know, after years of isolation, all of a sudden to find out that people really are interested in you and that people can relate to you in spite of the fact that sociology books call us antisocial and brand us as criminals, when actually the criminals are in the *Social Register*—well, we did relate to that, to the whole incident.

COMMENT

At the time of this interview I was deep in my book on prisons, *Kind and Usual Punishment*. The year before, I had published an article in the *Atlantic* about the California prison system, which had achieved a considerable underground circulation among the inmates. George Jackson, who for good reason had in general a deep mistrust of journalists and who thus far had rebuffed their efforts to interview him, had read the piece and sent word through his lawyer that he would welcome an interview by me.

I knew something of the prison administrators' opinion of Jackson from a confidential memorandum by L. H. Fudge, Associate Superintendent of a California prison camp, that was mailed to me in a plain envelope by—a convict trustee? A disaffected prison staff member? I shall never know. The memorandum might, I suppose, pass for what publishers' advertising departments call "a selling review" of *Soledad Brother*: "This book provides remarkable insight into the personality makeup of a highly dangerous sociopath.... This type individual is not uncommon in several of our institutions. Because of his potential and the growing numbers, it is imperative that we in Corrections know as much as we can about his personality makeup and are able to correctly identify his kind.... This is one of the most self-revealing and insightful books I have ever read concerning a criminal personality."

Among the prison officials quoted at length in my *Atlantic* article was James Park, Associate Warden at San Quentin—he had not, I gathered, been pleased with the piece nor with my rendition of his conversation. It was to him that I was obliged to apply for permission to interview Jackson, refused until Jackson's lawyer obtained a court order compelling Park to allow my visit.

When the court order came through, I telephoned Park to make arrangements for the interview. I could hear him over the phone fussing away at his secretary: "Where's that fucking court order for Jessica?" (Like *Mortuary Management* and Bennett Cerf, the Corrections crowd all called me "Jessica.") "Mr. Park," said I sternly, "don't you know it's a misdemeanor in California to use obscene language in the presence of women and children?" Which it is; a silly and sexist law that my husband is challenging in the courts, but that came in handy at that moment.

This is one of the very few interviews in which I used a tape recorder. I am mistrustful of these gadgets, which might break down at any moment and which necessitate tedious hours of transcription. But somehow—while I am on the whole confident of my ability to scribble down accurate notes of conversations—in the case of a person behind bars, helpless to challenge any possible misquotation, it seemed important to get the interview on tape. Fortunately George Jackson knew how to work the recorder. He took charge and it went off without a hitch.

When three months later Jackson was gunned down in the San Quentin shoot-out, his words, to which I had listened over and over again in the course of my laborious transcription of the interview, came back to me in his distinctive tone of voice: "And it's pretty clear that what they're saying is that 'First chance I get, nigger, I'm going to kill you.'"

June 1971

QUADRATURIN

Sigizmund Krzhizhanovsky

I

FROM OUTSIDE there came a soft knock at the door: once. Pause. And again—a bit louder and bonier: twice.

Sutulin, without rising from his bed, extended—as was his wont—a foot toward the knock, threaded a toe through the door handle, and pulled. The door swung open. On the threshold, head grazing the lintel, stood a tall, gray man the color of the dusk seeping in at the window.

Before Sutulin could set his feet on the floor the visitor stepped inside, wedged the door quietly back into its frame, and jabbing first one wall, then another, with a briefcase dangling from an apishly long arm, said, "Yes: a matchbox."

"What?"

"Your room, I say: it's a matchbox. How many square feet?"

"Eighty-six and a bit."

"Precisely. May I?"

And before Sutulin could open his mouth, the visitor sat down on the edge of the bed and hurriedly unbuckled his bulging briefcase. Lowering his voice almost to a whisper, he went on. "I'm here on business. You see, I, that is, we, are conducting, how shall I put it . . . well, experiments, I suppose. Under wraps for now. I won't hide the fact: a well-known foreign firm has an interest in our concern. You want the electric-light switch? No, don't bother: I'll only be a minute. So then: we have discovered—this is a secret now—an agent for biggerizing rooms. Well, won't you try it?"

The stranger's hand popped out of the briefcase and proffered Sutulin a narrow dark tube, not unlike a tube of paint, with a tightly screwed cap and a leaden seal. Sutulin fidgeted bewilderedly with the slippery tube and, though it was nearly dark in the room, made out on the label the clearly printed word: QUADRATURIN. When he raised his eyes, they came up against the fixed, unblinking stare of his interlocutor.

"So then, you'll take it? The price? Goodness, it's gratis. Just for advertising. Now if you'll"—the guest began quickly leafing through a sort of ledger he had produced from the same briefcase—"just sign this book (a short testimonial, so to say). A pencil? Have mine. Where? Here: column three. That's it."

His ledger clapped shut, the guest straightened up, wheeled around, stepped to the door... and a minute later Sutulin, having snapped on the light, was considering with puzzledly raised eyebrows the clearly embossed letters: QUADRATURIN.

On closer inspection it turned out that this zinc packet was tightly fitted—as is often done by the makers of patented agents—with a thin transparent paper whose ends were expertly glued together. Sutulin removed the paper sheath from the Quadraturin, unfurled the rolled-up text, which showed through the paper's transparent gloss, and read:

DIRECTIONS

Dissolve one teaspoon of the QUADRATURIN essence in one cup of water. Wet a piece of cotton wool or simply a clean rag with the solution; apply this to those of the room's internal walls designated for proliferspansion. This mixture leaves no stains, will not damage wallpaper, and even contributes—incidentally—to the extermination of bedbugs.

Thus far Sutulin had been only puzzled. Now his puzzlement was gradually overtaken by another feeling, strong and disturbing. He stood up and tried to pace from corner to corner, but the corners of this living cage were too close together: a walk amounted to almost nothing but turns, from toe to heel and back again. Sutulin stopped short, sat down, and closing his eyes, gave himself up to thoughts, which began: Why not ...? What if ...? Suppose ...? To his left, not three feet away from his ear, someone was driving an iron spike into the wall. The hammer kept slipping, banging, and aiming, it seemed, at Sutulin's head. Rubbing his temples, he opened his eyes: the black tube lay in the middle of the narrow table, which had managed somehow to insinuate itself between the bed, the windowsill, and the wall. Sutulin tore away the leaden seal, and the cap spun off in a spiral. From out of the round aperture came a bitterish gingery smell. The smell made his nostrils flare pleasantly.

"Hmm ... Let's try it. Although ..."

And, having removed his jacket, the possessor of Quadraturin proceeded to the experiment. Stool up against door, bed into middle of room, table on top of bed. Nudging across the floor a saucer of transparent liquid, its glassy surface gleaming with a slightly yellowish tinge, Sutulin crawled along after it, systematically dipping a handkerchief wound around a pencil into the Quadraturin and daubing the floorboards and patterned wallpaper. The room really was, as that man today had said, a matchbox. But Sutulin worked slowly and carefully, trying not to miss a single corner. This was rather difficult since the liquid really did evaporate in an instant or was absorbed (he couldn't tell which) without leaving even the slightest film; there was only its smell, increasingly pungent and spicy, making his head spin, confounding his fingers, and causing his knees, pinned to the floor, to tremble slightly. When he had finished with the floorboards and the bottom of the walls, Sutulin rose to his strangely weak and heavy feet and continued to work standing up. Now and then he had to add a little more of the essence. The tube was gradually emptying. It was already night outside. In the kitchen, to the right, a bolt came crashing down. The apartment was readying for bed. Trying not to make any noise, the experimenter, clutching the last of the essence, climbed up onto the bed and from the bed up onto the tottering table: only the ceiling remained to be Quadraturinized. But just then someone banged on the wall with his fist. "What's going on? People are trying to sleep, but he's . . ."

Turning around at the sound, Sutulin fumbled: the slippery tube spurted out of his hand and landed on the floor. Balancing carefully, Sutulin got down with his already drying brush, but it was too late. The tube was empty, and the rapidly fading spot around it smelled stupefyingly sweet. Grasping at the wall in his exhaustion (to fresh sounds of discontent from the left), he summoned his last bit of strength, put the furniture back where it belonged, and without undressing, fell into bed. A black sleep instantly descended on him from above: both tube and man were empty.

2

Two voices began in a whisper. Then by degrees of sonority—from piano to *mf*, from *mf* to *fff*—they cut into Sutulin's sleep.

"Outrageous. I don't want any new tenants popping out from under that skirt of yours . . . Put up with all that racket?!"

"Can't just dump it in the garbage . . ."

"I don't want to hear about it. You were told: no dogs, no cats, no children . . ." At which point there ensued such *fff* that Sutulin was ripped once and for all from his sleep; unable to part eyelids stitched together with exhaustion, he reached—as was his wont—for the edge of the table on which stood the clock. Then it began. His hand groped for a long time, grappling air: there was no clock and no table. Sutulin opened his eyes at once. In an instant he was sitting up, looking dazedly around the room. The table that usually stood right here, at the head of the bed, had moved off into the middle of a faintly familiar, large, but ungainly room.

Everything was the same: the skimpy, threadbare rug that had trailed after the table somewhere up ahead of him, and the photographs, and the stool, and the yellow patterns on the wallpaper. But they were all strangely spread out inside the expanded room cube.

"Quadraturin," thought Sutulin, "is terrific!"

And he immediately set about rearranging the furniture to fit the new space. But nothing worked: the abbreviated rug, when moved back beside the bed, exposed worn, bare floorboards; the table and the stool, pushed by habit against the head of the bed, had disencumbered an empty corner latticed with cobwebs and littered with shreds and tatters, once artfully masked by the corner's own crowdedness and the shadow of the table. With a triumphant but slightly frightened smile, Sutulin went all around his new, practically squared square, scrutinizing every detail. He noted with displeasure that the room had grown more in some places than in others: an external corner, the angle of which was now obtuse, had made the wall askew; Quadraturin, apparently, did not work as well on internal corners; carefully as Sutulin had applied the essence, the experiment had produced somewhat uneven results.

The apartment was beginning to stir. Out in the corridor, occupants shuffled to and fro. The bathroom door kept banging. Sutulin walked up to the threshold and turned the key to the right. Then, hands clasped behind his back, he tried pacing from corner to corner: it worked. Sutulin laughed with joy. How about that! At last! But then he thought: they may hear my footsteps—through the walls—on the right, on the left, at the back. For a minute he stood stock-still. Then he quickly bent down—his temples had suddenly begun to ache with yesterday's sharp thin pain—and, having removed his boots, gave himself up to the pleasure of a stroll, moving soundlessly about in only his socks.

"May I come in?"

The voice of the landlady. He was on the point of going to the door and unlocking it when he suddenly remembered: he mustn't. "I'm getting dressed. Wait a minute. I'll be right out."

"It's all very well, but it complicates things. Say I lock the door and take the key with me. What about the keyhole? And then there's the window: I'll have to get curtains. Today." The pain in his temples had become thinner and more nagging. Sutulin gathered up his papers in haste. It was time to go to the office. He dressed. Pushed the pain under his cap. And listened at the door: no one there. He quickly opened it. Quickly slipped out. Quickly turned the key. Now.

Waiting patiently in the entrance hall was the landlady.

"I wanted to talk to you about that girl, what's her name. Can you believe it, she's submitted an application to the House Committee saying she's—"

"I've heard. Go on."

"It's nothing to you. No one's going to take your eighty-six square feet away. But put yourself in my—"

"I'm in a hurry," he nodded, put on his cap, and flew down the stairs.

3

On his way home from the office, Sutulin paused in front of the window of a furniture dealer: the long curve of a couch, an extendable round table . . . it would be nice—but how could he carry them in past the eyes and the questions? They would guess, they couldn't help but guess . . .

He had to limit himself to the purchase of a yard of canary-yellow material (he did, after all, need a curtain). He didn't stop by the cafe: he had no appetite. He needed to get home—it would be easier there: he could reflect, look around, and make adjustments at leisure. Having unlocked the door to his room, Sutulin gazed about to see if anyone was looking: they weren't. He walked in. Then he switched on the light and stood there for a long time, his arms spread flat against the wall, his heart beating wildly: *this he had not expected*—not at all.

The Quadraturin was *still* working. During the eight or nine hours Sutulin had been out, it had pushed the walls at least another seven feet apart; the floorboards, stretched by invisible rods, rang out at his first step—like organ pipes. The entire room, distended and monstrously misshapen, was beginning to frighten and torment him. Without taking off his coat, Sutulin sat down on the stool and surveyed his spacious and at the same time oppressive coffin-shaped living box, trying to understand what had caused this unexpected effect. Then he remembered: he hadn't done the ceiling—the essence had run out. His living box was spreading only sideways, without rising even an inch upward.

"Stop. I have to stop this Quadraturinizing thing. Or I'll..." He pressed his palms to his temples and listened: the corrosive pain, lodged under his skull since morning, was still drilling away. Though the windows in the house opposite were dark, Sutulin took cover behind the yellow length of curtain. His head would not stop aching. He quietly undressed, snapped out the light, and got into bed. At first he slept, then he was awoken by a feeling of awkwardness. Wrapping the covers more tightly about him, Sutulin again dropped off, and once more an unpleasant sense of mooringlessness interfered with his sleep. He raised himself up on one palm and felt all around him with his free hand: the wall was gone. He struck a match. Umhmm: he blew out the flame and hugged his knees till his elbows cracked. "It's growing, damn it, it's still growing." Clenching his teeth, Sutulin crawled out of bed and, trying not to make any noise, gently edged first the front legs, then the back legs of the bed toward the receding wall. He felt a little shivery. Without turning the light on again, he went to look for his coat on that nail in the corner so as to wrap himself up more warmly. But there was no hook on the wall where it had been yesterday, and he had to feel around for several seconds before his hands chanced upon fur. Twice more during a night that was long and as nagging as the pain in his temples, Sutulin pressed his head and knees to the wall as he was falling asleep and, when he awoke, fiddled about with the legs of the bed again. In doing this—mechanically, meekly, lifelessly—he tried, though it was still dark outside, not to open his eyes: it was better that way.

4

Toward dusk the next evening, having served out his day, Sutulin was approaching the door to his room: he did not quicken his step and, upon entering, felt neither consternation nor horror. When the dim, sixteen-candle-power bulb lit up somewhere in the distance beneath the long low vault, its yellow rays struggling to reach the dark, ever-receding corners of the vast and dead, yet empty barrack, which only recently, before Quadraturin, had been a cramped but cozy, warm, and lived-in cubbyhole, he walked resignedly toward the yellow square of the window, now diminished by perspective; he tried to count his steps. From there, from a bed squeezed pitifully and fearfully in the corner by the window, he stared dully and wearily through deep-boring pain at the swaying shadows nestled against the floorboards, and at the smooth low overhang of the ceiling. "So, something forces its way out of a tube and can't stop squaring: a square squared, a square of squares squared. I've got to think faster than it: if I don't out-think it, it will outgrow me and . . ." And suddenly someone was hammering on the door, "Citizen Sutulin, are you in there?"

From the same faraway place came the muffled and barely audible voice of the landlady. "He's in there. Must be asleep."

Sutulin broke into a sweat: "What if I don't get there in time, and they go ahead and . . ." And, trying not to make a sound (let them think he was asleep), he slowly made his way through the darkness to the door. There.

"Who is it?"

"Oh, open up! Why's the door locked? Remeasuring Commission. We'll remeasure and leave."

Sutulin stood with his ear pressed to the door. Through the thin panel he could hear the clump of heavy boots. Figures were being mentioned, and room numbers.

"This room next. Open up!"

With one hand Sutulin gripped the knob of the electric-light switch and tried to twist it, as one might twist the head of a bird: the switch spattered light, then crackled, spun feebly around, and drooped down. Again someone hammered on the door: "Well!"

Sutulin turned the key to the left. A broad black shape squeezed itself into the doorway.

"Turn on the light."

"It's burned out."

Clutching at the door handle with his left hand and the bundle of wire with his right, he tried to hide the extended space from view. The black mass took a step back.

"Who's got a match? Give me that box. We'll have a look anyway. Do things right."

Suddenly the landlady began whining, "Oh, what is there to look at? Eighty-six square feet for the eighty-sixth time. Measuring the room won't make it any bigger. He's a quiet man, home from a long day at the office—and you won't let him rest: have to measure and remeasure. Whereas other people, who have no right to the space, but—"

"Ain't that the truth," the black mass muttered and, rocking from boot to boot, gently and even almost affectionately drew the door to the light. Sutulin was left alone on wobbling, cottony legs in the middle of the four-cornered, inexorably growing, and proliferating darkness.

5

He waited until their steps had died away, then quickly dressed and went out. They'd be back, to remeasure or check they hadn't undermeasured or whatever. He could finish thinking better here—from crossroad to crossroad. Toward night a wind came up: it rattled the bare frozen branches on the trees, shook the shadows loose, droned in the wires, and beat against walls, as if trying to knock them down. Hiding the needlelike pain in his temples from the wind's buffets, Sutulin went on, now diving into the shadows, now plunging into the lamplight. Suddenly, through the wind's rough thrusts, something softly and tenderly brushed against his elbow. He turned around. Beneath feathers batting against a black brim, a familiar face with provocatively half-closed eyes. And barely audible through the moaning air: "You know you know me. And you look right past me. You ought to bow. That's it."

Her slight figure, tossed back by the wind, perched on tenacious stiletto heels, was all insubordination and readiness for battle.

Sutulin tipped his hat. "But you were supposed to be going away. And you're still here? Then something must have prevented—"

"That's right—this."

And he felt a chamois finger touch his chest then dart back into the muff. He sought out the narrow pupils of her eyes beneath the dancing black feathers, and it seemed that one more look, one more touch, one more shock to his hot temples, and it would all come unthought, undone, and fall away. Meanwhile she, her face nearing his, said, "Let's go to your place. Like last time. Remember?"

With that, everything stopped.

"That's impossible."

She sought out the arm that had been pulled back and clung to it with tenacious chamois fingers.

"My place...isn't fit." He looked away, having again withdrawn both his arms and the pupils of his eyes.

"You mean to say it's cramped. My God, how silly you are. The more cramped it is..." The wind tore away the end of her phrase. Sutulin did not reply. "Or, perhaps you don't..."

When he reached the turning, he looked back: the woman was still standing there, pressing her muff to her bosom, like a shield; her narrow shoulders were shivering with cold; the wind cynically flicked her skirt and lifted up the lapels of her coat.

"Tomorrow. Everything tomorrow. But now..." And, quickening his pace, Sutulin turned resolutely back.

"Right now: while everyone's asleep. Collect my things (only the necessaries) and go. Run away. Leave the door wide open: let *them*. Why should I be the only one? Why not let *them*?"

The apartment was indeed sleepy and dark. Sutulin walked down the corridor, straight and to the right, opened the door with resolve, and as always, wanted to turn the light switch, but it spun feebly in his fingers, reminding him that the circuit had been broken. This was an annoying obstacle. But it couldn't be helped. Sutulin rummaged in his pockets and found a box of matches: it was almost empty. Good for three or four flares—that's all. He would have to husband both light and time. When he reached the coat pegs, he struck the first match: light crept in yellow radiuses through the black air. Sutulin purposely, overcoming temptation, concentrated on the illuminated scrap of wall and the coats and jackets hanging from hooks. He knew that there, behind his back, the dead, Quadraturinized space with its black corners was still spreading. He knew and did not look around. The match smoldered in his left hand, his right pulled things off hooks and flung them on the floor. He needed another flare; looking at the floor, he started toward the corner—if it was still a corner and if it was still there—where, by his calculations, the bed should have fetched up, but he accidentally held the flame under his breath—and again the black wilderness closed in. One last match remained: he struck it over and over: it would not light. One more time—and its crackling head fell off and slipped through his fingers. Then, having turned around, afraid to go any farther into the depths, he started back toward the bundle he had abandoned under the hooks. But he had made the turn, apparently, inexactly. He walked—heel to toe, heel to toe—holding his fingers out in front of him, and found nothing: neither the bundle, nor the hooks, nor even the walls. "I'll get there in the end. I must get there." His body was sticky with cold and sweat. His legs wobbled oddly. He squatted down, palms on the floorboards: "I shouldn't have come back. Now here I am alone, nowhere to turn." And suddenly it struck him: "I'm waiting here, but it's growing, I'm waiting, but it's . . ."

In their sleep and in their fear, the occupants of the quadratures adjacent to citizen Sutulin's eighty-six square feet couldn't make head or tail of the timbre and intonation of the cry that woke them in the middle of the night and compelled them to rush to the threshold of the Sutulin cell: for a man who is lost and dying in the wilderness to cry out is both futile and belated: but if even so—against all sense—he does cry out, then, most likely, *thus.*

1926
Translated from the Russian by Joanne Turnbull

FOR AS WITH ANIMALS, SO IT IS WITH MAN; THE ONE MUST DIE, THE OTHER LIKEWISE

Alfred Döblin

THE SLAUGHTERHOUSE in Berlin. The various structures, halls and pens are bounded in the north-east of the city, from Eldenaer Strasse, taking in Thaerstrasse and Landsberger Allee as far as Cothenius Strasse, along the ring road.

It covers an area of 47.88 hectares, or 187.5 acres. Not counting the buildings on the other side of Landsberger Allee it cost 27,093,492 marks to build, with the cattleyard accounting for 7,682,844 marks, and the slaughterhouse 19,410,648 marks.

Cattleyard, slaughterhouse and wholesale meat market make up one fully integrated economic entity. The administration is in the hands of the committee for stockyards and slaughterhouses, comprising two city officials, a member of the District Board, eleven councillors and three members of the public. It employs 258 officials, including vets, inspectors, stampers, assistant vets, assistant inspectors, clerical staff and maintenance workers. Traffic ordinance of 4 October 1900, general regulations governing the driving of cattle and the supply of feed. Tariff of fees: market fees, boxing fees, slaughtering fees, fees for the removal of feed troughs from the pork market hall.

Eldenaer Strasse is lined by dirty grey walls with barbed wire on top. The trees outside are bare, it is winter, they have secreted their sap in their roots and are waiting for spring. Butchers' carts draw up at a steady clip, yellow and red wheels, light horses. Behind one runs a skinny horse, from the pavement someone calls out, hey, Emil, what about the horse, 50 marks and a round for the eight of us, the horse goes a little crazy, trembles, nibbles one of the trees, the coachman tears it away, 50 marks and a round, Otto, else we go. The man smacks the horse on the cruppers: deal.

Yellow administration buildings, an obelisk for the war dead. And either side of that long halls with glass roofs, these are the pens, the waiting rooms. Outside notice boards: Property of the Association of Wholesale Butchers Berlin, Ltd. Post no bills: special permission only, the Board.

The long halls are fitted with numbered doors, 26, 27, 28, black openings for the animals to enter through. The cattle building, the pig building, the slaughter halls: courts of justice for the beasts, swinging axes, you won't leave here alive. Peaceful adjacent streets, Strassmann-, Liebig-, Proskauer Strasse, parks where people stroll. Close-knit communities, if someone here has a sore throat, the doctor will come running.

But on the other side, the rails of the circular railway extend for ten miles. The beasts are brought in from the provinces, ovine, bovine, porcine specimens from East Prussia, Pomerania, Brandenburg, West Prussia. They come mooing and bleating down the ramps. The pigs grunt and snuffle, they can't look where they're going, the drovers are after them, swinging sticks. They lie down in their pens, tight together, white, fat, snoring, sleeping. They have been made to walk a long way, then shaken up in rail cars, now the ground under their feet is steady, only the flagstones are cold, they wake up, seek each other's warmth. They are laid out in levels. Here's two fighting, the bay leaves them enough room for that, they butt heads, snap at each other's throats, turn in circles, gurgle, sometimes they are completely silent, gnashing in fear. In panic one scrambles over the bodies of the others, and the other gives chase, snaps, and those below start up, the two combatants fall, seek each other out.

A man in a canvas coat wanders through the passage, the bay is opened, he parts the combatants with a stick, the door is open, they push out, squealing, and a grunting and screaming begins. The funny white beasts are driven across courtyards, between halls, the droll little thighs, the funny curly tails, red and green scribbles on their backs. There is light, dear piggies, there is the floor, snuffle away at it, look for the few minutes that are left to you. No, you're right, we shouldn't work by the clock, snuffle and rootle to your heart's content. You will be slaughtered here, take a look at the slaughterhouse, it's for you. There are old abattoirs, but you are entering a new model. It's light, built of red brick, from the outside one might have guessed engineering works, shop or office premises, or a construction hall. I'll be going the other way, dear little piggies, because I'm a human, I'll be going through this door here, but we'll see each other soon enough.

Shoulder the door open, it's a swing door, on a spring. Whew, the steam in here. What are they steaming? It's like a Turkish bath, maybe that's what the pigs are here for. You're going somewhere, you can't see where, your glasses are misted over, perhaps you're naked, you're sweating out your rheumatism, cognac alone doesn't do the trick you know, you're shuffling along in your slippers. The steam is too thick, you can't see a sausage. Just squealing and gurgling and clattering, shouts, clatter of equipment, lids banging down. The pigs must be somewhere in here, they made a separate entrance. The dense white steam. There are the pigs, some are hanging up, they're already dead, they've been topped, they look almost ready to eat. There's a man with a hose, washing down the white split carcasses. They're hanging on iron stands, head down, some of the pigs are whole, their forelegs are in a wooden stock, a dead animal can't get up to any mischief, it can't even run away. Pigs' feet lie there in a pile, chopped off. Two men emerge from the fog carrying something, it's a cleaned opened animal on an iron spreader. They fasten the spreader to a hoist. Lots of their fellows come trundling along after, staring dully at the tiled floor.

You walk through the hall in fog. The stone flags are grooved, damp, and also bloodied. Between the stands the ranks of white, disembowelled animals. The killing bays must be at the back, it's from there you hear smacking sounds, crashing, squealing, screaming, gurgling, grunting sounds. There are big cauldrons there, which produce the steam. Men dunk the dead beasts in the boiling water, scald them, pull them out nice and white, a man scrapes off the outer skin with a knife, making the animal still whiter and very smooth. Very mild and white, deeply contented as after a strenuous bath, a successful operation or massage, the pigs lie out on wooden trestles in rows, they don't move in their sated calm, and in their new white tunics. They are all lying on their sides, on some you see the double row of tits, the number of breasts a sow has, they must be fertile animals. But they all of them have a straight red slash across the throat, right in the middle, which looks deeply suspicious.

More smacking sounds, a door is opened at the back, the steam clears, they drive in a new collection of pigs, running in, I've left through the sliding door at the front, funny pink animals, funny thighs, curly-wurly tails, the backs with coloured scribbles. And they're snuffling in this new bay. It's cold like the last one was, but there is something wet on the floor that they're unfamiliar with, something red and slippery. They rub their muzzles in it.

A pale young man with fair hair plastered to his head, a cigar in his mouth. Look at him, he will be the last human with whom you will have dealings! Don't think badly of him, he is only doing his job. He has official business with you. He is wearing rubber boots, trousers, shirt and braces. That's his official garb. He takes the cigar out of his mouth, lays it aside on a bracket in the wall, picks up a long-handled axe that was lying in the corner. This is the sign of his official rank, his power over you, like the detective's badge. He will produce his for you any moment now. There is a long wooden pole that the young man will raise to shoulder height over the little squealers who are contentedly snuffling and grunting and truffing. The man walks around, eyes lowered, looking, looking. There is a criminal investigation against a certain party, a certain party in the case of X versus Y—bamm! One ran in front of him, bamm, another one. The man is nimble, he has proved his authority, the axe has crashed down, dipped into the seething mob, with its blunt side against a skull, another skull. It's the work of a moment. Something continues to scrabble about on the floor. Treads water. Throws itself to the side. Knows no more. And lies there. The legs are busy, the head. But it's none of the pig's doing, it's the legs in their private capacity. Already a couple of men have looked across from the scalding room, it's time, they lift a slide to the killing bay, drag the animal out, whet the long blade on a stick, kneel down and shove it into its throat, then *skkrrk* a long cut, a very long cut across the throat, the animal is ripped open like a sack, deep, sawing cuts, it jerks, kicks, lashes out, it's unconscious, no more than unconscious, now more than unconscious, it squeals, and now the arteries in the throat are open. It is deeply unconscious, we are in the area of metaphysics now, of theology, my child, you no longer walk upon the earth, now we are wandering on clouds. Hurriedly bring up the shallow pan, the hot black blood streams into it, froths, makes bubbles, quickly, stir it. Within the body blood congeals, its purpose is to make obstructions, to dam up wounds. It's left the body, but it still wants to congeal. Just as a child on the operating table will go Mama, Mama, when Mama is nowhere around and it's going under in its ether mask, it keeps on going Mama till it is incapable of calling any more. *Skkrrik, skkrrak*, the arteries to left and right. Quickly stir. There, now the quivering stops. Now you're lying there pacified. We have come to the end of physiology and theology, this is where physics begins.

The man gets up off his knees. His knees hurt. The pig needs to be scalded, cleaned and dressed, that will happen blow by blow. The boss, feisty and well fed, walks around in the steam, with his pipe in his mouth, taking an occasional gander at an opened belly. On the wall by the swing doors hangs a poster: Gathering of Animal Shippers, Saalbau, Friedrichshain, Music: the Kermbach Boys. Outside are announcements for boxing matches. Germaniasäle, Chausseestrasse 110, tickets 1.50 to 10 marks. Four bouts on each bill.

Today's market numbers: 1,399 cattle, 2,700 calves, 4,654 sheep, 18,864 pigs. Market notes: prime cattle good, others steady. Calves smooth, sheep steady, pigs firm to begin with, then sluggish, fat pigs slow.

The wind blows through the driveway, and it's raining. Cattle low, men are driving along a large, roaring, horned herd. The animals are obstinate, keep heading off in wrong directions, the drovers run around with their sticks. In the middle of the gathering a bull tries to mount a cow, the cow runs off to left and right, the bull is in pursuit, and repeatedly tries to climb her withers.

A big white steer is driven into the slaughter hall. Here there is no steam, no bay as for the wee-weeing pigs. The big strong steer steps through the gate alone, between its drovers. The bloody hall lies before it, with dangling halves and quarters and chopped bones. The big steer has a wide forehead. It is driven forward to the slaughterer with kicks and blows. To straighten it out, the man gives it a tap on the hind leg with the flat of his axe. Then one of the drovers grabs it round the throat from below. The animal stands there, gives in astonishingly easily, as though it consented and, having seen everything, knows: this is its fate and there is no getting away from it. Possibly it takes the drover's movement for a caress, because it looks so friendly. It follows the pulling arms of the drover, bends its head aside, its muzzle up.

But then the knocker, with hammer upraised, is standing behind it. Don't look round. The hammer, picked up in both hands by the strongly built man, is behind it and above it, and then: wham, crashes down. The muscular strength of a powerful man like an iron wedge in its neck. And at that same moment—the hammer has not yet been taken back—the animal's four legs jerk apart, the whole heavy body seems to lift off. Then, as if it had no legs, the animal, the heavy body, lands splat on the floor, on its cramped stiffly protruding legs, lies there for a moment, and keels over onto its side. From right and left the knocker approaches him, gives him another tap on the head, to the temples, sleep, you'll not wake again. Then the fellow next to him takes the cigar out of his mouth, blows his nose, unsheathes his knife, it's as long as half a sword, and drops to his knees behind the animal, whose legs are already uncramping. It jerks in spasms, slings its rump this way and that. The slaughterer is looking for something on the floor, he doesn't apply the knife point, he calls for the bowl for blood. The blood is still circulating sluggishly, little moved by the beating of the mighty heart. The marrow is crushed, but the blood is still flowing through the veins, the lungs are breathing, the intestines moving. Now the knife will be applied, and the blood will jet out, I can picture it, a beam of it thick as my arm, black, lovely, jubilant blood. Then the whole merry crowd will leave the house, the guests will go dancing out, a tumult, and no more lovely meadows, warm shed, fragrant hay, gone, all gone, a void, an empty hole, darkness, here comes a new picture of the world. Wa-hey, a gentleman has come on the scene who has bought the house, a new road, improved economy, and he is having it torn down. They bring the big basin, press it against him, the mighty animal kicks its hind legs up in the air. The knife is jolted into its throat next to the windpipe, feels for the artery, these arteries are thick and well protected. And then it's open, another one, the flow, hot, streaming blackberry-red, the blood burbles over the knife, over the slaughterman's arm, the ecstatic blood, the hot blood, transformation is at hand, from the sun is come your blood, the sun has been hiding in your body, now look at it come out to play. The animal draws a colossal breath, as though it had been throttled, a colossal irritation, it gurgles, rattles. Yes, the beams are cracking. As the flanks are so terribly aquiver, a man comes to help. When a stone wants to fall, give it a push. The man jumps on the animal, on its body, with both feet, stands on it, balances, steps on the guts, bounces up and down, the blood is to be expelled quicker, all of it. And the gurgling gets louder, it's a long-drawn-out wheezing, with light futile tapping of the hind legs. The legs are waving now. Life is draining away, the breathing is stopping. Heavily the hips turn and slump. That's earth, that's gravity. The man bounces up. The other on the ground is already peeling back the skin from the neck.

Happy meadows, warm fuggy stall.

Translated from the German by Michael Hofmann

HELEN
Rachel Bespaloff

OF ALL the figures in the poem she is the severest, the most austere. Shrouded in her long white veils, Helen walks across the *Iliad* like a penitent; misfortune and beauty are consummate in her and lend majesty to her step. For this royal recluse freedom does not exist; the very slave who numbers the days of oppression on some calendar of hope is freer than she. What has Helen to hope for? Nothing short of the death of the Immortals would restore her freedom, since it is the gods, not her fellow men, who have dared to put her in bondage. Her fate does not depend on the outcome of the war; Paris or Menelaus may get her, but for her nothing can really change. She is the prisoner of the passions her beauty excited, and her passivity is, so to speak, their underside. Aphrodite rules her despotically; the goddess commands and Helen bows, whatever her private repugnance. Pleasure is extorted from her; this merely makes her humiliation the more cruel. Her only resource is to turn against herself a wrath too weak to spite the gods. She seems to live in horror of herself. "Why did I not die before?" is the lament that keeps rising to her lips. Homer is as implacable toward Helen as Tolstoy is toward Anna. Both women have run away from home thinking that they could abolish the past and capture the future in some unchanging essence of love. They awake in exile and feel nothing but a dull disgust for the shriveled ecstasy that has outlived their hope. The promise of freedom has been sloughed off in servitude; love does not obey the rules of love but yields to some more ancient and ruder law. Beauty and death have become neighbors and from their alliance springs a necessity akin to that of force. When

Helen and Anna come to and face their deteriorated dream, they can blame only themselves for having been the dupes of harsh Aphrodite. Everything they squandered comes back on them; everything they touch turns to dust or stone. In driving his heroine to suicide, Tolstoy goes beyond Christianity and rejoins Homer and the tragic poets. To them the hero's flaw is indistinguishable from the misery that arises from it. The sufferer bears it; he pays for it, but he cannot redeem it any more than he can live his life over. Clytemnestra, Orestes, and Oedipus are their crimes; they have no existence outside them. Later on, the philosophers, heirs of Odysseus, introduce the Trojan horse of dialectic into the realm of tragedy. Error takes the place of the tragic fault, and the responsibility for it rests with the individual alone. With Homer, punishment and expiation have the opposite effect; far from fixing responsibility, they dissolve it in the vast sea of human suffering and the diffuse guilt of the life-process itself. A flaw in a defective universe is not quite the same thing as a sin; remorse and grace have not yet made their appearance. But it is nonetheless true that this Greek idea of a diffuse guilt represents for Homer and the tragic poets the equivalent of the Christian idea of original sin. Fed on the same reality, charged with the same weight of experience, it contains the same appraisal of existence. It too acknowledges a fall, but a fall that has no date and has been preceded by no state of innocence and will be followed by no redemption; the fall, here, is a continuous one as the life-process itself which heads forever downward into death and the absurd. In proclaiming the innocence of Becoming, Nietzsche is as far from the ancients as he is from Christianity. Where Nietzsche wants to justify, Homer simply contemplates, and the only sound that he lets ring through his lines is the plaint of the hero. If the final responsibility for the tragic guilt rests on the mischievous gods, this does not mean that guilt is nonexistent. On the contrary, there is not a page in the *Iliad* that does not emphasize its irreducible character. So fully does Helen assume it that she does not even permit herself the comfort of self-defense. In Helen, purity and guilt mingle confusedly as they do in the vast heart of the warrior herd spread out on the plain at her feet.

Thus Helen, at Ilion, drags her ill luck along with a kind of somber humility that still makes no truce with the gods.* But is it really Aphrodite? Is it not rather the Asiatic Astarte who has trapped her? In a certain way, Helen's destiny prefigures that of Greece which, from the Trojan War to Alexander's conquests, was alternately submitting to and repelling the tremendous attraction of the Orient. What the exile misses in Paris' high dwelling is not the blond Achaian, arrogant Menelaus, son of a wild race of northern barbarians, but the rude, pure homeland—the familiar city, the child she used to fondle.

How tired she gets of the soft, weak ways of Aphrodite's protégé; he is a humiliation and a wound to her. "If the gods have decreed these evils for us, why could not I have had a husband who was capable of a feeling of revolt?" Here in hostile Troy, where boredom makes her despondent, Helen has no one to cling to but Hector, the least Oriental of Priam's sons, the most manly, the most Greek. There is a feeling of tenderness between them. Helen's presence is odious to everyone, and Hector is her only defender from the hatred she excites. Nobody can forgive the stranger for being the embodiment of the fatality that pursues the city. Innocent though she is, Helen feels the weight of these rebukes; she even seems to invite them, as though courting a just punishment for a crime she did not commit. She is all the more grateful, therefore, to the one person who shows her compassion without importuning her with lust. When Hector comes to scold Paris, Helen is worried about the dangers that threaten her brother-in-law. He is the only one to whom she speaks gently: "Meanwhile, come in, brother, and take this seat. Care assails your heart more than anyone else's, and that because of me, bitch that I am, and the folly of Alexander. Zeus has given us a hard lot, that later on we may be the subject of a song for men to come." These words weave a complicity between Hector and Helen that is something more than fraternal. With an unequaled insight, Homer hears in their talk an accent of intimacy which is attuned to the truth of

---

*And possibly this royal humility, in Helen and Oedipus, is what distinguishes the antique style from the Christian.

human relationships. This affection, on Helen's part at least, shields a deeper feeling, which Homer, listening, does not betray.

The exile's lament is the last to echo over Hector's remains; it bathes the end of the *Iliad* in the pure, desolate light of compassion. "This is now the twentieth year from the time I came away and left my native land; yet I have never heard a bad or a harsh word from you. So I weep for you and for my unhappy self too, with grief at heart. I have nobody else now in wide Troy to be kind or gentle to me; everybody shudders away from me." This, however, is not the moan of some humiliated creature at the mercy of her tormentors; it is the grief of a mortal at the mercy of gods who have laden her with dazzling graces, the better to balk her of the joy these gifts seemed to promise. No matter who wins in the end, Helen, unlike Andromache and the Trojan princesses, does not have to fear a life of slavery and forced labor "under the eyes of a harsh master." After twenty years, she is still the stake the war is being fought for, and the reward the winner will carry off. In the depths of her wretchedness, Helen still wears an air of majesty that keeps the world at a distance and flouts old age and death. The most beautiful of women seemed born for a radiant destiny; everything pointed that way; everything appeared to contribute to it. But, as it turns out, the gods only chose her to work misfortune on herself and on the two nations. Beauty is not a promise of happiness here; it is a burden and a curse. At the same time, it isolates and elevates; it has something preservative in it that wards off outrage and shame. Hence its sacred character—to use the word in its original, ambiguous sense—on the one hand, life-giving, exalting; on the other, accursed and dread. The Helen the two armies are contending for will never be Paris' any more than she has been Menelaus'; the Trojans cannot own her any more than the Greeks could. Beauty, captured, remains elusive. It deserts alike those who beget, or contemplate, or desire it. Homer endows it with the inexorability of force or fate. Like force, it subjugates and destroys—exalts and releases. It is not by some chance, arising out of her life's vicissitudes, that Helen has come to be the cause of the war and its stake; a deeper necessity has brought her there to join the apparition of beauty with the unleashing of rage. Beside the warriors and above them, Helen is the calm and the bitterness that spring up in the thick of battle, casting their cool shadow over victories and defeats alike, over the living and the thousands of dead. For, if force degrades itself in the insignificance of Becoming (one arrow from Paris' bow puts an end to the might of Achilles), beauty alone transcends all contingencies, including those that brought it to flower. The origins of Leda's daughter are lost in fable, her end in legend. In immortal appearance the world of Being is maintained and protected.

Homer carefully abstains from the description of beauty, as though this might constitute a forbidden anticipation of bliss. The shade of Helen's eyes, of Thetis' tresses, the line of Andromache's shoulders— these details are kept from us. No singularity, no particularity is brought to our notice; yet we see these women; we would recognize them. One wonders by what impalpable means Homer manages to give us such a sense of the plastic reality of his characters. Incorruptible, Helen's beauty passes from life into the poem, from flesh into marble, its pulse still throbbing. The statue's mouth utters a human cry, and from the empty eyes gush "tender tears." When Helen climbs the ramparts of Troy to watch the fight between Paris and Menelaus, one can almost feel the loftiness of her step. By the Scaean gates, the Trojan elders are holding council. At the sight of her, "the good orators" fall silent, struck to the heart. They cannot help finding her beautiful. And this beauty frightens them like a bad omen, a warning of death. "She has terribly the look, close-up, of the immortal goddesses.... But even so, whatever she may be, let her set sail and go away. Let her not be left here to be a scourge to us and our sons hereafter." Here—and this is unusual—the poet himself, speaking through Priam, lifts his voice to exonerate beauty and proclaim it innocent of man's misfortunes. "I do not blame you. I blame the gods, who launched this Achaian war, full of tears, upon me." The real culprits, and the only ones, are the gods, who live "exempt from care," while men are consumed with sorrow. The curse which turns beauty into destructive fatality does not originate in the human heart. The diffuse guilt of Becoming pools into a single sin, the one sin condemned and explicitly stigmatized by Homer: the happy carelessness of the Immortals.

There follows a scene of starry serenity in which the human accent, however, is still audible. Priam asks Helen to tell him the names of the most famous of the Achaian warriors that he can see in the enemy camp. The battlefield is quiet; a few steps away from each other, the two armies stand face-to-face awaiting the single combat that will decide the outcome of the war. Here, at the very peak of the *Iliad*, is one of those pauses, those moments of contemplation, when the spell of Becoming is broken, and the world of action, with all its fury, dips into peace. The plain where the warrior herd was raging is no more than a tranquil mirage to Helen and the old king.

No doubt this is where Nietzsche listened to the dialogue between Beauty and Wisdom, set above life but very close to it. "Pushed, pressed, constrained, tracked down by torment," come at length to the place where, around him, everything "turned strange and solitary," he had a vision of Helen (or Ariadne), high and inaccessible against the blue sky.

Meanwhile Helen stands helplessly watching the men who are going to do battle for her. She is there still, since nations that brave each other for markets, for raw materials, rich lands, and their treasures, are fighting, first and forever, for Helen.

Translated from the French by Mary McCarthy

BILLIE HOLIDAY

Elizabeth Hardwick

"THE UNSPEAKABLE vices of Mecca are a scandal to all Islam and constant source of wonder to pious pilgrims." As a pilgrim to Mecca, I lived at the Hotel Schuyler on West 45th Street in Manhattan, lived with a red-cheeked, homosexual young man from Kentucky. We had known each other all our lives. Our friendship was a violent one and we were as obsessive, critical, jealous, and cruel as any couple. Often I lay awake all night in a rage over some delinquency of his during the day. His coercive neatness inflamed me at times, as if his habits were not his right but instead a dangerous poison to life, like the slow seepage from the hotel stove. His clothes were laid out on the bed for the next day; and worst of all he had an unyielding need to brush his teeth immediately after dinner in the evening. This finally meant that no fortuitous invitation, no lovely possibility arising unannounced could be accepted without a concentrated uneasiness of mind. These holy habits ruined his sex life, even though he was, like the tolling of a time bell, to be seen every Saturday night at certain gay bars, drinking his ration of beer.

My friend had, back in Kentucky, developed a passion for jazz. This study seized him and he brought to it the methodical, intense, dogmatic anxiety of his nature. I learned this passion from him. It is a curious learning that cuts into your flesh, leaving a scar, a longing never satisfied, a wound of feeling hard to live with. It can be distressing to listen to jazz when one is troubled, alone, with the "wrong" person. Things can happen in your life that cause you to give it up altogether. Yet, under its dominion, it may be said that one is more likely to commit suicide listening to "Them There Eyes" than to Opus 132. What is it? "... the sea itself, or is it youth alone?"

We lived there in the center of Manhattan, believing the very placing of the hotel to be an overwhelming beneficence. To live in the obscuring jungle of the midst of things: close to—what? Within walking distance of all those places one never walked to. But it was history, wasn't it? The acrimonious twilight fell in the hollows between the gray and red buildings. Inside the hotel was a sort of underbrush, a swampy footing for the irregular. The brooding inconsequence of the old hotel dwellers, their delusions and disappearances. They lived as if in a house recently burglarized, wires cut, their world vandalized, by themselves, and cheerfully enough, also. Do not imagine they received nothing in return. They got a lot, I tell you. They were lifted by insolence above their car loans, their surly arrears, their misspent matrimonies.

The small, futile shops around us explained how little we know of ourselves and how perplexing are our souvenirs and icons. I remember strangers to the city, in a daze, making decisions, exchanging coins and bills for the incurious curiosities, the unexceptional novelties. Sixth Avenue lies buried in the drawers, bureaus, boxes, attics, and cellars of grandchildren. There, blackening, are the dead watches, the long, oval rings for the little finger, the smooth pieces of polished wood shaped into a long-chinned African head, the key rings of the Empire State building. And for us, there were the blaring shops, open most of the night, where one could buy old, scratched, worn-thin jazz records—Vocalion, Okeh, and Brunswick labels. Our hands sliced through the cases until the skin around our fingers bled.

Yes, there were the records, priceless flotsam they seemed to us then. And the shifty jazz clubs on 52nd Street. The Onyx, the Down Beat, the Three Deuces. At the curb, getting out of a taxi, or at the White Rose Bar drinking, there "they" were, the great performers with their worn, brown faces, enigmatic in the early evening, their coughs, their broken lips and yellow eyes; their clothes, crisp and bright and hard as the bone-fibered feathers of a bird. And there she was—the "bizarre deity," Billie Holiday.

At night in the cold winter moonlight, around 1943, the city pageantry was of a benign sort. Young adolescents were then asleep and the threat was only in the landscape, aesthetic. Dirty slush in the gutters, a lost black overshoe, a pair of white panties, perhaps thrown from a passing car. Murderous dissipation went with the music, inseparable, skin and bone. And always her luminous self-destruction.

She was fat the first time we saw her, large, brilliantly beautiful, fat. She seemed for this moment that never again returned to be almost a matron, someone real and sensible who carried money to the bank, signed papers, had curtains made to match, dresses hung and shoes in pairs, gold and silver, black and white, ready. What a strange, betraying apparition that was, madness, because never was any woman less a wife or mother, less attached; not even a daughter could she easily appear to be. Little called to mind the pitiful sweetness of a young girl. No, she was glittering, somber, and solitary, although of course never alone, never. Stately, sinister, and absolutely determined.

The creamy lips, the oily eyelids, the violent perfume—and in her voice the tropical l's and r's. Her presence, her singing created a large, swelling anxiety. Long red fingernails and the sound of electrified guitars. Here was a woman who had never been a Christian.

To speak as part of the white audience of "knowing" this baroque and puzzling phantom is an immoderation; and yet there are many persons, discrete and reasonable, who have little splinters of memory that seem to have been *personal*. At times they have remembered an exchange of some sort. And always the lascivious gardenia, worn like a large, white, beautiful ear, the heavy laugh, marvelous teeth, and the splendid archaic head, dragged up from the Aegean. Sometimes she dyed her hair red and the curls lay flat against her skull, like dried blood.

*

Early in the week the clubs were *dead*, as they spoke of it. And the chill of failure inhabited the place, visible in the cold eyes of the owners. These men, always changing, were weary with futile calculations. They often held their ownership so briefly that one could scarcely believe the ink dry on the license. They started out with the embezzler's hope and moved swiftly to the bankrupt's torpor. The bartenders —thin, watchful, stubbornly crooked, resentful, silent thieves. Wandering soldiers, drunk and worried, musicians, and a few people, couples, hideously looking into each other's eyes, as if they were safe.

My friend and I, peculiar and tense, experienced during the quiet nights a tainted joy. Then, showing our fidelity, it seemed that a sort of motif would reveal itself, that under the glaze ancient patterns from a lost world were to be discovered. The mind strains to recover the blank spaces in history, and our pale, gray-green eyes looked into her swimming, dark, inconstant pools—and got back nothing.

In her presence on these tranquil nights it was possible to experience the depths of her disbelief, to feel sometimes the mean, horrible freedom of a thorough suspicion of destiny. And yet the heart always drew back from the power of her will and its engagement with disaster. An inclination bred upon punishing experiences compelled her to live gregariously and without affections. Her talents and the brilliance of her mind contended with the strength of the emptiness. Nothing should degrade this genuine nihilism; and so, in a sense, it is almost a dishonor to imagine that she lived in the lyrics of her songs.

Her message was otherwise. It was *style*. That was her meaning from the time she began at fifteen. It does not change the victory of her great effort, of the miraculous discovery or retrieval from darkness of pure style, to know that it was exercised on "I love my man, tell the world I do...." How strange it was to me, almost unbalancing, to be sure that she did not love any man, or anyone. Also often one had the freezing perception that her own people, those around her, feared her. One thing she was ashamed of—or confused by, rather— that she was not sentimental.

*

In my youth, at home in Kentucky, there was a dance place just out-side of town called Joyland Park. In the summer the great bands arrived, Ellington, Louis Armstrong, Chick Webb, sometimes for a Friday and Saturday or merely for one night. When I speak of the great bands it must not be taken to mean that we thought of them as such. No, they were part of the summer nights and the hot dog stands, the fetid swimming pool heavy with chlorine, the screaming roller coaster, the old rain-splintered picnic tables, the broken iron swings. And the bands were also part of Southern drunkenness, couples drinking coke and whisky, vomiting, being unfaithful, love-lorn, frantic. The black musicians, with their cumbersome instruments, their tuxedos, were simply there to beat out time for the stumbling, cuddling fox-trotting of the period.

The band busses, parked in the field, the caravans in which they suffered the litter of cigarettes and bottles, the hot, streaking highways, all night, or resting for a few hours in the black quarters: the Via Dolorosa of show business. They arrived at last, nowhere, to audiences large or small, often with us depending upon the calendar of the Park, the other occasions from which the crowd would spill over into the dance hall. Ellington's band. And what were we doing, standing close, murmuring the lyrics?

At our high school dances in the winter, small, cheap, local events. We had our curls, red taffeta dresses, satin shoes with their new dye fading in the rain puddles; and most of all we were dressed in our ferocious hope for popularity. This was a stifling blanket, an airless tent; gasping, grinning, we stood anxious-eyed, next to the piano, hovering about Fats Waller who had come from Cincinnati for the occasion. Requests, perfidious glances, drunken teenagers, nodding teacher-chaperones: these we offered to the music, looking upon it, I suppose, as something inevitable, effortlessly pushing up from the common soil.

On 52nd Street: "Yeah, I remember your town," she said, without inflection.

And I remember her dog, Boxer. She was one of those women who admire large, overwhelming, impressive dogs and who give to them a care and courteous punctuality denied everything else. Several times we waited in panic for her in the bar of the Hotel Braddock in Harlem. (My friend, furious and tense with his new, hated work in "public relations," was now trying without success to get her name in Winchell's column. Today we were waiting to take her downtown to sit for the beautiful photographs Robin Carson took of her.) At the Braddock, the porters took plates of meat for the dog to her room. Soon, one of her friends, appearing almost like a child, so easily broken were others by the powerful, energetic horrors of her life, one of those young people would take the great dog to the street. These animals, asleep in dressing rooms, were like sculptured treasures, fit for the tomb of a queen.

The sheer enormity of her vices. The outrageousness of them. For the grand destruction one must be worthy. Her ruthless talent and the opulent devastation. Onto the heaviest addiction to heroin she piled up the rocks of her tomb with a prodigiousness of Scotch and brandy. She was never at any hour of the day or night free of these consumptions, never except when she was asleep. And there did not seem to be any pleading need to quit, to modify. With cold anger she spoke of various cures that had been forced upon her, and she would say, bearing down heavily, as sure of her rights as if she had been robbed, "And I paid for it myself." Out of a term at the Federal Women's Prison in West Virginia she stepped, puffy from a diet of potatoes, onto the stage of Town Hall to pick up some money and start up again the very day of release.

Still, even with her, authenticity was occasionally disrupted. An invitation for chili—improbable command. We went up to a street in Harlem just as the winter sun was turning black. Darkened windows with thin bands of watchful light above the sills. Inside the halls were dark and empty, filled only with the scent of dust. We, our faces bleached from the cold, in our thin coats, black gloves, had clinging to us the evangelical diffidence of bell-ringing members of a religious sect, a determination glacial, timid, and yet pedantic. Our frozen alarm and fascination carried us into the void of the dead tenement. The house was under a police ban and when we entered, whispering her name, the policeman stared at us with furious incredulity. She was hounded by the police, but for once the occasion was not hers. Somewhere, upstairs, behind another door there had been a catastrophe.

Her own records played over and over on the turntable; everything else was quiet. All of her living places were temporary in the purest meaning of the term. But she filled even a black hotel room with a stinging, demonic weight. At the moment she was living with a trumpet player who was just becoming known and who soon after faded altogether. He was as thin as a stick and his lovely, round, light face, with frightened, shiny, round eyes, looked like a sacrifice impaled upon the stalk of his neck. His younger brother came out of the bedroom. He stood before us, wavering between confusing possibilities. Tiny, thin, perhaps in his twenties, the young man was engrossed in a blur of functions. He was a sort of hectic Hermes, working in Hades, now buying cigarettes, now darting back to the bedroom, now almost inaudible on the phone, ordering or disposing of something in a light, shaking voice.

"Lady's a little behind. She's over-scheduled herself." Groans and coughs from the bedroom. In the peach-shaded lights, the wan rosiness of a beaten sofa was visible. A shell, still flushed from the birth of some crustacean, was filled with cigarette ends. A stocking on the floor. And the record player, on and on, with the bright clarity of her songs. Smoke and perfume and somewhere a heart pounding.

One winter she wore a great lynx coat and in it she moved, menacing and handsome as a Cossack, pacing about in the trap of her vitality. Quarrelsome dreams sometimes rushed through her speech, and accounts of wounds she had inflicted with broken glass. And at the White Rose Bar, a thousand cigarettes punctuated her appearances, which, not only in their brilliance but in the fact of their taking place at all, had about them the aspect of magic. Waiting and waiting: that was what the pursuit of her was. One felt like an old carriage horse standing at the entrance, ready for the cold midnight race through the park. She was always behind a closed door—the fate of those addicted to whatever. And then at last she must come forward, emerge in powders and Vaseline, hair twisted with a curling iron, gloves of satin or silk jersey, flowers—the expensive martyrdom of the "entertainer."

At that time not so many of her records were in print and she was seldom heard on the radio because her voice did not accord with popular taste then. The appearances in night clubs were a necessity. It was a burden to be there night after night, although not a burden to sing, once she had started, in her own way. She knew she could do it, that she had mastered it all, but why not ask the question: Is this all there is? Her work took on, gradually, a destructive cast, as it so often does with the greatly gifted who are doomed to repeat endlessly their own heights of inspiration.

She was late for her mother's funeral. At last she arrived, ferociously appropriate in a black turban. A number of jazz musicians were there. The late morning light fell mercilessly on their unsteady, night faces. In the daytime these people, all except Billie, had a furtive, suburban aspect, like family men who work the night shift. The marks of a fractured domesticity, signals of a real life that is itself almost a secret existence for the performer, were drifting about the little church, adding to the awkward unreality.

Her mother, Sadie Holiday, was short and sentimental, bewildered to be the bearer of such news to the world. She made efforts to *sneak* into Billie's life, but there was no place and no need for her. She was set up from time to time in small restaurants which she ran without any talent and failed in quickly. She never achieved the aim of her life, the professional dream, which was to be "Billie's dresser." The two women bore no resemblance, neither of face nor of body. The daughter was profoundly intelligent and found the tragic use for it in the cunning of destruction. The mother seemed to face each day with the bald hopefulness of a baby and end each evening in a baffled little cry of disappointment. Sadie and Billie Holiday were a violation, a rift in the statistics of life. The great singer was one of those for whom the word *changeling* was invented. She shared the changeling's spectacular destiny and was acquainted with malevolent forces.

She lived to be forty-four; or should it better be said she died at forty-four. Of "enormous complications." Was it a long or a short life? The "highs" she sought with such concentration of course remained a mystery. "Ah, I fault Jimmy for all that," someone said once in a taxi, naming her first husband, Jimmy Monroe, a fabulous Harlem club owner when she was young.

Once she came to see us in the Hotel Schuyler, accompanied by someone. We sat there in the neat squalor and there was nothing to do and nothing to say and she did not wish to eat. In the anxious gap, I felt the deepest melancholy in her black eyes, an abyss into which every question had fallen without an answer. She died in misery from the erosions and poisons of her fervent, felonious narcotism. The police were at the hospital bedside, vigilant lest she, in a coma, manage a last chemical inner migration.

Her whole life had taken place in the dark. The spotlight shone down on the black, hushed circle in a café; the moon slowly slid through the clouds. Night-working, smiling, in make-up, in long, silky dresses, singing over and over, again and again. The aim of it all is just to be drifting off to sleep when the first rays of the sun's brightness threaten the theatrical eyelids.

YEREVAN

Vasily Grossman

THE TRAIN arrived in Yerevan on the morning of November 3. No one was there to meet me, though I had sent a telegram in advance to Martirosyan, the writer whose book I had come to translate. I had been certain he would be there; I had even imagined that other Armenian writers would also be coming to meet me. And so there I was on the platform, under a warm, pale-blue sky, wearing a thick woolen scarf, a cloth cap, and a new autumn coat I had just bought in order to look respectable in Armenia. Muscovite experts in sartorial matters had looked me up and down and said, "Well, it's hardly chic, but it'll do for a translator." In one hand I had a case, quite a heavy one—I was, after all, going to be in Armenia for two months. In the other I had a bag with a heavy manuscript—a word-for-word translation of an epic novel by a prominent Armenian writer about the construction of a copper-smelting plant.

The exclamations of joy had died down and dark eyes were no longer gleaming all around me; my fellow passengers and the hundreds of people who had come to meet them had all hurried away to line up for taxis. The Moscow–Yerevan train had crawled off to the yards; the murky, rain-stained windows and the dusty green flanks of coaches that, after nearly three thousand kilometers, looked tired and sweaty—everything had now disappeared. Everything around me was unfamiliar, and my heart sank—the last little piece of Moscow had slipped away from me.

I saw a large square in front of the station, and a huge half-naked young man on a bronze horse. His sword was drawn, and I realized this must be David of Sasun.* I was struck by the power of this statue: David himself, his steed, his sword—everything was huge, full of movement and strength.

I stood in the spacious square and wondered why no one had come to meet me. Arrogance? Forgetfulness? Eastern indolence? Some muddle with the telegram? I looked around the square, glancing up at the magnificent monument.... The power of David and his steed, the movement captured in the bronze—suddenly all this seemed too much. It was not a legend realized in bronze but a bronze advertisement for a legend.

I was upset. Should I go straight to the hotel? Without a document, I wouldn't be let in. Should I trail around the Armenian capital, under the hot sun, wearing a warm coat, a cap, and a thick scarf? A stranger wandering through an alien city always seems sad and absurd. The young and fashionable love nothing more than to laugh at some old countrywoman passing through Moscow in her rustic felt boots, or at some old Yakut walking through Theater Square in a fur jacket on a sultry August afternoon.

Thank heavens none of my fellow passengers had seen me. Yesterday I had haughtily rejected their attempts to tell me how to go by bus to the hotel. They had understood that I was being met by someone with a car.

A few minutes later I was in line for the left-luggage office, standing in the cool half dark. There was no sign of any artificial fur coats here, only a sad young woman with a docile child; a young lad in a trade-school forage cap; a young lieutenant, evidently from a village, who had the eyes of a child and who seemed unused to his country's vast spaces; and an old man with a suitcase made of wood.

Now I am walking through the square. No one so much as glances at me: I'm just a man in a jacket. I'm just someone going for a walk; I've gone out to buy some flatbread or half a liter of beer; I'm on my way to the clinic for some kind of treatment. No one imagines that

---

*The legendary hero of *The Daredevils of Sasun*, a medieval epic about the expulsion of Arab invaders.

I've only just arrived, that I'm feeling lost, and that I can only half remember the address of the one person I know in Yerevan, the writer Martirosyan.

I board a bus. For some reason I feel awkward about admitting I don't know the price of a ticket. I give the conductor a ruble. He gestures at me: Haven't I got any change? I shake my head, even though I have several small coins in my pocket. The price turns out to be the same as in Moscow.

Your first minutes on the streets of an unfamiliar city are always special; what happens in later months or years can never supplant them. These minutes are filled with the visual equivalent of nuclear energy, a kind of nuclear power of attention. With penetrating insight and an all-pervading excitement, you absorb a huge universe—houses, trees, faces of passersby, signs, squares, smells, dust, cats and dogs, the color of the sky. During these minutes, like an omnipotent God, you bring a new world into being; you create, you build inside yourself a whole city with all its streets and squares, with its courtyards and patios, with its sparrows, with its thousands of years of history, with its food shops and its shops for manufactured goods, with its opera house and its canteens. This city that suddenly arises from nonbeing is a special city; it differs from the city that exists in reality—it is the city of a particular person. Its autumn leaves have their own unique way of rustling; there is something special about the smell of its dust, about the way its young boys fire their slingshots.

And it takes only a few minutes, not even hours, to accomplish this miracle of creation. And when a man dies, there dies with him a unique, unrepeatable world that he himself has created—a whole universe with its own oceans and mountains, with its own sky. These oceans and this sky are strikingly similar to the billions of oceans and skies in the minds of others; this universe is strikingly similar to the one and only universe that exists in its own right, regardless of humanity. But these mountains, these waves, this particular grass, and this particular pea soup have something unique about them, something that has come into being only recently; they have their own tints, their own quiet splashing and rustling—they are part of a particular universe that lives in the soul of the man who has created it.

And so there I was, sitting in a bus, walking across a square, looking at the titanic bronze Stalin and at houses, built from pink and yellow-gray tufa, that reproduce the contours of ancient Armenian churches with a grace that seems entirely natural; there I was, creating my own special Yerevan—a Yerevan remarkably similar to the Yerevan in the external world, a Yerevan remarkably similar to the city present in the minds of the thousands of other people walking about on the streets, and at the same time distinct from all these other Yerevans. It was my own Yerevan, my own unrepeatable Yerevan. The autumn leaves of its plane trees rustled in their own peculiar way; its sparrows were shouting in their own peculiar way.

I was in the main square. On each side was a large building built from pink tufa: the Intourist hotel Armenia, for Armenians from the diaspora coming to visit their motherland; the Soviet of the National Economy, responsible for everything to do with Armenian marble, basalt, tufa, copper, aluminum, cognac, and electricity; the architecturally perfect Soviet of Ministers; and the post office, where my heart would later race anxiously when I went to pick up letters sent general delivery. I came to the main boulevard, where the sparrows were shouting wildly, in Armenian, among the brown leaves of the plane trees. I passed the wonderful Yerevan market, with its heaps of fruit and vegetables in every color—yellow, red, orange, white, and blue-black—with the velvet of its peaches, the Baltic amber of its grapes, its juicy red-orange persimmons, its pomegranates and chestnuts, its mighty eighteen-inch-long radishes that seemed to belong to some phallic cult, its garlands of *churchkhela*,* its hills of cabbages and dunes of walnuts, its fiery peppers, its fragrant and spicy green leaves.

I already knew that it was Tamanyan who had created the architectural style of the new Yerevan, and that he had drawn his inspiration from ancient Armenian churches; I knew he had resurrected an

---

*Traditional candies popular throughout the Caucasus.

ancient ornamental pattern depicting a bunch of grapes and the head of an eagle. . . . Later, people showed me the very finest creations of Armenian architects; they took me to see a street of detached houses, every one of which was a masterpiece. But, considering them of no interest, these people never showed me the old buildings; nor did they show me the inner courtyards hidden behind the façades both of the temple-like modern buildings and of the squat nineteenth-century buildings that had marched into Yerevan along with the Russian infantry. All this, however, I had already seen—on my very first day in Yerevan.

The inner yard! What constitutes the kernel, the heart and soul of Yerevan is not its churches or government buildings, not its railway stations, not its theater or its concert hall, nor its three-story palace of a department store. No, what constitutes the soul of Yerevan are its inner courtyards. Flat roofs, long staircases, short flights of steps, little corridors and balconies, terraces of all sizes, plane trees, a fig tree, a climbing vine, a little table, small benches, passages, verandas—everything fits harmoniously together, one thing leading into another, one thing emerging from another. Linking all the balconies and verandas, like arteries and nerve fibers, are hundreds of long lines on which the copious and motley linen of the inhabitants of Yerevan has been hung out to dry. Here are the sheets on which the black-browed men and women sleep and make children; here are the vast, sail-like brassieres of hero-mothers; here are the shirts of little girls; here are the underpants, discolored in the crotch, of Armenian old men; here are lace veils, swaddling clothes, and little babies' trousers. Here we see the city as a living organism, stripped of its outer skin. Here we see all of Eastern life: the tenderness of the heart, the peristalsis of the gut, the firing of synapses, the power of both blood kinship and the ties that link everyone born in the same town or village. Old men click their worry beads and exchange leisurely smiles; children get up to mischief; smoke rises from braziers; quince and peach preserves simmer in copper pans; washing tubs disappear in clouds of steam; green-eyed cats watch their mistresses pluck chickens. We are not far from Turkey. We are not far from Persia.

The inner yard! It links different eras: the present, when a four-engined Ilyushin-18 can take you from Moscow to Yerevan in a few hours, and the days of camel paths and caravansaries.

And so I go on building my own Yerevan. I grind up, crush, absorb, and inhale its basalt and its rose-colored tufa, its asphalt and its cobblestones, the glass of its shop windows, its monuments to Stalin and Lenin, its monuments to Abovyan, Shaumyan, and Charents, the countless portraits of Anastas Mikoyan; I absorb and inhale faces, accents, the frenzied roar of cars being driven at speed by frenzied drivers. I see a lot of people with big noses, a lot of faces covered in black stubble; I understand that it can't be easy to shave iron beards.

I see today's Yerevan with its factories, its huge, tall blocks of new apartments for workers, its splendid opera house, its magnificent pink schools, its academic institutions, its precious repository for books and manuscripts—the Matenadaran—and its famous Academy of Sciences. The academy looks graceful and harmonious.

I see Mount Ararat—it stands high in the blue sky. With its gentle, tender contours, it seems to grow not out of the earth but out of the sky, as if it has condensed from its white clouds and its deep blue. It is this snowy mountain, this bluish-white sunlit mountain that shone in the eyes of those who wrote the Bible.

The young and fashionable of this city love black suits. The shops are well supplied; there is plenty of butter, sausages, and meat. And the young women are lovely, though some of them really do have terribly big noses. One thing astonishes me: An old man or woman has only to raise their hand and a bus driver will stop for them; people here are kind and compassionate. Pretty young women walk along the pavement, clicking their thin high heels; dandies in hats lead sheep they have bought for the impending holiday; the sheep click their little hooves on the pavement, and the young women click their fashionable little heels; amid the fine buildings and the neon lights, the sheep smell their death. Some of them try to resist, to dig their little hooves in; afraid of dirtying their clothes, the dandies push the sheep, trying to get them to move; the sheep, full of the anguish of their coming death, lie down on the pavement; the behatted dandies, still afraid of dirtying their clothes, lift them up; the anguished sheep scatter their little black peas. Women with kind faces are carrying chickens and turkeys by their legs; the birds' heads hang down. These little heads must be swollen and painful, and the birds arch their necks in order, at least slightly, to reduce their sufferings. Their round pupils look at Yerevan without reproach. There too—in the birds' confused and spinning little heads—a city of pink tufa is coming into being.

Lord and creator, I wander through the streets of Yerevan; I build Yerevan in my soul. Yerevan—this city that Armenians say has existed for two thousand seven hundred years; this city that was invaded by both Mongols and Persians; this city that was visited by Greek merchants and occupied by Paskevich's army;* this city that, only three hours earlier, did not exist at all.

But then this creator, this almighty ruler begins to feel anxious; he starts glancing around uneasily.

Whom can I ask? Many of the people around me do not speak Russian—I feel shy, embarrassed to address them. The lord and master is tongue-tied. And so I enter a courtyard. But no—not a chance. This courtyard is nothing like our own deserted Russian yards—it is an Eastern courtyard, an Eastern inner yard, and I am at once scrutinized by dozens of pairs of eyes. I hurry back out onto the street. Very soon, however, I enter another courtyard. My anxiety is growing— I am no longer meditating on how, in the East, the inner yard is the heart and soul of life. But it truly *is* the heart and soul of life—and so, once again, I go back out onto the street. What am I to do?

I rush into a third courtyard—and am filled with despair. I see a network of little staircases and balconies, an old man sipping coffee from a little cup, a group of women who break off their conversation to look at me. I smile confusedly and turn back. Everywhere I look,

---

*Ivan Paskevich (1782–1856) was an important general in the tsarist army. His successes as second in command, and then as commander in chief, of the Russian forces during the war with Persia (1826–1828) included the liberation of most of Armenia from Persian rule.

there is life! What am I to do? There is nothing poetic about my thoughts now. Should I try to find Martirosyan as quickly as possible? But what help would that be? I can't turn up in his house and, ignoring his attempts to introduce me to his wife and family, ignoring everyone's questions, make a dash for the toilet. I've heard that Armenian intellectuals are fond of gossip. I can't burst into the apartment of one of the masters of Armenian prose and trample people underfoot as I dash towards the water closet. I'd never be able to live it down—people would be joking about this throughout my stay in Armenia. No, it was out of the question. And so—I jump into a half-empty tram. For three kopeks I acquire a ticket. I sit myself down on the hard seat, and for a while I breathe more freely. No longer am I a lord and creator—I am the slave of a base need. This need controls me; it has power over my thoughts and my soul. It has fettered my proud brain.

The whole world—architecture, the outlines of mountains, plants and trees, people's customs and habits—everything is now subordinated to a single longing.

I see tall boxlike buildings; I see squares; I see a grocery store, a television shop, a bakery, a building site; I see a bridge, a deep gorge, houses clinging to its stone slopes, quick foaming water far down below. Everything is new to me; I am seeing everything for the first time. But no longer is the creator's power of thought constructing an entire capital city—old quarters and new quarters at once. The creator's thought is now obstinately focused on a single goal—yet open to all possible ways of achieving it. How, in a given building, are the toilets arranged? The construction sites are still largely unmechanized and there are crowds of workers everywhere—just what I don't want. Behind every pile of bricks I'll find people, people, and still more people.... But if I get out by the bridge and stand on top of the cliff, I might get dizzy. My blood pressure feels terribly high.... But the torrent at the bottom of the gorge is white with foam. It looks beautiful!

A children's park.... Hopeless! You can see right through it from every side. The trees are mere twigs; they must have only just been planted. Even an infant would feel awkward behind a tree as small as these.

And then smoking chimneys—a factory with an entire settlement around it. . . . Districts like this are densely populated; the little houses are close together and there is a family in every room.

Then there's a grating of wheels, and the tram makes a sharp turn. The road has come to an end; now there is only wasteland and scree. Nearly all the passengers get out; only two others are left, both unshaven, their faces covered in black stubble. One has a long nose, the other a snub Mongolian nose. And me. The conductress gives me a searching look. She walks down the car to the driver and says a few quick words to him in Armenian. Evidently, she is sharing her suspicions with him. Yes, she glances around at me: What is this strange man after—this strange man in glasses? What is he doing at the terminus, amid a wasteland of clay and scree?

In a moment the driver will walk up to me, and then, out of nowhere, a policeman will appear. What will I say? That I'm from Moscow, that this is my first time in Yerevan? And that, in order to get to know the city, I needed to see these wastelands and scrap heaps? I'll get flustered, of course. I won't admit the truth; I won't say why I've made this journey to the city's outskirts. And it really will all look very strange indeed: A man leaves his things in the left-luggage office, no one turns up to meet him, he wanders about the city for hours, he doesn't register his arrival at any official institution; he makes no attempt to get a hotel room or even a bed in the House of the Collective Farmer. Instead, he makes his way to some outlying district where there is nothing but pits and scrap heaps. Yes, it's all very strange indeed, very perplexing. Or rather, it's all only too obvious.

Then, with my back to the wall, terror-stricken, I will admit the truth. I will admit the base and absurd need that has driven me to the outskirts of the Armenian capital. But no one will believe me— by then I will have told so many lies that the truth will seem like a joke. By then it will be only too obvious that I'm a saboteur—an old wolf of a spy who has finally given himself away. . . .

The tram has reached the end of the line, and no one has stopped me. I dash into some wasteland and find a safe place, out of sight among the ditches and scree....

Happiness. Do I need to describe this feeling? For thousands of years poets have been striving to convey on paper the nature of happiness....

All I will say here is that what I felt was not the proud happiness of a creator, the happiness of a thinker whose omnipotent mind has created its own unique and inimitable reality. It was a quiet happiness that is equally accessible to a sheep, a bull, a human being, or a macaque. Need I have gone all the way to Mount Ararat to experience it?

Translated from the Russian by Robert and Elizabeth Chandler

KARDAMYLI: BYZANTIUM RESTORED

Patrick Leigh Fermor

THE QUIET charm of Kardamyli grew with each passing hour. Most unexpectedly, we discovered a little hotel consisting of a few rooms over a grocer's shop owned by Socrates Phaliréas, the cousin, it turned out, of a distinguished sculptor-friend in Athens. Equally unexpectedly, it was, in its unflamboyant way, very comfortable. No planks were spread here with hair-shirt blankets for a stylite's penance, but springs and soft mattresses and a wicker chair or two waited for tired limbs in old and mellow rooms; and the kind, deep voice of the gigantic owner, a civilized and easy-going host, sitting down now and then for a chat, induced in all such a lack of hurry that the teeth of time and urgency and haste seemed all to have been drawn.

The same leisurely spell pervades the whole of this far-away little town. Cooled in summer by the breeze from the gulf, the great screen of the Taygetus shuts out intruding winds from the north and the east; no tramontana can reach it. It is like those Elysian confines of the world where Homer says that life is easiest for men; where no snow falls, no strong winds blow nor rain comes down, but the melodious west wind blows for ever from the sea to bring coolness to those who live there. I was very much tempted to become one of them, to settle in this small hotel for months with books and writing-paper; the thought has often recurred. The *Guide Bleu* only spares it half a line, mentioning little beyond the existence of its four hundred and ninety inhabitants. It is better so. It is too inaccessible and there is too little to do there, fortunately, for it ever to be seriously endangered by tourism. No wonder the nereids made it their home.

Returning from a long bathe beyond the forest of reeds, we saw a boy carrying a large silver fish by the tail: a *salpa*. (I haven't discovered its usual name.) I bought it, and, while it was being cooked, we sat under a mulberry tree, whose trunk was whitewashed right up to the start of the branches, on a terrace outside one of the few taverns. Like us, a few fishermen under their great hats were watching the sun sinking over the Messenian mountains, on the other side of which, sixteen leagues away, lay Pylos. A miniature mole ran out, and, alongside it, gently rocking with each sigh of the green transparent water, caiques were tethered a few yards above their shadows on the pebbly bottom. Oleanders leaned over a flat layer of rock across which the sea flowed with just enough impetus to net the surface with a frail white reticulation of foam which slid softly away and dissolved while a new one formed. A small distance from the shore rocks jutted, one bearing a whitewashed church, the other a miniature ruined fort. The sea's surface was striped with gold which turned as the sun dipped into pale sulphur shot with lilac. Beyond it the unruffled gulf sailed unhindered to the darkening peninsula opposite.

Thinking of our grilling fish, our minds strayed back to Kalamata (now hidden at the gleaming gulf's end), several years before.

It was midsummer in that glaring white town, and the heat was explosive. Some public holiday was in progress—could it have been the feast of St. John the Baptist which marks the summer solstice?—and the waterfront was crowded with celebrating citizens in liquefaction. The excitement of a holiday and the madness of a heat wave hung in the air. The stone flags of the water's edge, where Joan and Xan Fielding and I sat down to dinner, flung back the heat like a casserole with the lid off. On a sudden, silent, decision we stepped down fully dressed into the sea carrying the iron table a few yards out and then our three chairs, on which, up to our waists in cool water, we sat round the neatly laid table-top, which now seemed by magic to be levitated three inches above the water. The waiter, arriving a moment later, gazed with surprise at the empty space on the quay; then, observing us with a quickly-masked flicker of pleasure, he stepped unhesitatingly into the sea, advanced waist deep with a butler's gravity, and, saying nothing more than "Dinner-time," placed our meal before us—three beautifully grilled *kephali*, piping hot, and with their golden brown scales sparkling. To enjoy their marine flavour to the utmost, we dipped each by its tail for a second into the sea at our elbow... Diverted by this spectacle, the diners on the quay sent us can upon can of retsina till the table was crowded. A dozen boats soon gathered there, the craft radiating from the table's circumference like the petals of a marguerite. Leaning from their gently rocking boats, the fishermen helped us out with this sudden flux of wine, and by the time the moon and the Dog-Star rose over this odd symposium, a mandoline had appeared and *manga* songs in praise of hashish rose into the swooning night:

"When the hookah glows and bubbles,"

wailed the fishermen,

"Brothers, not a word! Take heed!
"Behold the *mangas* all around us
"Puffing at the eastern weed..."

I woke up thinking of the Mourtzini and the Palaeologi. It occurred to me, drinking mountain-tea in the street, that I had clean forgotten to ask when the Mourtzinos family had died out. "But it hasn't," Mr. Phaliréas said. "Strati, the last of them, lives just down the road."

Evstratios Mourtzinos was sitting in his doorway weaving, out of split cane and string, a huge globular fish-trap more complex than any compass design or abstract composition of geometrical wire. The reel of twine revolved on the floor, the thread unwinding between his big toe and its neighbour as the airy sphere turned and shifted in his skilful brown fingers with a dazzling interplay of symmetrical parabolas. The sunlight streamed through the rust-coloured loops and canopies of drying nets. A tang of salt, tar, seaweed and warm cork hung in the air. Cut reeds were stacked in sheaves, two canaries sung in a cage in the rafters, our host's wife was slicing onions into a copper saucepan. Mourtzinos shrugged his shoulders with a smile at my rather absurd questions and his shy and lean face, which brine and the sun's glare had cured to a deep russet, wore an expression of dubious amusement. "That's what they say," he said, "but we don't know anything about it. They are just old stories. . . ." He poured out hospitable glasses of ouzo, and the conversation switched to the difficulties of finding a market for fish: there was so much competition. There is a special delight in this early-morning drinking in Greece.

Old stories, indeed. But supposing every link were verified, each shaky detail proved? Supposing this modest and distinguished looking fisherman were really heir of the Palaeologi, descendant of Constantine XI and of Michael VIII the Liberator, successor to Alexis Comnène and Basil the Bulgar-Slayer and Leo the Isaurian and Justinian and Theodosius and St. Constantine the Great? And, for that matter, to Diocletian and Heliogabalus and Marcus Aurelius, to the Antonines, the Flavians, the Claudians and the Julians, all the way back to the Throne of Augustus Caesar on the Palatine, where Romulus had laid the earliest foundations of Rome? . . . The generous strength of a second glass of ouzo accelerated these cogitations. It was just the face for a constitutional monarch, if only Byzantium were free. For the sheer luxury of credulity I lulled all scepticism to sleep and, parallel to an unexacting discourse of currents and baits and shoals, a kind of fairy-tale began assembling in my mind: "Once upon a time, in a far-away land, a poor fisherman and his wife lived by the sea-shore. . . . One day a stranger from the city of Byzantium knocked on the door and begged for alms. The old couple laid meat and drink before him . . ." Here the mood and period painlessly changed into a hypothetic future and the stranger had a queer story to tell: the process of Westernization in Turkey, the study of European letters, of the classics and the humanities had borne such fruit that the Turks, in token of friendship and historical appropriateness, had decided to give the Byzantine Empire back to the Greeks and withdraw to the Central Asian steppes beyond the Volga from which they originally came, in order to plant their newly-won civilization in the Mongol wilderness. . . . The Greeks were streaming back into Constantinople and Asia Minor. Immense flotillas were dropping anchor off Smyrna and Adana and Halicarnassus and Alexandretta. The seaboard villages were coming back to life; joyful concourses of Greeks were streaming into Adrianople, Rhodosto, Broussa, Nicaea, Caesaraea, Iconium, Antioch and Trebizond. The sound of rejoicing rang through eastern Thrace and banners with the Cross and the double-headed eagle and the Four Betas back-to-back were fluttering over Cappadocia and Karamania and Pontus and Bithynia and Paphlagonia and the Taurus mountains. . . .

But in the City itself, the throne of the Emperors was vacant. . . .

Stratis, our host, had put the fish-trap on the ground to pour out a third round of ouzo. Mrs. Mourtzinos chopped up an octopus-tentacle and arranged the cross-sections on a plate. Stratis, to illustrate his tale, was measuring off a distance by placing his right hand in the crook of his left elbow, "a grey mullet that long," he was saying, "weighing five okas if it weighed a dram. . . ."

Then, in the rebuilt palace of Blachernae, the search for the heir had begun. What a crackling of parchment and chrysobuls, what clashing of seals and unfolding of scrolls! What furious wagging of beards and flourishes of scholarly forefingers! The Cantacuzeni, though the most authenticated of the claimants, were turned down; they were descendants only from the last emperor but four. . . . Dozens of doubtful Palaeologi were sent packing . . . the Stephanopoli de Comnène of Corsica, the Melissino-Comnènes of Athens were regretfully declined. Tactful letters had to be written to the Argyropoli; a polite firmness was needed, too, with the Courtney family of Powderham Castle in Devonshire, kinsmen of Pierre de Courtenai, who, in 1218, was Frankish Emperor of Constantinople; and a Lascaris maniac from Saragossa was constantly hanging about the gates. . . . Envoys returned empty-handed from Barbados and the London docks. . . . Some Russian families allied to Ivan the Terrible and the Palaeologue Princess Anastasia Tzarogorodskaia had to be considered. . . . Then all at once a new casket of documents came to light and a foreign emissary was despatched hot foot to the Peloponnese; over the

Taygetus to the forgotten hamlet of Kardamyli.... By now all doubt
had vanished. The Emperor Eustratius leant forward to refill the
glasses with ouzo for the fifth time. The Basilissa shooed away a
speckled hen which had wandered indoors after crumbs. On a sunny
doorstep, stroking a marmalade cat, sat the small Diadoch and Des-
pot of Mistra.

Our host heaved a sigh ... "The trouble with dyes made from pine-
cones," he went on—"the ordinary brown kind—is that the fish can
see the nets a mile off. They swim away! But you have to use them or
the twine rots in a week. Now, the new *white* dyes in Europe would
solve all that! But you would hunt in vain for them in the ships'
chandlers of Kalamata and Gytheion...."

The recognition over, the rest seemed like a dream. The removal
of the threadbare garments, the donning of the cloth-of-gold dalmat-
ics, the diamond-studded girdles, the purple cloaks. All three were
shod with purple buskins embroidered with bicephalous eagles, and
when the sword and the sceptre had been proffered and the glittering
diadem with its hanging pearls, the little party descended to a waiting ship. The fifth ouzo carried us, in a ruffle of white foam, across
the Aegean archipelago and at every island a score of vessels joined
the convoy. By the time we entered the Hellespont, it stretched from
Troy to Sestos and Abydos ... on we went, past the islands of the
shining Propontis until, like a magical city hanging in mid-air, Constantinople appeared beyond our bows, its towers and bastions glittering, its countless domes and cupolas bubbling among pinnacles
and dark sheaves of cypresses, all of them climbing to the single great
dome topped with the flashing cross that Constantine had seen in a
vision on the Milvian bridge. There, by the Golden Gate, in the heart
of a mighty concourse, waited the lords of Byzantium: the lesser
Caesars and Despots and Sebastocrators, the Grand Logothete in his
globular headgear, the Counts of the Palace, the Sword Bearer, the
Chartophylax, the Great Duke, the thalassocrats and polemarchs,
the Strateges of the Cretan archers, of the hoplites and the peltasts
and the cataphracts; the Silentiaries, the Count of the Excubitors,
the governors of the Asian Themes, the Clissourarchs, the Grand

Eunuch, and (for by now all Byzantine history had melted into a single anachronistic maelstrom) the Prefects of Sicily and Nubia and Ethiopia and Egypt and Armenia, the Exarchs of Ravenna and Carthage, the Nomarch of Tarentum, the Catapan of Bari, the Abbot of Studium. As a reward for bringing good tidings, I had by this time assumed the Captaincy of the Varangian Guard; and there they were, beyond the galleons and the quinqueremes, in coruscating ranks of winged helmets, clashing their battle-axes in homage; you could tell they were Anglo-Saxons by their long thick plaits and their flaxen whiskers.... Bells clanged. Semantra hammered and cannon thundered as the Emperor stepped ashore; then, with a sudden reek of naphtha, Greek fire roared saluting in a hundred blood-red parabolas from the warships' brazen beaks. As he passed through the Golden Gate a continual paean of cheering rose from the hordes which darkened the battlement of the Theodosian Walls. Every window and roof-top was a-bristle with citizens and as the great company processed along the purple-carpeted street from the Arcadian to the Amastrian Square, I saw that all the minarets had vanished.... We crossed the Philadelphia and passed under the Statue of the Winds. Now, instead of the minarets, statuary crowded the skyline. A population of ivory and marble gleamed overhead and, among the fluttering of a thousand silken banners, above the awnings and the crossed festoons of olive-leaves and bay, the sky was bright with silver and gold and garlanded chryselephantine.... Each carpeted step seemed to carry us into a denser rose-coloured rain of petals softly falling.

The heat had become stifling. In the packed square of Constantine, a Serbian furrier fell from a roof-top and broke his neck; an astrologer from Ctesiphon, a Spanish coppersmith and a money-lender from the Persian Gulf were trampled to death; a Bactrian lancer fainted, and, as we proceeded round the Triple Delphic Serpent of the Hippodrome, the voices of the Blues and the Greens, for once in concord, lifted a long howl of applause. The Imperial horses neighed in their stables, the hunting cheetahs strained yelping at their silver chains. Mechanical gold lions roared in the throne room, gold birds on the jewelled branches of artificial trees set up a tinkling and a twitter.

The general hysteria penetrated the public jail: in dark cells, mono-physites and bogomils and iconoclasts rattled their fetters across the dungeon bars. High in the glare on his Corinthian capital, a capering stylite, immobile for three decades, hammered his calabash with a wooden spoon....

Mrs. Mourtzinos spooned a couple of onions and potatoes out of the pot, laid them before us and sprinkled them with a pinch of rock salt. "When we were a couple of hours off Cerigo," Stratis observed, splashing out the ouzo, "the wind grew stronger—a real *meltemi*—a roaring *boucadoura*!—so we hauled the sails down, and made every-thing fast...."

There, before the great bronze doors of St. Sophia, gigantic in his pontificalia, stood Athenagoras the Oecumenical Patriarch, whom I saw a few months before in the Phanar; surrounded now with all the Patriarchs and Archbishops of the East, the Holy Synod and all the pomp of Orthodoxy in brocade vestments of scarlet and purple and gold and lilac and sea blue and emerald green: a forest of gold pastoral staves topped with their twin coiling serpents, a hundred yard-long beards cascading beneath a hundred onion-mitres crusted with gems; and, as in the old Greek song about the City's fall, the great fane rang with sixty clanging bells and four hundred gongs, with a priest for every bell and a deacon for every priest. The proces-sion advanced, and the coruscating penumbra, the flickering jungle of hanging lamps and the bright groves and the undergrowth of candles swallowed them. Marble and porphyry and lapis-lazuli soared on all sides, a myriad glimmering haloes indicated the entire mosaic hagiography of the Orient and, high above, suspended as though on a chain from heaven and ribbed to its summit like the concavity of an immense celestial umbrella, floated the golden dome. Through the prostrate swarm of his subjects and the fog of incense the imperial theocrat advanced to the iconostasis. The great basilica rang with the anthem of the Cherubim and as the Emperor stood on the right of the Katholikon and the Patriarch on the left, a voice as though from an archangel's mouth sounded from the dome, followed by the fanfare of scores of long shafted trumpets, while across Byzantium the heralds proclaimed the Emperor Eustratius, Servant of God, King of Kings, Most August Caesar and Basileus and Autocrator of Constantinople and New Rome. The whole City was shaken by an unending, ear-splitting roar. Entwined in whorls of incense, the pillars turned in their sockets, and tears of felicity ran down the mosaic Virgin's and the cold ikons' cheeks....

Leaning forward urgently, Strati crossed himself. "*Holy Virgin and all the Saints!*" he said. "I was never in a worse situation! It was pitch dark and pouring with rain, the mast and the rudder were broken, the bung was lost, and the waves were the size of a house. There I was, on all fours in the bilge water, baling for life, in the Straits between the Elaphonisi and Cape Malea!..."

...the whole of Constantinople seemed to be rising on a dazzling golden cloud and the central dome began to revolve as the redoubled clamour of the Byzantines hoisted it aloft. Loud with bells and gongs, with cannon flashing from the walls and a cloud-borne fleet firing long crimson radii of Greek fire, the entire visionary city, turning in faster and faster spirals, sailed to a blinding and unconjecturable zenith.... The rain had turned to hail, the wind had risen to a scream; the boat had broken and sunk and, through the ink-black storm, Strati was swimming for life towards the thunderous rocks of Laconia....

...The bottle was empty....

The schoolmaster's shadow darkened the doorway. "You'd better hurry," he said, "the caique for Areopolis is just leaving." We all rose to our feet, upsetting, in our farewells, a basket of freshly cut bait and a couple of tridents which fell to the floor with a clatter. We stepped out into the sobering glare of noon.

YVETTE

Gillian Rose

YVETTE and I planned to visit Jerusalem together, where she was born and grew up. I very much wanted to go to Israel with Yvette, who was teaching me biblical and modern Hebrew, capital and cursive script. But she died before we could realise our dreams.

Once I arrived late for a taxi at Yvette's flat in Harrington Road, Brighton. The flat was perched high above a vociferous fire-escape, which I always tried to dampen on ascending in order to surprise her. On this occasion I'd booked the taxi to fetch me from her place, since I wanted to deliver a volume to her and then fly on somewhere else. My mind went completely blank when the impatient driver remarked blandly, "There was an old woman at the address you gave me. She didn't know nothing about a taxi." An "old woman"? Who? Yvette? Preposterous!

While I copied out Rilke's *Elegies* for Yvette, Yvette sent me Yeats's "John Kinsella's Lament for Mrs Mary Moore":

> *None other knows what pleasures man*
> *At table or in bed.*
> What shall I do for pretty girls
> Now my Old Bawd is dead?

I suppose Yvette's looks could be misleading, for she was canny and crafty enough to disappear into the environment when it suited her purpose. From the moment that, unobserved, I first noticed and watched her, as she paced up and down the platform at Preston Park Station in Brighton, I knew that I was in the presence of a superior being. Green tights, a shapeless dark skirt and a mop of nondescript grey hair were but transparent media for the piercing intelligence in evident amused communication with itself, and warranting, on each turn at both ends of the platform, a grim but irrepressible smile, which spread slowly over her bare, unmade-up, delicate features.

This lucid apparition came to me many times—crossing the Level in Brighton, in the corridors of the School of European Studies, as well as frequently at that same station platform—before I found myself being introduced to her at Julius Carlebach's home, and the supernatural being began to acquire a measure of the natural.

That evening at Julius's was memorable for another reason. It was the occasion of my initiation into the anti-supernatural character of Judaism: into how *non-belief in God* defines Judaism and how change in that compass registers the varieties of Jewish modernity. The more liberal Judaism becomes, the less the orientation by Halachah, the law, and the greater the emphasis on individual faith in God. Julius sat at the head of the table in a dining-room which was museum and mausoleum of the Carlebach family's distinguished and dreadful history. Portraits of his ancestors presided. Between Solomon Carlebach, Rabbi of Lübeck, Julius's grandfather, mentioned in Thomas Mann's *Dr Faustus*, and Julius's cousin, Shlomo Carlebach, the singing Rabbi of Manhattan's Upper West Side, Julius's father, Joseph Carlebach, the famous Rabbi of Hamburg, accompanied his congregation from Hamburg to their death outside Riga, with his wife and the four youngest of their nine children. The square in Hamburg where his synagogue stood has recently been renamed Carlebach Platz. In his acceptance speech in Hamburg, when Julius received the honour on behalf of his family, he pointed out to his audience that they were assembled in the same school hall where he had stood, a fifteen-year-old schoolboy, on 10 November 1938, the day after *Kristallnacht*, when the Gestapo came and told the children that they had four weeks to leave Germany. "You could hear people collapse internally," Julius commented on his adult audience. What happened to those children?

At dinner, Julius explained, "An Orthodox Jew doesn't have to worry about whether he believes in God or not. As long as he observes

the law." Subsequently, I became familiar with the notoriously in-
scrutable Midrash: "Would that they would forsake Me, but obey
my Torah." When we parted that evening, Yvette and I had agreed
that I would visit her.

Yvette's dowdy and unselfconscious bearing was unable to conceal
her visceral vocation as the Lover—not the Beloved: she was predator
not prey. I had picked this up immediately that first time I spied on
her from my station hide-out. The main room of her small granny-flat
was furnished so that it conjured the atmosphere of Jerusalem's Ben
Yehuda Street. Teeming with colourful artifacts, against the backdrop
of the holy city, it re-created in miniature the bazaars of Eastern
Europe, displaying the wares of so many destroyed folk cultures. From
every available space, photographs of Yvette's five children and ten
grandchildren listed tenderly towards her. We invariably sat opposite
each other at the solid table by the window, high above the tree-lined
road, and Yvette expounded to me her philosophy of love. Yvette was
sixty-five years old when I first began to get to know her, and she had,
concurrently, three lovers:

> What lively lad most pleasured me
> Of all that with me lay?
> I answer that I gave my soul
> And loved in misery,
> But had great pleasure with a lad
> That I loved bodily.
>
> Flinging from his arms I laughed
> To think his passion such
> He fancied that I gave a soul
> Did but our bodies touch,
> And laughed upon his breast to think
> Beast gave beast as much.

When I protested at this ceremony of lust, Yvette's reply was prepared:
Yeats's "Last Confession" was elaborated by Swinburne:

No thorns go as deep as a rose's,
And love is more cruel than lust.

Yvette described my idea of creative closeness in relationships as a "total" and, by implication, totalitarian attitude. However, she insisted that while the number of her former lovers was too great to count, she had only been in love five times. This was an important distinction to her, and she appreciated having it confirmed by Miriam, her youngest child and only daughter.

Yvette was formidably well read. She had been married to an academic who taught English at the Open University, but now, in the mid-1980s, she was working as a secretary at the University of Sussex. Yvette regularly attended lectures and conferences, and she always posed with studied diffidence the most well-aimed critical questions, which presupposed her command of whatever literature was at stake. She was, however, deeply Francophile, and her staples were Proust—she reread *À la Recherche* in its entirety, once a year, in her antique, slightly foxed Pléiade edition—and Maupassant, all the passages and stories expurgated from school editions. She also had a sly but ardent passion for the novels of Ivy Compton-Burnett. And these authors, whom she inhabited, knowing them to be both enticing and rebarbative, were the source and confirmation of her philosophy of human relationships.

One Sunday, with the rain singing out of the secular silence, I met Yvette by chance walking in the unusually deserted Preston Park. We recognised each other with pleasure from afar. Yvette came up close to me and put her hand on my arm. I already knew that her daughter, Miriam, after years of not being able to conceive, including an ectopic pregnancy, with the consequent loss of one of her fallopian tubes, was now, at long last, expecting. Yvette said in a factual and unemotional tone of voice, "I have cancer of the breast. I have to wait for an operation." She paused to gauge my response, which was guided by her evident dispassion, and then she added, "Miriam and I are now two ladies-in-waiting."

Yvette was divorced from her husband. It had been he who had initiated the decisive break after they had had five children together. Yvette stressed that the shock of their unanticipated separation did not derive from the closeness of their tumultuous family life, but from the fact that their partnership had always sustained much extra-marital activity on both sides. Several small children would be deposited in the coping hands of Nanny as Yvette snatched a furtive and hurried rendezvous with her current liaison. "I loved my man," she would defiantly assert of her former husband. Although she felt that she and her daughter Miriam, in particular, had been utterly deserted by him, she refused to rewrite history. Coming from a family in which my mother divorced both of her husbands, and, in addition, denied that she ever loved them, I found Yvette's aggressive vulnerability refreshing.

Yvette was the most enthusiastic and inventive grandmother. She couldn't spend enough time with her grandchildren, and she was especially close to Miriam's two children, who lived downstairs in the main body of the spacious Victorian house that Yvette had bequeathed to her daughter. She frequently visited her favourite son and his wife in Southampton with their older children. Another son would visit from London with his Sephardi wife and their two children, and the remaining two sons lived in Israel and Australia.

Yvette was completely devoted to pleasure without guilt. This was what made her such an attentive and encouraging confidante. She would listen with rapt attention to my confessions of pain and rage, but invariably dismiss my scruples, overcoming the nihilism of the emotions by affirming the validity of every tortuous and torturing desire. Although I was thus tutored by her, I watched with squeamish propriety as Yvette playfully squeezed her three-year-old grandson's balls and penis. "Aren't children meant to emerge to independence with a residue of resentment from the fact that it is the mother who accidentally arouses but explicitly forbids genital pleasure?" I ventured with theoretical pedantry in remembrance of Freud, and of the narrow border between child care and child abuse. Yvette positively relished my staid inhibitions, which she dismissed airily as contrary to the universal and sacred spirit of lust. A Grand Mother indeed.

In the far, dark corner of Yvette's main room there stood a heavy veneered chest of drawers with a pride of family photographs jostling on top. The three bottom compartments of this tallboy were jammed full with pornographic material, which, one day, after I'd known her for quite a while, Yvette showed to me. The photographs were almost entirely of women, clad in enough to titillate, and revealing proud genitals in various *contrapposto* positions. Yvette possessed very little male pornography, not because it is less available, but because it didn't interest her.

When I remarked one day, in a different context, that I couldn't reconcile her grandmotherly identity with her prodigious sexuality, she looked sadly and wisely at me as the one corrupted by unnatural practices: "Have you forgotten the connection between sex and children?" She was, of course, partly right.

Yvette's inexhaustible animus could be traced to her unsentimental disapproval of her own mother, as a mother and as an Israeli. According to Yvette, her mother, now in her nineties and living in a home in Jerusalem, had barred her children from loving or esteeming their father. Yvette's infinite fury at this ban had bestowed on her the lifelong celebration of lustful love. This vocation was inseparable from the rage at her mother, but also, and deeper still, it was inseparable from her secret concurrence with her mother concerning the intellectual inferiority of the male. Her contempt was overlaid, and therefore indiscernible to the untrained eye, with a much more explicit contempt for the resentful ruses of preyed-upon females.

To capture her distance from her mother as an Israeli, Yvette gives over the narrative voice to her for the space of a story. Yvette had, after all, run away in her early twenties with a one-legged Englishman, a "goy," as she would say. I cannot find a published version of this jumble tale, but one probably exists in Hebrew or Yiddish.

A LEGEND ABOUT THE BAAL SHEM TOV (BESHT)—
THE BEARER OF A GOOD NAME
In the remote Polish village where he lived, there is a widow—
shall we call her Katrilevska for she is *not* Jewish. She has several

mouths to feed and is hopeless and helpless. A coarse-looking peasant enters her hovel and ascertains her needs. First, he brings her firewood, fills up her stove and lights it. Then he goes back, returning with two pails of water on his shoulders and now she can boil some coffee. Lastly he brings her a warm loaf. All this at 4 a.m., and all the while the peasant hums a song in a foreign tongue, but it is very sweet. He bids her farewell and disappears. It is the Besht, and he was humming *tehilim*, and was back in his house just after 4 a.m., in time to pray *shakhrit*.

The crucial thing is that Yvette's mother recited this story with disapprobation—or, I wonder, was it heard with disdain by the young Israeli children?

Yvette had two major recurrences of cancer before she died. After the first, relatively minor operation, a nip in the breast, which she valiantly displayed to select visitors, and several courses of chemotherapy, Yvette fell *in love*—in love, according to her own criterion—hopelessly and helplessly in love. But no Besht ever came to save her or even to console her. The object of this serious passion was thirty years her junior, a colleague of my generation. Clever, charming, promiscuous and superficial, he enjoyed Yvette's friendship, but was genuinely disconcerted by her remorseless ardour. Yvette was monstrous: she pursued him with myriad love letters, phone calls, messages pinned to his door, unsolicited visitations. I taunted her, "Yvette, if you were a man, your actions would be seen as gross harassment." On a later occasion, her violent blandishments unabated, I asked her, archly, what she would do with him, were he, miraculously, to succumb? Yvette replied without a fraction of hesitation, "I would chew him up and spit him out."

A whole generation of young women and men were bereaved by Yvette's death. She made new friends up to the end, and she gave people, young and old, her courage to face the terrors of desire in themselves and to ease off the unstable alleviation of attributing to the Beloved our desire for those terrors. She could impart this wisdom because it grew out of the folly that she was still endlessly contesting in herself. And the cure for an unhappy love affair was always the pleasures of the ensuing one.

Yvette practised the *ars moriendi*; I had long known that she would. The day before she died, her spirit intact, she listened with a look of beatitude on her simplified face to the story that I had brought with me from Leamington Spa, where I had just moved, to the Brighton hospice, where she lay in a room that formed a hard crystal of light, exposed to the raucous and merciless spring. It was a love story, and when I had finished relating it to her, and had sat quietly with her for several hours, she finally spoke out of the suffused silence, "You are now going to leave." Then, in her own way, she gave me her blessing: "You know how I feel. You know how I feel. Nothing has changed. Nothing has changed. All the very best. All the very best." I bent over her and kissed her on the lips several times, her lips reaching mine each time before mine touched hers.

Among the many pieces of unlined file paper, cut into thirds and covered with Yvette's old-fashioned typewriting, I found another fragment of Swinburne:

> From too much love of living,
>   From hope and fear set free,
> We thank with brief thanksgiving
>   Whatever gods may be
>
> That no man lives for ever,
> That dead men rise up never;
> That even the weariest river
>   Winds somewhere safe to sea.

I believe that I did in some sense visit Israel with Yvette, that through knowing her, I somehow reached the soul of that land of blessings and curses.

IN THE GREAT CITY OF PHOENIX

Tove Jansson

AFTER a long bus trip through Arizona, Jonna and Mari came late in the evening to the great city of Phoenix and checked into the first hotel they could find near the bus station.

It was called the Majestic, a heavy building from the 1910s with an air of shabby pretension. The lobby with its long mahogany counters beneath dusty potted palms, the broad staircase up to the gloom of the upper floors, the row of stiff, velvet sofas—everything was too grand, everything except the desk clerk, who was tiny under his wreath of white hair. He gave them their room key and a form to fill out and said, "The elevator closes in twenty minutes."

The elevator operator was asleep. He was even older than the desk clerk. He pushed the button for the third floor and sat back down on his velvet chair. The elevator was a huge ornamented bronze cage and it rattled upward very slowly.

Jonna and Mari entered a static, desolate room with way too much furniture and went to bed without unpacking. But they couldn't sleep. They relived the bus trip again and again, through shifting landscapes of desert and snowy mountains, cities without names, white salt lakes, and brief pauses in little towns they knew nothing about and to which they would never return. The trip went on and on, leaving everything behind, hour after hour, a long, long day in a silver-blue Greyhound bus.

"Are you asleep?" Jonna asked.

"No."

"We can get our films developed here. I've been filming blind for a month and haven't any idea what I've got."

"Are you sure it was a good idea to shoot through the bus window? I think we were going too fast."

"I know," Jonna said. And, after a while, "But it was so pretty."

They left the films to be developed, which would take a couple of days.

"Why is the city so empty?" Mari asked.

"Empty?" repeated the man behind the camera counter. "I never thought about it. But I suppose it's because most people live outside of town and drive in to work and then back home."

When Jonna and Mari came back to their room, they noticed a change, a small but sweeping change. It was their first encounter with the invisible chambermaid, Verity. Verity's presence in the hotel room was powerful. It was everywhere. She had reorganized their travelers' lives in her own way. This Verity was an obvious perfectionist and at the same time a conspicuous free spirit. She had laid out Jonna's and Mari's belongings symmetrically but with a certain humor; had unpacked their travel mementos and arranged them on the dresser in a caravan whose placement did not lack irony; had placed their slippers with the noses touching and spread out their nightgowns so the sleeves were holding hands. On their pillows she'd put books she'd found and liked—or perhaps disliked—using their stones from Death Valley as bookmarks. Those ugly stones must have amused her greatly. She had given the room a face.

Jonna said, "Someone's having fun with us."

The next evening, the mirror was decorated with their Indian souvenirs. Verity had washed and ironed everything she thought needed washing and ironing and placed it in symmetrical piles, and in the middle of the table was a large bunch of artificial flowers, which, if they remembered correctly, had previously adorned the lobby.

"I wonder," Mari said. "I wonder if she does this in all the rooms, and is it to cheer up the hotel guests or herself? How does she have the time? Is she just teasing the other chambermaids?"

"We'll see," said Jonna.

They met Verity in the corridor. She was large, with red cheeks and a lot of black hair. She laughed out loud and said, "I'm Verity. Were you surprised?"

"Very much," replied Jonna politely. "We wondered what made you so playful?"

"I thought you looked like fun," Verity said.

And so, quite naturally, they began to be friends with Verity. Every day she was interested to know if Jonna's films had come back. No, they hadn't. It would take a whole week before Jonna and Mari could travel on to Tucson.

Verity was amazed. "Why Tucson, of all places? It's just another town, except it's the closest city on the map. Why do you have to keep traveling, here or there or somewhere else? Is there such a big difference? You've got your health and each other's company. Moreover, now you've got me. For that matter, you should meet the residents. They can be very interesting if you take them the right way."

"The residents?"

"Pensioners, of course. Aren't you pensioners yourselves? Why else would you have come to the Majestic?"

"Nonsense," said Jonna, somewhat sharply, and headed for the stairs.

Verity said, "But aren't you going to take the elevator? Albert likes people to take his elevator. I'm going down myself."

Albert stood up and pressed the button for the ground floor.

"Hi, Albert," said Verity. "How are the legs?"

"The left one's working better," Albert said.

"And how's the birthday coming?"

"I don't know yet. But it's all I think about, all the time."

In the lobby, Verity explained. "Albert's going to be eighty, and he's terribly anxious about his birthday. Should he invite all the residents or just the ones he likes and then the others will be hurt? By the way, would you like to have some fun this evening? Of course everyone goes to bed early at the Majestic..."

"Not us," Jonna said. "But this city is empty and quiet in the evenings. You know that."

Verity looked at her for a moment, almost sternly. "Don't talk like a tourist. I'll take you to Annie's bar. I'll come and get you when I've finished work."

It was a very small bar, long and narrow with a pool table in the back. Annie herself tended the bar, the jukebox played constantly, and people came in steadily and greeted one another in passing as if they'd seen each other an hour ago, which perhaps they had. No ladies among the clientele.

Verity said, "Now you're going to have Annie's banana drink, an Annie Special, her treat. Tell her you like it, then you can get a real drink to chase it. Annie's my friend. She's got two kids and she's a single mother."

"On the house," Annie said. "And where do you come from? Finland? Oh, I didn't think you were allowed to travel to other countries..." She turned her smile toward new customers, but after a while she came back and wanted to give them another Banana Special. They had to toast Finland.

"In that case, Annie, I think we'll need some vodka," Verity said. "Am I right?"

Somebody played the current hit, "A Horse with No Name," and Annie poured vodka into three small glasses, raised a quick, invisible glass of her own, and disappeared to take care of other customers. Jonna opened her tape recorder, and a Stetson to their right hollered, "Hey, Annie! They're stealing our music!"

"They like it!" Annie hollered back. "How did it go with that job?"

"Nothing came of it. How are the kids?"

"Fine. Willy's had a sore throat, so John's bound to catch it. Getting sitters is hopeless."

The bar had grown crowded.

"Give these ladies some space!" Annie yelled. "They're from Finland."

Verity turned to the Stetson and told him cheerfully that her new friends, among other curious undertakings, had traveled a great distance out of the city "in order to see a cactus garden, of all things—cactus that doesn't even flower—and there's an entrance fee!"

"Very bad," said the Stetson sadly. "Pure weeds. I cleaned out a whole patch of them at the Robinsons' last week. They didn't pay much."

"Let me show you something interesting," said their neighbor to the left. "Look, a wonderful little item that ought to sell like nobody's business, but doesn't." He put three small plastic dogs on the bar, one pink, one green, one yellow, and the dogs began marching side by side, the green one in the lead. Mari looked at Jonna, but Jonna shook her head. It meant, no, he's not trying to sell them, he just wants to amuse us.

The friendly crowding, the jukebox, the pool balls clicking from the curtained-off section of the room, a sudden laugh in the even flood of conversation, a voice being raised to object or explain, and people coming in the whole time and somehow finding space. Annie worked as if possessed but with no trace of nerves, her smile was her own, and the fact that she was hurrying did not mean time was short.

They left the bar and walked back to the hotel. The broad street was empty, and there were lights in only a few windows.

"The cactus garden," Mari said. "That was nothing to laugh at. It was done with great care, with great love! Just sand and more sand, all the plants prickly and gray—they were as tall as statues or so tiny they had to put up barriers so people wouldn't step on them, and everything had its name on a visiting card. It was a brave garden." She added, "Verity, you're brave yourself."

"What do you mean?"

"This city. And the hotel."

"Why do you take everything so seriously?" Verity asked. "Cactuses like sand, they grow, they do all right. Visiting cards, that's dumb! And I'm doing all right myself. At the Majestic I know all the codgers and all their tricks and dodges, and I know Annie, and now I know you. I've got everything I need. And Phoenix is just the place where I happen to live, right? What's so remarkable about that?"

The desk clerk woke up when they came in.

"Verity," he said, "you'll have to take the stairs, you know. But the elevator will be running again tomorrow."

The elevator was decorated with bows of black ribbon. As they were climbing the stairs, Verity explained. "Albert died this afternoon, on the second floor. So we're paying our respects."

"Oh, I'm so sorry," Mari said.

"No need to be sorry. He never had to face that birthday he was so worried about. Jonna, when will your films be ready?"

"Tomorrow."

"And then you're going on to Tucson?"

"Yes."

"There's probably no Annie's bar in Tucson. I've heard unpleasant things about that town, I really have."

In the room, Verity had put all the shoes she could find in marching order toward the door and turned the flower vase upside down. The curtains were drawn, and the suitcase lay open. Verity had been explicit.

Jonna's films were ready the next day. They could see the bus trip across Arizona on the camera store's picture screen, a small device that the owner had placed on the counter for the convenience of tourists. Jonna and Mari watched in silence. It was dreadful. An incoherent, flickering stream of pictures sliced to bits by telephone poles, pine trees, fences. The landscape tipped over and came up straight again and hurried on. It was a mess.

"Thanks," said Jonna. "I think that's enough. I haven't actually had this camera very long."

He smiled at her.

"But the Grand Canyon," Mari said. "Can't we see just a little bit, please?"

And the Grand Canyon made its entrance in the majesty of a fiery dawn. Jonna had held the camera steady and taken time. It was beautiful.

They walked back to the hotel and ran into Verity in the corridor. "Are they good?" she asked at once.

"Very good," Mari said.

"And you're sure you want to go to Tucson tomorrow?"

"Yes."

"Tucson is a horrible place, believe me. There's nothing there to film." Verity turned on her heel and continued down the corridor, calling back over her shoulder, "I'll see you at Annie's this evening!"

Nothing had changed at Annie's bar. The regulars were there and greeted them in a careless, friendly way. They each had a Banana Special on the house. The pool players were hard at it, and the jukebox was playing "A Horse with No Name."

"Business as usual," said Mari and smiled at Verity. But Verity didn't want to talk. The man with the plastic dogs was there. The green, the pink, and the yellow had their race across the bar.

"Take them with you," he said. "They're great for making bets when things get slow."

On their way home, Verity said, "I forgot to ask Annie if John caught that sore throat. When does your bus leave?"

"Eight o'clock."

When they came to the Majestic, a fire truck screamed by through the empty streets. It was a windy night, but very warm.

Verity said, "Shall we say goodbye right now and get it over with?"

"Let's do," said Jonna.

In the room, Jonna opened her tape recorder. "Listen to this," she said. "I think it'll be good."

The jukebox through a torrent of people talking, Annie's bright voice, pool balls clicking, the jingle of the cash register—a pause, then their steps on the sidewalk; finally the fire engine and silence.

"But why are you crying?" Jonna said.

"I don't really know. Maybe the fire truck..."

Jonna said, "We'll send a pretty postcard to Verity from Tucson. And one to Annie."

"There aren't any pretty cards of Tucson! It's a dreadful place!"

"We could stay here for a while?"

"No," Mari said. "You can't repeat. It's the wrong ending."

"Of course. Writers," Jonna said and counted out the next day's vitamins into two small glasses.

Translated from the Swedish by Thomas Teal

VICUÑA PORTO

Antonio di Benedetto

VICUÑA Porto was like the river; he grew with the rains.

Water poured down upon the earth from the torrid sky and the current would swell. Meanwhile, Vicuña Porto seemed to emanate from the diligently irrigated soil.

If a cow got lost, the blame lay with the river that gluttonously licked up everything in its path. If a merchant died, eviscerated in his bed, Porto must have done it.

With each year—and two had gone by—Vicuña Porto loomed larger. He was a multitudinous man and the city feared him.

It lived in dread of him but without putting up a garrote. Until the conflagration that took one block, then two, then three. Every man listened to the fire consuming the doorposts as if they were his own bones.

The city formed a resolution: It would hunt Vicuña down.

But some said it was the season of his arrival, while others said it was the time when he left, and none could say whether he was in the city or not. A futile search was made within the city limits. Then an armed brigade was mustered to pursue Vicuña and his men, bring him to ground in his lair, and bring about his death.

I requested a place in that legion.

No one knew why.

No one had ever seen Vicuña or had any notion of where his tracks lay. He chose his own name; no one gave it to him.

Vicuña . . . and a time long past. Vicuña . . . and the Corregidor. I knew his name. I knew his face!

I

The Gobernador, my hand in his, lingered endlessly over our leave-taking, incredulous as he was that I was departing for the north, precisely opposite the direction in which I had always yearned to go.

With all the solemnity of his post radiating from his cheeks, he told me at last that "Su Majestad shall celebrate this return to arms, and even more than that: a victory he is well able to reward."

This was the necessary promise. It corresponded to the obvious fact that a daring feat of arms in the service of public order would place me in the monarch's hand, to be set down in a position more to my liking.

Triumph would come in a single round, amid great applause. Vicuña Porto could not disguise himself as a landowner, settler, or peon on a yerba maté plantation. Wherever we met him, I would know him.

He had served me when I was Corregidor. Disloyal, he fomented rebellion among the Indians and instigated looting. He was never caught; the clamor of his exploits was hushed by his departure for other regions, and so the lands under my supervision were pacified.

The regiment's officer in chief did not hand over command to me. He told me I would have full authority, but the squadron would have at its head an officer on active duty, taken from among the troops themselves.

This was a mark of disdain, cloaked in respect. A mere precaution, he told me, to ensure my security and minimize certain concerns, given that soldiers encamped in the wild grow hostile and lazy.

The two of us—the officer in chief, whose name was Capitán Parrilla, and myself—left the barracks with only a small escort. Most of the twenty-five men had marched ahead earlier that morning with a large herd of horses, ten relief horses for each man, and cattle for our sustenance.

Hence there was no parade, march-past, or celebration of any sort to send us off, though I would have longed for one, perhaps so my Diego could see me.

A restless cow with very long horns was energetically attempting to escape from the herd as four soldiers feigned powerlessness to subjugate her. They wanted an excuse to give rein to their horses and break out of the trudging march.

That was our welcome: dust and partial disorder.

We moved to the head of the column, Parrilla in ill humor.

I swiveled around in the saddle to look back, wanting to give notice to the city that when I returned I would only be passing through. A head, Vicuña Porto's, would be my ticket to the better destiny that neither civil merit, intermediaries, nor supplication had gained me.

But between ourselves and the city were the soldiers and the herd. There was no option but to look forward.

So, forward then.

2

After the flatlands—outer limit of the brief excursions on horseback that people from the city sometimes took—the forest began. We skirted past.

The sun shone its torch in our faces. The forest seemed airy, welcoming, and cool, but remained over there, to one side of us, our margin as we were its.

Then it seemed to follow us, ceaselessly flowing alongside.

I was drowsy, falling asleep. Hipólito Parrilla was not a man for talk, or so his conduct indicated.

This was not the case. Until we reached the freshwater lake, he hadn't wanted to make himself thirsty with conversation. Dust gets into an open mouth.

At the lake he had us drink. First men, then horses, then cows—the order of importance imposed by those who drank first.

He permitted neither maté nor asado. He demanded that we devote our utmost efforts to the march while we were still fresh, our strength not yet drained.

The soldiers chewed on ground-up charquí. I didn't want to do that, not yet.

The captain had a most uneven character.

By day he maintained a rigor so extreme that we were forbidden to break even briefly for some restorative stew. At nightfall, we settled among the ruins of Pitun, where an asado was prepared that he and I, served by one of the men, ate at a separate fire. His full stomach visibly protruding, he grew merry. I could not join in his mood—sleep was gathering me in—so he walked over to the troops.

He sang with the soldiers and authorized aguardiente.

In the morning, when the reveille sounded and I looked about me, a decline in the number of our men was apparent.

A search was made.

The men were lying in the deep trenches the Jesuit priests had made a century earlier to keep the Indians from fleeing into the forest.

Parrilla ordered that all who were drunk be whipped. But very few were sober and the punishments were light and quick so as not to delay our departure.

Once again I kept my distance from the soldiers, reluctant to witness this tedious and flagrantly unjust flogging, in punishment for what the jefe himself had authorized.

Before we entered Ypané, Parrilla stood up on his horse in the native fashion and harangued the troops, warning that if they repeated their disorderly conduct in the town they would be whipped not on their backs but lower down, and riding would become a torture.

A speech imparting the plan for this expedition to the expeditionary force would, I thought, have been more in keeping with the situation. No one, it seemed, quite knew what that plan was.

I was nonplussed. Parrilla—who could have been my comrade and, up to a point, my equal—took no interest in me. He was a man who did not know what he wanted, sometimes aloof, at other times expansive, and both to excess. I held apart from the troops and had not so much as exchanged a glance with a single soldier. I paid no attention to them, except for the four or five who appeared before me without my seeking them out: the one who served our food, the one who saw to my horses, a few others.

In Ypané, Parrilla grew obstinate in unjustified suspicions. It was patently obvious that Vicuña Porto could not have taken refuge in that town, so small, impoverished, and peaceful.

The local priest and administrator claimed to have heard nothing but distant rumors of the bandit's existence and to have neither seen him nor suffered from his misdeeds. Dissatisfied with their report, Parrilla ordered the entire population of whites and natives to gather in front of the church.

It was the season for planting—what, I don't know. Indians scratched the shallow surface of the soil with the bleached bone of a cow or horse; they had no better tools nor were they aware that such tools existed. Others, behind them, planted the seeds. Still others, following the almost imperceptible furrows, covered them over, also using the most primitive tools.

But before these last could arrive, birds dived down to the earth in dispute with the men, to rob the seeds. Of every five seeds planted, three were left. And I foresaw that the three that remained would be eaten by insects and worms that came later, after farmers and birds of prey had both moved on.

I asked one of the Indians we herded from the fields to the church about the yield of the harvests—his daily bread. He did not understand.

I needed no answer from him.

Ventura Prieto had given me the answer, years earlier, though he never spoke of it to me.

3

That afternoon, we entered the region of the Mbaya Indians.

We could no longer ride in the vanguard. Parrilla sent a scout ahead of us. He went alone, as custom dictated, so there would be no conversation to distract him.

I was thirsty. My mouth seemed filled with flour.

Vegetation betrayed the presence of a marsh.

I thought Parrilla would give order to disperse and drink. To the contrary, observing that certain of the relief horses were attempting to break from the herd and wet their mouths, he ordered them held back.

To me, he deigned to explain. "These waters may be insalubrious."

An argument that might have persuaded one other than myself. But I harbored a suspicion that the captain was imposing greater sacrifices than were necessary in the aim of grinding down my resistance, and for that reason alone.

Then came my provocation.

I asked for his flask of aguardiente. I was not similarly equipped.

I drank two swigs without returning it to him. Two more: four. Two more: four, five, six.

My scalp began to sting. Waxing loquacious with the captain as he watched in annoyance, I told him this was caused by the sun.

I asked whether his family had a heraldic emblem. He answered that it did. I told him that the tree and the tower appear in my family's coat of arms. He made no comment. I then inquired as to whether there figured, in the Parrilla family coat of arms, the implement used for grilling meat, commonly known as a *parrilla*.

Parrilla exploded with a lash of his whip to my mount's croup. The horse was as taken by surprise as I was and gave two mighty bounds; the second threw me to the ground.

Parrilla dismounted and reached me before I was able to stand up. My head was burning with rage and aguardiente.

He took me by the shoulders, assisting me as I rose to my feet. I flailed in an effort to hit him in the face. In a tone both vehement and sincere, he said, "Can't a man blaze up in anger and make a mistake, then repent and be pardoned?"

Behind us, some hundred varas away, the relief horses trotted. The soldiers followed.

They could not know what had happened.

Perhaps they thought it an accident or misstep, a sudden fit of nerves from the brute I was mounted on.

One horseman can ride next to another at a trot, without either ever looking at the other's face.

4

The sun, in the final quarter of the sky, halted in its transit.

The grass would be our blanket that night.

I helped trample down the ground. For the first time, I mingled with the soldiers.

I was agitated and bitter. I tried to convince myself of my own lucidity, but in truth I was in such a daze that the men going to and fro with me at our task seemed to float in midair.

Flatten grass, and a viper that neither escapes nor is trampled to death by a horse, will attack, to defend itself.

Not wanting to bite the pastern or fetlock, it climbed up the animal's leg. I could have reached it after it passed the knee, as it uncoiled to bite the breast.

But I was unaware of it until the horse bucked and I risked another humiliating spill.

The reins slipped from me and I clung to the mane.

Bitten, the horse broke into a gallop while the viper, losing its hold, dangled by a single tooth from the chest. The long body whipped at the victim's flanks. The danger—the reason for my terror—was that it could break free, spiral through the air, and twine about my leg.

The quadruped stumbled, I rolled over its head, and the men came to my rescue.

There was a threat of rain. A straw shack was built for Parrilla and me, which forced us into even greater unwanted proximity.

Before sleeping, I went out into the dark to attend to my bodily needs.

The guard dogs tracked me a moment, nostrils alert to any nearby wild beasts. They sniffed and let me by. I had been recognized; my scent would be the only watchword necessary for my return.

I was in a position that would have made self-defense rather awkward when I heard the dry grass crunch at my back.

Footsteps.

A dampness at my temples.

Footsteps, heavy ones, those of a large animal. I was nailed to the spot, absolutely defenseless, as if in a trance. It would pass in a second, I told myself, leaving me another instant for delay after that, for if I flee like this, they'll see me arrive in a way that.... And the dogs behind me and....

But now it was too late to flee.

I turned, and in the time it took to move my head I knew that this was not the footstep of a beast; it lacked wariness.

A man.

A calm man.

He said, as if delivering a witticism, "This whole wide country for the two of us and we've ended up choosing the same spot."

*

When it was time to go back, he asked if we could stay a bit longer.

He said, "Señor Doctor, there's no moon, and we'd call attention to ourselves if we struck a light. My face can't be seen, and therefore it behooves me to speak my name."

I was expecting the name. I knew it already.

"Vicuña Porto."

I did not react. I sensed a dagger in his hands.

It was him if he said as much, thereby risking his life. His voice summoned up my table, my office, my horse, my sword, my daily round of duties in another land. We were there in search of him, so it was not unreasonable for him to be there. But I did not understand how he could have approached without being seen, and still less how he had managed to identify me in the blackness of night.

He had revealed himself, and now undoubtedly waited to see what I would do. I was petrified with amazement at my singular destiny. I had fallen into his hands. All I could do was fear some treacherous blow.

I did not speak, and he prodded me, "Perhaps the Señor Doctor doesn't know me, doesn't recognize Vicuña Porto?"

I hastened to say I did, for the tone of the question was midway between jest and warning. And when I'd said that yes, I knew him, he commented, as if regretfully, "You know me, *vaya*! How unfortunate!"

Was he allowing me a final word, before sacrificing me?

I jumped back, not to take out a weapon but to escape. But I had a strange premonition that I was only delivering myself to my murderer, someone stationed behind me with a knife, ready to cut my throat. Porto's cry would be the other man's command....

And so, after jumping back, I jumped forward, a maneuver that Porto took for an attack. He stuck out a foot, I fell facedown, and he threw himself upon me, his knees pressing me flat as he dug a sharp point into my neck.

"*Piedad*," I begged.

"Hand over your weapons," he ordered.

I told him my knife was in my boot. He seemed to grasp that I had not meant to attack him; the pressure on my legs diminished and I no longer felt the sharp metal on my neck.

But he continued to straddle me while slapping me vigorously about the head. "You don't know me, you don't know me," he said. "Su merced does not know me."

He was through with hitting me. He stood up.

I lay sprawled on the grassy earth.

I knew he was standing over me, observing my movements.

After a time, we both calmed down.

As if to breathe a little, as if to test me, he walked in a circle around me, never taking his eyes off of me.

I looked toward the campfire. It was far away. If I tried to flee, Vicuña Porto, murderous knife in hand, would catch me.

As I watched, someone in the camp rose to his feet by the fire, a black, ecstatic figure silhouetted against the blaze.

It disappeared.

It reappeared, surrounded by dogs, as if it knew precisely where to find me.

Vicuña Porto stepped toward me, warning me anew. "You don't know me, eh? You don't know me."

But he did not leave. He stayed at my side and ordered me to get up and go meet the man coming toward us.

I admired his temerity. He would confront the soldier and kill him, I thought. What he might do with me after that I hardly imagined.

We walked side by side.

The dogs raced forward.

The sentry let out the precautionary cry.

"Señor Don Diegooooo!"

Vicuña Porto answered on my behalf, "Here we are. . . ."

*

Vicuña Porto was a soldier in the legion sent in pursuit of Vicuña Porto.

Translated from the Spanish by Esther Allen

THE FLESH-MAN FROM FAR WIDE

David R. Bunch

I HAD JUST nailed the mice down lightly by their tails to the struggle board, was considering how happy is happy, and was right on the point of rising from my hip-snuggie chair to go fetch forth the new-metal cat when my warner set up a din. I raced to my Viewer Wall where the weapon thumbs all were, set the peep scope to max-sweep and looked out, wide-ranging the blue plastic hills. And I saw this guy, this shape, this little bent-down thing coming not from the Valley of the White Witch, my main area of danger now, but coming from the Plains of Far Wide, from which I had not had a visitor for nigh on to five eras.

Was he sad, oh, was he sad! He came on, this little toad-down man, tap-tap, mince-mince, step-walk-step, but with tense carefulness in his slowness, as if every inch-mince were some slipping up on a bird. It made me itch just to see him, and to think how walking should be, great striding, big reaching, tall up with steel things clanking long-down by your side and other weapons in leather with which to defy your world. And your wagons coming up with maces and hatchets on end. Though I go not that way myself, truth to say, for I am of Moderan, where people have "replacements." I walk with a hitch worse than most, an inch-along kind of going, clop-clip-clap-clop, over the plastic yards, what little I walk, for I still have bugs in the hinges. I was an Early, you know, one of the first of Moderan. But I remember. Something in the pale green blood of my flesh-strips recalls how walking should be—a great going out with maces to pound up your enemies' heads, and a crunchy bloody jelly underfoot from the bones and juices of things too little even to be glanced at under your iron-clad feet.

But this guy! Hummph. He came like a lily. Yes, a white lily with bell-cone head bent down. I wondered why my warner even bothered with him. But yes, I knew why my warner bothered with him. My warner tells me of all movement toward my Stronghold, and sometimes the lilies—"Stand by for decontamination!" He was at my Outer Wall now, at the Screening Gate, so I directed my decontaminators and weapons probers to give him the rub-a-dub. To be truthful, two large metal hands had leaped out of the Wall to seize him and hold him directly in front of the Screening Gate, so my call to "Stand by for decontamination!" was merely a courtesy blab. When the Decontamination and the Weapons Report both gave him a clean bill I thumbed the gates back in all my eleven steel walls and let the lily man mince through.

"Hello, and welcome, strange traveler from Far Wide."

He stood trembling in his soft-rag shoes, seeming hard put on how actually to stop his inch-mince walk. "Forgive me," he said, "if I seem nervous." And he looked at me out of the blue of his flesh-ball eyes while he tugged at a cup-shaped red beard. And I was appalled at the "replacements" he had disallowed, the parts of himself he had clung to. For one wild blinding moment I was almost willing to bet that he had his real heart, even. But then I thought ah, no, not at this late year and in Moderan. "This walking," he continued, "keeps going. You see, it takes awhile to quiet. You know, getting here at last, I cannot, all of me, believe I am really here. My mind says yes! My poor legs keep thinking there's still walking to do. But I'm here!"

"You're here," I echoed, and I wondered, what next? what goes? I thought of the mice I had nailed and the new cat waiting and I was impatient to get on with my Joys. But then, a visitor is a visitor, and a host most likely is a victim. "Have you eaten? Have you had your introven?"

"I've eaten." He eyed at me strange-wide. "I didn't have introven."

I began to feel more uneasy by the minute. He just stood there vibrating slightly on thin legs, with those blue-flesh-ball eyes peeking my way, and he seemed to be waiting for me to react. "I'm here!" he said again. And I said, "Yes," not knowing what else to say. "Would you wish to tell me about your trip," I asked, "the trials and tribulations?"

Then he started his recital. It was mostly a dreary long tune of hard going, of almost baseless hopes concerning what he hoped to find, of how he had kept coming, of how he had almost quit in the Spoce Mountains, of how something up ahead had kept him trying, something like a gleam of light through a break in an iron wall. "Get over the wall," he said, "and you have won it, all that light. Over the wall!" He looked at me as though this was surely my time to react.

"Why did you almost quit in the Spoce Mountains?"

"Why did I almost quit in the Spoce Mountains!? Have you ever tried the Spoce Mountains?" I had to admit that I had not. "If you have never tried the Spoce Mountains—" He fell in to a fit of shaking that was more vivid than using many words. "Where are all the others?" he asked when the shaking had stopped a little.

"All the others? What are you talking about?"

"Oh, yes. There must be great groups here. There must be long lists waiting." His white cone-shaped face lit up. "Oh, they're in the Smile Room. That's it, isn't it?"

My big steel fingers itched to crush him then like juicing a little worm. There was something about him, so soft, so trustful and pleading and so all against my ideas of the iron mace and the big arm-swing walk. "There's no Smile Room here," I blurted. "And no long lists waiting."

Unwilling to be crushed he smiled that pure little smile. "Oh, it must be such a wonderful machine. And so big! After all the other machines, the One, the ONE—finally!"

Great leaping lead balls bouncing on bare-flesh toes! What had we here? A nut? Or was he just lost from home? "Mister," I said, "I don't know what you're driving at. This is my home. It's where I wall out danger. It's where I wall in fun. My kind of fun. It's a Stronghold."

At the sound of that last word his blue eyes dipped over and down in his white-wash face; his head fell forward like trying to follow the eyes to where they were falling. And out of a great but invisible cloud that seemed to wrap him round his stricken mouth gaped wide. "A

Stronghold! All this way I've come and it is a Stronghold! You have not the Happiness Machine at a Stronghold. It could not be.

"Oh, it is what kept me going—the hope of it. I was told. In the misty dangerous weird Spoce Mountains when the big wet-wing Gloon Glays jumped me and struck me down with their beaks I arose and kept coming. And on one very sullen rain-washed hapless morning I awoke in a white circle of the long-tusk wart-skin woebegawn-gawns, and oh it would have been so much easier, so very much less exacting, to have feigned sleep while they tore me and opened my soul case with death. But no! I stood up, I remembered prophecy. I drew my cloak around me. I walked. I walked on. I left them staring with empty teeth. I thought of my destination. And now— It was a dream! I am fooled! Take me to your Happiness Machine!"

He was becoming hysterical. He blabbed as how he wanted to go and sit in some machine gauged to beauty and truth and love and be happy. He was breaking down. I saw I must rally him for one more try, to get him beyond my Walls. "Mister," I said, "you have, no doubt, known the big clouds and the sun failing and the rain-washed gray dawn of the hopeless time. You have—I believe it—stood up in disaster amid adversity's singing knives and all you had going for you was what you had brought along. There were no armies massing for you on other fields, no uncles raising funds in far countries across seas; perhaps there were no children, even, coming for Daddy in the Spoce Mountains, and with death not even one widow to claim the body and weep it toward the sun. And yet you defied all this, somehow got out of disaster's tightening ring and moved on down. I admire you. I truly am sorry I do not have what you want. And though you are a kind of fool, by my way of thinking, to go running around in flesh looking for a pure something that perhaps does not exist, I wish you luck as I thumb the gates back and make way for your progress. You may find, up ahead somewhere, across a lot of mountains, and barren land, these Happiness Machines for which you cry." He trembled when I spoke of mountains, but he moved out through the gates.

And though I was sure he would find nothing the way he was going, I have not been entirely able to forget him. What would prompt such a creature, obviously ill-equipped for any great achievement, to hope for the ultimate and impossibly-great achievement, happiness? And such an odd way to expect it, happiness dispensed by some magic machine gauged to beauty and truth and love. In a resplendent place at the end of a long trip.

To hear him talk you'd think happiness could be based on lily-weak things. How weird. Power is joy; strength is pleasure; put your trust only in the thick wall with the viewer and the warner. But sometimes, in spite of myself, I think of this little flesh-ridden man and wonder where he is.

And when I'm at my ease, feeding my flesh-strips the complicated fluids of the introven, knowing I can live practically forever with the help of the new-metal alloys, a vague uneasiness comes over me and I try to evaluate my life. With the machines that serve me all buzzing underneath my Stronghold and working fine—yes, I am satisfied, I am adequate. And when I want a little more than quiet satisfaction, I can probe out and destroy one of my neighbor's Walls perhaps, or a piece of his warner. And then we will fight lustily at each other for a little while from our Strongholds, pushing the destruction buttons at each other in a kind of high glee. Or I can just keep home and work out some little sadistic pleasure on my own. And on the terms the flesh-man wanted—truth, beauty, love—I'm practically sure there is no Happiness Machine out there anywhere at all. I'm almost sure there isn't.

THE EARTHGOD AND THE FOX

Kenji Miyazawa

ON THE northern edge of a stretch of open land the ground rose in a slight hillock. The hillock was covered entirely with spike-eared grass, and right in the middle of it stood a single, beautiful female birch tree.

The tree was not actually very big, but her trunk gleamed a glossy black and her branches spread out gracefully. In May her pale flowers were like clouds, while in autumn she shed leaves of gold and crimson and many other colors.

All the birds, from birds of passage such as the cuckoo and the shrike right down to the tiny wren and the white-eye, would come to perch in the tree. But if a young hawk or some other large bird was there, the smaller birds would spy him from afar and refuse to go anywhere near.

The tree had two friends. One was the earthgod, who lived in the middle of a marshy hollow about five hundred paces away, and the other was a brown fox, who always appeared from somewhere in the southern part of the plain.

Of the two of them it was the fox, perhaps, that the birch tree preferred. The earthgod, in spite of his imposing name, was too wild, with hair hanging unkempt like a bundle of ragged cotton thread, bloodshot eyes, and clothes that dangled about him like bits of seaweed. He always went barefoot, and his nails were long and black. The fox, on the other hand, was very refined and almost never made people angry or offended.

The only thing was that, if you compared them really carefully, the earthgod was honest, whereas the fox was, perhaps, just a bit dishonest.

It was an evening at the beginning of summer. The birch tree was covered with soft new leaves, which filled the air around them with a delightful fragrance. The Milky Way stretched whitish across the sky, and the stars were winking and blinking and switching themselves on and off all over the firmament.

On such a night, then, the fox came to pay the birch tree a visit, bringing with him a book of poetry. He was wearing a dark blue suit fresh from the tailor's, and his light brown leather shoes squeaked slightly as he walked.

"What a peaceful night," he said.

"Oh, yes!" breathed the birch tree.

"Do you see Scorpio crawling across the sky over there? In ancient China, you know, they used to call the biggest star in the constellation the 'Fire Star.'"

"Would that be the same as Mars?"

"Dear me, no. Not Mars. Mars is a *planet*. This one is a real star."

"Then what's the difference between a planet and a star?"

"Why, a planet can't shine by itself. In other words, it has to have light from somewhere else before it can be seen. A star is the kind that shines by itself. The sun, now, is a star, of course. It looks big and dazzling to us, but if you saw it from very far away, it would only look like a small star, just the same as all the others."

"Good heavens! So the sun is only one of the stars, is it? Then I suppose the sky must have an awful lot of suns—no, stars—oh, silly me, *suns*, of course."

The fox smiled magnanimously. "You might put it like that," he said.

"I wonder why some stars are red, and some yellow, and some green?"

The fox smiled magnanimously again and folded his arms grandly across his chest. The book of poetry under his arm dangled perilously, but somehow stopped just short of falling.

"Well, you see," he said, "at first all the stars were like big, fluffy clouds. There are still lots of them like that in the sky. There are some in Andromeda, some in Orion, and some in the Hunting Dogs. Some of them are spiral-shaped and some are in rings the shape of fishes' mouths."

"I'd love to see them sometime. Stars the shape of fishes' mouths—how splendid!"

"Oh, they are, I can tell you. I saw them at the observatory."

"My word! I'd love to see them myself."

"I'll show you them. As a matter of fact, I've a telescope on order from Germany. It'll be here sometime before next spring, so I'll let you have a look as soon as it comes."

The fox had spoken without thinking, but the very next moment he was saying to himself, "Oh dear, if I haven't gone and told my only friend another fib again. But I only said it to please her, I really didn't mean any harm by it. Later on, I'll tell her the truth."

The fox was quiet for a while, occupied with such thoughts, but the birch tree was too delighted to notice.

"I'm so happy!" she said. "You're always so kind to me."

"Oh, quite," said the fox rather dejectedly. "You know I'd do anything for you. Would you care to read this book of poetry, by the way? It's by a man called Heine. It's only a translation, of course, but it's not at all bad."

"Oh! May I really borrow it?"

"By all means. Take as long as you like over it. . . . Well, I must say goodbye now. Dear me, though, I feel there's something I forgot to say."

"Yes, about the color of the stars."

"Ah, of course! But let's leave that until next time, shall we? I mustn't overstay my welcome."

"Oh, that doesn't matter."

"Anyway, I'll be coming again soon. Goodbye to you, then. I'll leave the book with you. Goodbye."

The fox set off briskly homeward. And the birch tree, her leaves rustling in a south wind that sprang up just then, took up the book of verse and turned the pages in the light of the faint glow from the Milky Way and the stars that dotted the sky. The book contained "Lorelei" and many other beautiful poems by Heine, and the birch tree read on and on through the night. Not until past three, when Taurus was already beginning to climb in the east above the plain, did she begin to get even slightly drowsy.

Dawn broke, and the sun rose in the heavens. The dew glittered on the grass, and the flowers bloomed with all their might. Slowly, slowly, from the northeast, bathed in morning sunlight as though he had poured molten copper all over himself, came the earthgod. He walked slowly, quite slowly, with his arms folded soberly across his chest.

Somehow, the birch tree felt rather put out, but even so she shimmered her bright green leaves in the earthgod's direction as he came, so that her shadow went flutter, flutter where it fell on the grass. The earthgod came up quietly and stopped in front of her.

"Good morning to you, Birch Tree."

"Good morning."

"D'you know, Birch Tree, there are lots of things I don't understand when I come to think about them. We don't really know very much, do we?"

"What kind of things?"

"Well, there's grass, for instance. Why should it be green, when it comes out of dark brown soil? And then there are the yellow and white flowers. It's all beyond me."

"Mightn't it be that the seeds of the grass have green or white inside them already?" said the birch tree.

"Yes. Yes, I suppose that's possible," he said. "But even so, it's beyond me. Take the toadstools in autumn, now. They come straight out of the earth without any seeds or anything. And they come up in red and yellow and all kinds of colors. I just don't understand it!"

"How would it be if you asked Mr. Fox?" said the birch tree, who was still too excited about last night's talk to know any better.

The earthgod's face changed color abruptly, and he clenched his fists.

"What's that? Fox? What's the fox been saying?"

"Oh," said the birch tree in a faltering voice, "he didn't say anything, really. It was just that I thought he might know."

"And what makes you think a fox has got anything to teach a god, eh?"

By now the birch tree was so unnerved that she could only quiver and quiver. The earthgod paced about with his arms folded over his chest, grinding his teeth loudly all the while. Even the grass shivered with fear wherever his jet-black shadow fell on it.

"That fox is a blight on the face of the earth!" he said. "Not a word of truth in him. Servile, cowardly, and terribly envious into the bargain!"

"It will soon be time for the yearly festival at your shrine, won't it?" said the birch tree, regaining her composure at last.

The earthgod's expression softened slightly.

"That's right," he said. "Today's the third of the month, so there are only six days to go."

But then he thought for a while and suddenly burst out again.

"Human beings, though, are a useless lot! They don't bring a single offering for my festival nowadays. Why, the next one that sets foot on my territory, I'll drag down to the bottom of the swamp for his pains!"

He stood there gnashing his teeth noisily. The birch tree, alarmed at finding that her attempts to soothe him had had just the opposite effect again, was past doing anything except fluttering her leaves in the breeze. For a while the earthgod strode about grinding his teeth, his arms folded high across his chest and his whole body seeming to blaze as the sunlight poured down on him. But the more he thought about it, the crosser he seemed to get. In the end he could bear it no longer and with a great howl stormed off home to his hollow.

The place where the earthgod lived was a dank and chilly swamp grown all over with moss, clover, stumpy reeds, and here and there a

194 · KENJI MIYAZAWA

thistle or a dreadfully twisted willow tree. There were soggy places where the water seeped through in rusty patches. You only had to look at it to tell that it was all muddy and somehow frightening.

On a patch like a small island right in the middle of it stood the earthgod's shrine, which was about six feet high and made of logs.

Back on this island, the earthgod stretched himself out full length on the ground beside his shrine and scratched long and hard at his dark, scraggy legs.

Just then he noticed a bird flying through the sky right above his head, so he sat up straight and shouted "Shoo!" The bird wobbled in alarm and for a moment seemed about to fall, then fled into the distance, gradually losing height as it went, as though its wings were paralyzed.

The earthgod gave a little laugh and was getting to his feet when he happened to glance toward the hillock, not far away, where the birch tree grew. And instantly his rage returned: his face turned pale, his body went as stiff as a poker, and he began tearing at his wild head of hair.

A solitary woodcutter on his way to work on Mt. Mitsumori came up from the south of the hollow, striding along the narrow path that skirted its edge. He seemed to know all about the earthgod, for every now and then he glanced anxiously in the direction of the shrine. But he could not, of course, see anybody there.

When the earthgod caught sight of the woodcutter, he flushed with pleasure. He stretched his arm out toward him, then grasped his own wrist with his other hand and made as though to pull it back. And, strange to say, the woodcutter, who thought he was still walking along the path, found himself gradually moving deeper and deeper into the hollow. He quickened his pace in alarm, his face turned pale, his mouth opened, and he began to gasp.

Slowly the earthgod twisted his wrist. And as he did so, the woodcutter slowly began to turn in circles. At this he grew more and more alarmed, until finally he was going round and round on the same spot, panting desperately all the while. His one idea seemed to be to get out of the hollow as quickly as he could, but for all his efforts he stayed, circling, where he was. In the end he began to sob and, flinging up his arms, broke into a run.

This seemed to delight the earthgod. He just grinned and watched without getting up from the ground, until before long the woodcutter, who by now was giddy and exhausted, collapsed in the water. Then the earthgod got slowly to his feet. With long strides he squelched his way to where the woodcutter lay and, picking him up, flung him over onto the grassy ground. The woodcutter landed in the grass with a thud. He groaned once and stirred, but still did not come to.

The earthgod laughed loudly. His laughter rose up into the sky in great mysterious waves. Reaching the sky, the sound bounced back down again to the place where the birch tree stood. The birch tree turned suddenly so pale that the sunlight shone green through her leaves, and she began to quiver frantically.

The earthgod tore at his hair with both hands. "It's all because of the fox that I feel so miserable," he told himself. "Or rather, the birch tree. No, the fox and the birch tree. That's why I suffer so much. If only I didn't mind about the tree, I'd mind even less about the fox. I may be nobody much, but I *am* a god after all, and it's disgraceful that I should have to bother myself about a mere fox. But the awful thing is, I do. Why don't I forget all about the birch tree, then? Because I can't. How splendid it was this morning when she went pale and trembled! I was wrong to bully a wretched human being just to work off my temper, but it can't be helped. No one can tell what somebody'll do when he gets really cross."

So dreadfully sad did he feel that he beat at the air in despair. Another bird came flying through the sky, but this time the earthgod just watched it go in silence.

From far, far away came the sound of cavalry at their maneuvers, with a crackling of rifle fire like salt being thrown on flames. From the sky, the blue light poured down in waves. This must have done the woodcutter good, for he came to, sat up timidly, and peered about him. The next moment he was up and running like an arrow shot from a bow. Away he ran in the direction of Mt. Mitsumori.

Watching him, the earthgod gave a great laugh again. Again his laughter soared up to the blue sky and hurtled back down to the birch tree below. Again the tree's leaves went pale and trembled delicately, so delicately that you would scarcely have noticed.

The earthgod walked aimlessly round and round his shrine till finally, when he seemed to feel more settled, he suddenly darted inside.

It was a misty night in August. The earthgod was so terribly lonely and so dreadfully cross that he left his shrine on an impulse and started walking. Almost before he realized it, his feet were taking him toward the birch tree. He couldn't say why, but whenever he thought of her, his heart seemed to turn over and he felt intolerably sad. Nowadays he was much easier in his mind than before, and he had done his best not to think about either the fox or the birch tree. But, try as he might, they kept coming into his head. Every day he would tell himself over and over again, "You're a god, after all. What can a mere birch tree mean to you?" But still he felt awfully sad. The memory of the fox, in particular, hurt till it seemed his whole body was on fire.

Wrapped in his own thoughts, the earthgod drew nearer and nearer the birch tree. Finally it dawned on him quite clearly that he was on his way to see her, and his heart began to dance for joy. It had been a long time. She might well have missed him. In fact, the more he thought about it the surer he felt it was so. If this really was the case, then he was very sorry he had neglected her. His heart danced as he strode on through the grass. But before long his stride faltered and he stopped dead; a great blue wave of sadness had suddenly washed over him. The fox was there before him. It was quite dark by now, but he could hear the fox's voice coming through the mist, which was glowing in the vague light of the moon.

"Why, of course," he was saying, "just because something agrees with the laws of symmetry is not to say that it is beautiful. That's nothing more than a dead beauty."

"How right you are," came the birch tree's soft voice.

"True beauty is not something rigid and fossilized. People talk of observing the laws of symmetry, but it's enough so long as the *spirit* of symmetry is present."

"Oh, yes, I'm sure it is," came the birch tree's gentle voice again.

But now the earthgod felt as though red flames were licking his whole body. His breath came in short gasps, and he really thought he couldn't bear it any longer. "What are you so miserable about?" he asked himself crossly. "What is this, after all, but a bit of talk between a birch tree and a fox out in the open country? You call yourself a god, to let things like this upset you?"

But the fox was talking again:

"So all books on art touch on this aspect."

"Do you have many books on art, then?" asked the birch tree.

"Oh, not such an enormous number. I suppose most of them are in English, German, and Japanese. There's a new one in Italian, but it hasn't come yet."

"What a fine library it must be!"

"No, no. Just a few scattered volumes, really. And besides, I use the place for my studies too, so it's rather a mess, what with a microscope in one corner and the London *Times* lying over there, and a marble bust of Caesar here. . . ."

"Oh, but it sounds wonderful! Really wonderful!"

There was a little sniff from the fox that might have been either modesty or pride, then everything was quiet for a while.

By now the earthgod was quite beside himself. From what the fox said, it seemed the fox was actually more impressive than he was himself. He could no longer console himself with the thought that he was a god if nothing else. It was frightful. He felt like rushing over and tearing the fox in two. He told himself that one should never even think such things. But then, what was he to do? Hadn't he let the fox get the better of him? He clutched at his breast in distress.

"Has the telescope you once mentioned come yet?" started the birch tree again.

"The telescope I mentioned? Oh, no, it hasn't arrived yet. I keep expecting it, but the shipping routes are terribly busy. As soon as it comes, I'll bring it along for you to see. I really must show you the rings around Venus, for one thing. They're so beautiful."

At this, the earthgod clapped his hands over his ears and fled away toward the north. He had suddenly felt frightened at the thought of what he might do if he stayed there any longer.

He ran on and on in a straight line. When he finally collapsed out of breath, he found himself at the foot of Mt. Mitsumori.

He rolled about in the grass, tearing at his hair. Then he began to cry in a loud voice. The sound rose up into the sky, where it echoed like thunder out of season and made itself heard all over the plain. He wept and wept until dawn, when, tired out, he finally wandered vacantly back to his shrine.

Time passed, and autumn came at last. The birch tree was still green, but on the grass round about golden ears had already formed and were glinting in the breeze, and here and there the berries of lilies of the valley showed ripe and red.

One transparent, golden autumn day found the earthgod in the very best of tempers. All the unpleasant things he had been feeling since the summer seemed somehow to have dissolved into a kind of mist that hovered in only the vaguest of rings over his head. The odd, cross-grained streak in him had quite disappeared, too. He felt that if the birch tree wanted to talk to the fox, well, she could, and that if the two of them enjoyed chatting together, it was a very good thing for them both. He would let the birch tree know how he felt today. With a light heart and his head full of such thoughts, the earthgod set off to visit her.

The birch tree saw him coming in the distance and, as usual, trembled anxiously as she waited for him to arrive.

The earthgod came up and greeted her cheerfully.

"Good morning, Birch Tree. A lovely day we're having!"

"Good morning, Earthgod. Yes, lovely, isn't it?"

"What a blessing the sun is, to be sure! There he is up there, red in the spring, white in the summer, and yellow in the autumn. And when he turns yellow in the autumn, the grapes turn purple. Ah, a blessing indeed!"

"How true."

"D'you know, today I feel much better. I've had all sorts of trials since the summer, but this morning at last something suddenly lifted from my mind."

The birch tree wanted to reply, but for some reason a great weight seemed to be bearing down on her, and she remained silent.

"The way I feel now, I'd willingly die for anybody. I'd even take the place of a worm if it had to die and didn't want to." He gazed far off into the blue sky as he spoke, his eyes dark and splendid.

Again the birch tree wanted to reply, but again something heavy seemed to weigh her down, and she barely managed to sigh.

It was then that the fox appeared.

When the fox saw the earthgod there, he started and turned pale. But he could hardly go back, so, trembling slightly, he went right up to where the birch tree stood.

"Good morning, Birch Tree," said the fox. "I believe that's the earthgod I see there, isn't it?" He was wearing his light brown leather shoes and a brown raincoat and was still in his summer hat.

"Yes, I'm the earthgod. Lovely weather, isn't it?" He spoke without a shadow on his mind.

"I must apologize for coming when you have a visitor," said the fox to the birch tree, his face pale with jealousy. "Here's the book I promised you the other day. Oh, and I'll show you the telescope one evening when the sky's clear. Goodbye."

"Oh, thank you...," began the birch tree, but the fox had already set off toward home without so much as a nod to the other visitor. The birch tree blanched and began to quiver again.

For a while, the earthgod gazed blankly at the fox's retreating form. Then he caught a sudden glint of sunlight on the fox's brown leather shoes amidst the grass, and he came to himself with a start. The next moment, something seemed to click in his brain. The fox was marching steadily into the distance, swaggering almost defiantly as he went. The earthgod began to seethe with rage. His face turned a dreadful dark color. He'd show him what was what, that fox with his art books and his telescopes!

He was up and after him in a flash. The birch tree's branches began to shake all at once in panic. Sensing something wrong, the fox himself glanced around casually, only to see the earthgod, black all over, rushing after him like a hurricane. Off went the fox like the wind, his face white and his mouth twisted with fear.

To the earthgod, the grass about him seemed to be burning like white fire. Even the bright blue sky had suddenly become a yawning black pit with crimson flames burning and roaring in its depths.

They ran snorting and panting like two railway trains. The fox ran as in a dream, and all the while part of his brain kept saying, "This is the end. This is the end. Telescope. Telescope. Telescope."

A small hummock of bare earth lay ahead. The fox dashed around it so as to get to the round hole at its base. He ducked his head, and was diving into the hole, his back legs flicking up as he went, when the earthgod finally pounced on him from behind. The next moment he lay all twisted, with his head drooping over the earthgod's hand and his lips puckered as though smiling slightly.

The earthgod flung the fox down on the ground and stamped on his soft, yielding body four or five times. Then he plunged into the fox's hole. It was quite bare and dark, though the red clay of the floor had been trodden down hard and neat.

The earthgod went outside again, feeling rather strange, with his mouth all slack and crooked. Then he tried putting a hand inside the pocket of the fox's raincoat as he lay there limp and lifeless. The pocket contained two brown burrs, the kind foxes comb their fur with. From the earthgod's open mouth came the most extraordinary sound, and he burst into tears.

The tears fell like rain on the fox, and the fox lay there dead, with his head lolling limper and limper and the faintest of smiles on his face.

Translated from the Japanese by John Bester

AN ESCAPED MAN

Victor Serge

A MAN was squatting in front of a fire of twigs cooking some siz-zling, red meat hanging from a sort of tripod. As his eyes opened, Rodion saw that man from behind. On his head he wore a fur cap made of a bristly animal-skin. Rodion's first thought was mingled with saliva, for the grilled meat was giving off its pungent smell in the sunlight. Rodion recognized the golden sand on which he was lying—naked, exhausted, in a vast warmth. The man, as if sensing that glance on the back of his neck, spun around on his bare heels. Rodion saw a low forehead over which hung curly hair the colour of dirty straw, a wide mouth, a fleshy nose marked by a scar, and crafty, little pointed eyes as blue as the sky.

"So you're back?"

Rodion recognized the sing-song accent of the Black-Lands folk in the man's speech.

"Thank you," he said simply, and he added, after a pause, "comrade."

"You can take your comrades and shove 'em up your arse. What kind of comrade are you to me, you poor half-drowned fool? What makes you think I'm not going to turn you in to earn the bounty? You think it's not obvious you escaped from the camp? Which brigade were you in? The Yagoda Brigade? The Enthusiasts' Brigade? Trium-phant Socialism? Screw the lot of them, citizen. If you don't want me to chuck your arse back in the water, you better not call me comrade. In this country, you'll learn there's no more anything: neither social-ism, nor capitalism, bunch of syphilitic whores. There's only you and me, and if that makes one too many, the question will be easy to settle without consulting the masses..."

As he delivered this half-mocking, half-angry monologue, the man was carefully broiling the meat. Rodion, comforted by his deep bass voice, tried his limbs: they were working, almost painful. A sudden confidence in the universe made him cordial.

"I'm sorry. Thank you anyway. That smells good."

"That smells of broiled wolf-cub," explained the man. "I killed it this morning in its lair. It bit me on the thumb, the little rascal. I didn't think it was so quick. There are lots of them here. I'm a wolf to the wolves, I am. I catch their scent, I lie in wait for them, I know all their tricks, and they haven't learned mine yet. You see, I'm the more cunning in this class struggle ... So I eat them. (*His eyes were laughing.*) I spot the lair. When the she-wolf goes off to hunt, I sneak up. Gotta work fast. I whistle, I imitate the little growling sounds the she-wolf makes, like this, listen ... I don't know whether it makes them nervous or charms them. The wolf-cub comes up; he shows the end of his snout, all pink and grey, then a suspicious puppy eye. I whistle again to give them confidence. I let him see my left hand, that intrigues him. He's never seen a human hand, he can't suspect that it is made to kill in a thousand ways. They're innocent, wolf-cubs, they're fools, and my hand looks like a harmless animal, it's pink. So he licks his chops and he jumps at it; to play, I think, for he's not yet strong enough to be mean; but I've got another hand, I have, and I break the wolf-cub's neck with this ..."

This: a piece of flint similar in every respect to the weapons of prehistoric cave-men.

"That's my productive system. I don't need any cooperatives, I don't."

With his fingers the man took a pinch of coarse salt and sprinkled it over a slice of meat which he practically threw in Rodion's face. "There, eat." Rodion was so weak that he attacked that sand-covered meat with his teeth, right on the sand, without even trying to take it in his hands, so as to move as little as possible ... Time passed, perhaps a long time. The wolf-cub's flesh had a delicious taste of blood, a taste of sunlight, a taste of life.

"How did you pull me out of the water?" asked Rodion at last.

Sitting with his legs tucked under him, Samoyed-fashion, the man went on devouring broiled meat, which he held with both hands. Bones cracked under his teeth. His hair was hanging over his forehead and eyes. His eyes sparkled with good humour: less, though, than his teeth. He replied only after a long while, after he had spat onto the sand some chewed tendons and some little crunched bones whose marrow he had sucked.

"First ask why," he said cheerfully. "Maybe I was more interested in your bundle than your pretty face. If you had had a good pair of boots I'm not sure I wouldn't have thrown you back into the water. What is your life going to be good for? I don't need it, and the entire world doesn't give a damn, believe me, just like I don't give a damn. I really don't know why I didn't just let you sink and drift slowly down to the White Sea. Maybe that would have been better for you, one more drowned man never hurt anybody. And nobody will ever ask him for his passport. Maybe I needed your company, arsehole. Not for long."

Rodion was listening in a dream. Such utter translucence reigned on the green fringe of the bushes. He asked:

"What's your name?"

The man shrugged his shoulders. "Ivan."

"Ivan Nobody?"

"Exactly." Ivan got up, sated, smiling a funny smile of well-being. He walked around for a while between sand and sky. He filled the vast landscape: his low forehead, his rounded shoulders, his heavy jaw, his vigilant little eyes, their blue cheerfulness sharpened by sly-ness. Stockily built, broad and heavy, giving an impression of enormous strength now that he was standing up, dressed more or less like a hunter from the Taiga. He returned toward Rodion, who lay naked, limbs outstretched, shivering. From his full height he looked down at Rodion and suddenly declaimed in a joking schoolboy's voice:

Diadia! diadia! our nets
Have pulled in the body of a drowned man. . . .

"That's from Pushkin," said Rodion, at the edge of unconsciousness.

"And Shakespeare?" said Ivan, with an imperceptible trace of mockery, "do you know that name?"

"No . . . I've only read Hegel, Hegel . . ."

"Possible. But you have fever, my drowned man."

How much warmth there was in his voice now . . . Rodion, feeling faint, closed his eyes. The man kneeled down next to him and with both hands began covering the lad's naked body with sand. Rodion felt that material warmth over all his flesh. His features relaxed. His childish face emerged from the sand. The light, passing through his eyelids and his sleep, extinguished all thought within him. He was coming back to life.

. . . He spent several days with the man, Ivan, who said he did not know the name of the river nor that of the other river whose junction Rodion had to find, a two or three day's walk upstream. There, big rafts loaded with logs were always floating downstream; by riding on one for three days you get to a town, a town without a name or memories either, for this man was wary of men, of language, of numbers, of memories. "Rivers have no names in nature," he said mischievously. "Drowned men don't have names at the bottom of the water, and they all have the same blue faces. The wolves don't know that they are wolves. That's the way things are . . ." He led Rodion to his lair, a comfortable burrow, large and quite dry, which had been dug right into the earth of the steppe. It was well exposed to the sun, yet well hidden by the bushes, and it was so well laid out that Rodion thought several men must have worked on it. Two cavalry coats and two heavy winter quilts made a comfortable bed. As he fell asleep there for the first time, Rodion felt a fear: why shouldn't Ivan smash my head in tonight? And he immediately answered himself: a refugee from a firing-squad and a refugee from a drowning—we were made to sleep together underground. What good would my death be to him? What good is my life to me? Nothing has any importance. No more problems. The simplicity of things made him slightly dizzy. The earth was vast, vast . . .

They parted without shaking hands or pronouncing any useless phrases. Both were taciturn, probably because the sky was white and heavy that day. Nothing to say to each other on the edge of the beach where a gloomy heath began. Rodion set off toward the dark line of distant mountains. Ivan was holding a stump of a carbine with a sawed-off barrel and a sawed-off stock, which dangled at the end of his arm. When Rodion was about a hundred metres away, Ivan raised up that mutilated weapon and shook it up and down over his head for a long while. He seemed to be sending incomprehensible signals. Rodion, who was walking rapidly, turned around several times to answer him by waving his cap.

The other nameless river was wider. A stunning breadth of heavenly blue flowed between sheer cragged cliffs of purplish-blue rocks. Tree trunks were floating in it. A wisp of smoke curled up over a patch of woods. From that point on, Rodion's whole being was expectant, on the lookout. Hidden on the bank, which was covered with tall reeds pointed like swords, he watched the majestic passage of a huge, well-constructed raft carrying a complete building made of logs. The men aboard were talking very loudly in a language he didn't understand, Finnish, or Samoyed or Syzran or Mari. They were blond men, rather well dressed in sweaters and old rusty leather—probably Communists. The next raft appeared several hours later, just before sunset, through a cloud of gnats. It was small, less heavily laden. Two young lads were steering it, standing, with long poles. Rodion hailed them; they came in to shore with a sort of indifference, welcomed him aboard without saying a word, and handed him a pole. All this took place automatically. As soon as the sun had set, the rocks took on the colour of blackened blood; the river became hostile, the gnat-bites painful. Then the two lads broke into an old convicts' song:

> We go on, dragging our chains
> Down the road of sorrows
> We go on, dragging our hearts

To the end of our bitter fate
One night we will escape
Beautiful girl, you will love us
And then they will pinch us again
Beautiful girl, you will cry for us

They kept repeating this stanza—the only one they knew—until they could no longer go on: from fatigue, from dull sadness. Rodion sang along with them as he worked his pole, for they needed to pay strict attention in order to prevent the current from dashing them against the rocks. At critical moments the three lads, leaning out over the dark waters, would arch their backs, absorbing the impact against their chests with a single gasp, and one of them swore. When the moon rose they again took up the song of chains and sorrows, of love and heartbreak, until the hour when, exhausted, they moored in a sort of creek in order to sleep. At dawn, Rodion told the two lads he had money, and they sold him a hunk of black bread for three roubles. As a precaution he left them a few hours upstream from the town. He leaped adroitly onto the bank. The two lads, having turned their backs, never saw him again. The surface of the water was shimmering, totally calm, and the motionless shrubs were reflected in it, emerald green.

"An escaped man," said one, "God go with him."

"An escaped man," echoed the other in reply, "The Devil take him."

The town began with a row of poor log houses standing in little yards enclosed by dilapidated fences. A little girl bounded out, barefoot. Her feet were black. Rodion halted, enchanted. He felt naïve joy, tinged with another feeling—bitter, almost terrible—as he gazed at those familiar houses, always the same, with thatched or planked roofs so weather-beaten that you could see daylight through them. What town was this? He didn't dare ask. He mingled with the crowd, searching for a street-sign, a notice posted by the local Soviet. But this was a town without street-signs, without posters, perhaps without a name, an ordinary little town with ruined churches: the same empty cooperatives as everywhere, a line of people in front of the closed shop of the *Tabak-Trust*, a miserable market-place where everything—the horses' long drooping heads, the people's faces, the rare sacks of grain—had the same colour of dried mud . . . On the red gauze banner strung across the main street, Rodion, who did not wish to read them, made out two faded rain-washed words: *Enthusiasm, Industrialization* . . .

His hungry wanderings led him to a vast building-site bristling with scaffolds and tall skeletal walls of red brick. Trucks were jouncing drunkenly through mud-puddles without even startling the little, resigned horses harnessed to ancient carts. Casks of cement were bursting through a rail fence, and men were bustling clumsily about among the trucks, the horses, the carts, the cement, the scaffoldings. On a door Rodion read: *Now hiring: labourers, masons, carpenters, stucco-workers and others—bed and soup.* He pushed open the door. Inside it smelled of cheap tobacco, fresh lime, manure, benzine; it was full of hoarse voices arguing about an incident involving a missing cart-load, a drunken driver, twenty-seven roubles, the Control Commission. Rodion asked for a job as a mason-tender.

"Fine. If you know the work, we'll give you a chance to prove it in the second brigade, 'Socialist Emulation.' Its output is nineteen percent higher than the average for the plan. Three roubles and sixty-five kopecks a day and soup from the technicians' canteen—you're lucky. Only you better meet the quota. We carry out the plan here, brother: we don't want any loafers. If you don't work out, tomorrow I'll send you over to the fourth, the gold-brickers brigade: black-list, two roubles forty-five, and sour-cabbage soup—Diarrhoea Brand."

"I'll meet the quota," said Rodion with an imperceptible touch of self-mockery. "I'm class-conscious, citizen. What are we building here?"

"District Headquarters for State Security, comrade proletarian. So the work must be done properly, you understand. There's competition with the prisoners' brigades."

The crew that Rodion joined included a woman who taught him to carry the maximum load of solidly-stacked bricks on his back and shoulders, to carry them to the top of the scaffolding fast enough so that the masons of the fifth prisoners' brigade never paused for an instant in their methodical labours. There was no time to breathe, to exchange a few words, or to smoke, and anyway smoking was forbidden, and anyway you lost your taste for everything. To keep up your spirits, you chewed bad tobacco—twenty cigarettes for sixty-five kopecks. The woman must have been about thirty. She hid in order to drink. When she saw Rodion's face drenched with sweat, pinched like the face of a dying man, she joined him on a shaky platform from which you could see a soft landscape of humble roofs and light-green prairies blending off into the horizons. The woman held her brandy-bottle out to Rodion.

"Drink fast! If the brigade-leader catches us we're sure to get fined...."

Rodion, racked with fatigue, avidly absorbed that liquid fire. His legs never stopped shaking under him, but he felt savagely strong and lucid: he saw reality with the intensity of a dream. The woman was flat-chested and the hard, deep-lined features of her face expressed wear and resistance. Her eyes were sunken and surrounded by dark shadows.

"Feeling better?" she asked. The corners of the grey kerchief knotted under her chin were fluttering in the breeze. Her tall form stood out over the scaffolding, and behind her there was nothing but airy space, plains, and Russian earth, the tortured earth of the Revolution, its black waters, its clouded waters, its clear waters, its frozen waters, its deadly waters, its invigorating waters, its enchanted forests, its mud, its impoverished villages, its countless living prisoners, its countless executed ones in graves, its construction sites, its masses, its solitudes and all the seeds germinating in its womb. Rodion saw it all, ineffably. All—even the germinating seeds, since they too are real. And that the woman drinking brandy from the bottle at that instant was truly, totally, a human being. He was entranced to see it so clearly.

"Listen," he said softly, "do you know what we are? Have you ever thought about it?" She considered him with astonishment. And her direct iron-blue gaze was tinged with fear.

1936–1938
Translated from the French by Richard Greeman

I'M WAITING FOR THE FERRY

Kabir

I'm waiting for the ferry,
But where are we going,
And is there a paradise anyway?

Besides,
What will I,
Who see you everywhere,

Do there?
I'm okay where I am, says Kabir.
Spare me the trip.

Translated from the Hindi by Arvind Krishna Mehrotra

CHRONOLOGICAL LIST OF NYRB CLASSICS

1999

Peasants and Other Stories
ANTON CHEKHOV
Translated from the Russian by
Constance Garnett
Selected and with an introduction
by Edmund Wilson

A High Wind in Jamaica
RICHARD HUGHES
Introduction by Francine Prose

My Dog Tulip
J. R. ACKERLEY
Introduction by Elizabeth
Marshall Thomas

My Father and Myself
J. R. ACKERLEY
Introduction by W. H. Auden

*Lolly Willowes, or, The Loving
Huntsman*
SYLVIA TOWNSEND WARNER
Introduction by Alison Lurie

The Living Thoughts of Kierkegaard
SØREN KIERKEGAARD
Edited and with an introduction
by W. H. Auden

Contempt
ALBERTO MORAVIA
Translated from the Italian by
Angus Davidson
Introduction by Tim Parks

Boredom
ALBERTO MORAVIA
Translated from the Italian by
Angus Davidson
Introduction by William Weaver

Prison Memoirs of an Anarchist
ALEXANDER BERKMAN
Introduction by John William
Ward

Jakob von Gunten
ROBERT WALSER
Translated from the German
and with an introduction by
Christopher Middleton

Asterisk (*) indicates an NYRB Classics Original. Dagger (†) indicates no longer in print.

The Winners†
JULIO CORTÁZAR
Translated from the Spanish by
Elaine Kerrigan
Introduction by Alastair Reid

The Other House
HENRY JAMES
Introduction by Louis Begley

Herself Surprised†
JOYCE CARY
Introduction by Brad Leithauser

To Be a Pilgrim†
JOYCE CARY
Introduction by Brad Leithauser

The Horse's Mouth†
JOYCE CARY
Introduction by Brad Leithauser

A Handbook on Hanging
CHARLES DUFF
Introduction by Christopher
Hitchens

2000

Memoirs of My Nervous Illness
DANIEL PAUL SCHREBER
Translated from the German and
edited by Ida Macalpine and
Richard A. Hunter
Introduction by Rosemary
Dinnage

*Hindoo Holiday: An Indian
Journey*
J. R. ACKERLEY
Introduction by Eliot Weinberger

We Think the World of You
J. R. ACKERLEY
Introduction by P. N. Furbank

The Wooden Shepherdess
RICHARD HUGHES
Introduction by Hilary Mantel

The Stories of J. F. Powers
J. F. POWERS
Introduction by Denis Donoghue

Morte D'Urban
J. F. POWERS
Introduction by Elizabeth
Hardwick

Wheat That Springeth Green
J. F. POWERS
Introduction by Katherine A.
Powers

The Fierce and Beautiful World†
ANDREY PLATONOV
Translated from the Russian by
Joseph Barnes
Introduction by Tatyana Tolstaya

Memoirs
LORENZO DA PONTE
Translated from the Italian by
Elisabeth Abbott
Preface by Charles Rosen
Edited, annotated, and with an
introduction by Arthur Livingston

The Fox in the Attic
RICHARD HUGHES
Introduction by Hilary Mantel

Manservant and Maidservant
IVY COMPTON-BURNETT
Introduction by Diane Johnson

A House and Its Head
IVY COMPTON-BURNETT
Afterword by Francine Prose

The Haunted Looking Glass
Ghost Stories chosen and
illustrated by Edward Gorey

The Root and the Flower
L. H. MYERS
Introduction by Penelope
Fitzgerald

The Quest for Corvo:
An Experiment in Biography
A. J. A. SYMONS
Introduction by A. S. Byatt

Hadrian the Seventh
FR. ROLFE (BARON CORVO)
Introduction by Alexander
Theroux

Madame de Pompadour
NANCY MITFORD
Introduction by Amanda Foreman

The Anatomy of Melancholy
ROBERT BURTON
Edited and with an introduction
by Holbrook Jackson
With a new introduction by
William H. Gass

Letty Fox: Her Luck†
CHRISTINA STEAD
Introduction by Tim Parks

Exploits and Adventures of
Brigadier Gerard
ARTHUR CONAN DOYLE
Introduction by George
MacDonald Fraser

The Golovlyov Family
SHCHEDRIN
Translated from the Russian by
Natalie Duddington
Introduction by James Wood

The Radiance of the King
CAMARA LAYE
Translated from the French by
James Kirkup
Introduction by Toni Morrison

Eustace and Hilda: A Trilogy
L. P. HARTLEY
Introduction by Anita Brookner

Sleepless Nights
ELIZABETH HARDWICK
Introduction by Geoffrey O'Brien

Seduction and Betrayal: Women
and Literature
ELIZABETH HARDWICK
Introduction by Joan Didion

A Way of Life, Like Any Other
DARCY O'BRIEN
Introduction by Seamus Heaney

Renoir, My Father
JEAN RENOIR
Translated from the French by
Randolph and Dorothy Weaver
Introduction by Robert L. Herbert

*The Autobiography of an Unknown
Indian*
NIRAD C. CHAUDHURI
Introduction by Ian Jack

As a Man Grows Older
ITALO SVEVO
Translated from the Italian by
Beryl de Zoete
Introduction by James Lasdun

Letters: Summer 1926
BORIS PASTERNAK,
MARINA TSVETAEVA, and
RAINER MARIA RILKE
Edited by Yevgeny Pasternak,
Yelena Pasternak, and Konstantin
M. Azadovsky
Translated by Margaret Wettlin,
Walter Arndt, and Jamey
Gambrell
Preface by Susan Sontag

Mr. Fortune
SYLVIA TOWNSEND WARNER
Introduction by Adam Mars-Jones

The Selected Works of Cesare Pavese
CESARE PAVESE
Translated from the Italian and
with an introduction by R. W. Flint

An African in Greenland
TÉTÉ-MICHEL KPOMASSIE
Translated from the French by
James Kirkup
Introduction by A. Alvarez

The Life of Henry Brulard
STENDHAL
Translated from the French and
with an introduction by John
Sturrock
Preface by Lydia Davis

2002

On the Yard
MALCOLM BRALY
Introduction by Jonathan Lethem

Selected Stories†
ROBERT WALSER
Translated from the German by
Christopher Middleton and others
Foreword by Susan Sontag

*The Adventures and Misadventures
of Maqroll*
ÁLVARO MUTIS
Translated from the Spanish by
Edith Grossman
Introduction by Francisco
Goldman

Mawrdew Czgowchwz
JAMES MCCOURT
Introduction by Wayne
Koestenbaum

Shadows of Carcosa: Tales of Cosmic Horror*
H. P. LOVECRAFT AND OTHERS
Edited by D. Thin

The Book of My Life
GIROLAMO CARDANO
Translated from the Latin by Jean Stoner
Introduction by Anthony Grafton

Troubles
J. G. FARRELL
Introduction by John Banville

The Moon and the Bonfires*
CESARE PAVESE
Translated from the Italian by R. W. Flint
Introduction by Mark Rudman

Paris Stories*
MAVIS GALLANT
Selected and with an introduction by Michael Ondaatje

A Sorrow Beyond Dreams: A Life Story†
PETER HANDKE
Translated from the German by Ralph Manheim
Introduction by Jeffrey Eugenides

The Private Memoirs and Confessions of a Justified Sinner
JAMES HOGG
Introduction by Margot Livesey

In the Freud Archives
JANET MALCOLM
With an afterword by the author

The Fountain Overflows
REBECCA WEST
Introduction by Andrea Barrett

2003

Prisoner of Love
JEAN GENET
Translated from the French by Barbara Bray
Introduction by Ahdaf Soueif

We Always Treat Women Too Well
RAYMOND QUENEAU
Translated from the French by Barbara Wright
Introduction by John Updike

Witch Grass
RAYMOND QUENEAU
Translated from the French and with an introduction by Barbara Wright

The Vet's Daughter
BARBARA COMYNS
Foreword by Kathryn Davis

Walter Benjamin: The Story of a Friendship
GERSHOM SCHOLEM
Translated from the German by Harry Zohn
Introduction by Lee Siegel

Mouchette
GEORGES BERNANOS
Translated from the French by
J. C. Whitehouse
Introduction by Fanny Howe

Warlock
OAKLEY HALL
Introduction by Robert Stone

*The New York Stories of Henry James**
HENRY JAMES
Selected and with an introduction
by Colm Tóibín

*Chess Story**
STEFAN ZWEIG
Translated from the German by
Joel Rotenberg
Introduction by Peter Gay

What's for Dinner?
JAMES SCHUYLER
Afterword by James McCourt

2006

*English, August: An Indian Story**
UPAMANYU CHATTERJEE
Introduction by Akhil Sharma

Conundrum
JAN MORRIS

Life and Fate
VASILY GROSSMAN
Translated from the Russian and
with an introduction by Robert
Chandler

Roumeli: Travels in Northern Greece
PATRICK LEIGH FERMOR
Introduction by Patricia Storace

Mani: Travels in the Southern Peloponnese
PATRICK LEIGH FERMOR
Introduction by Michael Gorra

Stoner
JOHN WILLIAMS
Introduction by John McGahern

Beware of Pity
STEFAN ZWEIG
Translated from the German by
Phyllis and Trevor Blewitt
Introduction by Joan Acocella

The Big Clock
KENNETH FEARING
Introduction by Nicholas
Christopher

Red Lights†
GEORGES SIMENON
Translated from the French by
Norman Denny
Introduction by Anita Brookner

*The Jeffersonian Transformation:
Passages from the "History"**
HENRY ADAMS
Introduction by Garry Wills

Soul and Other Stories*
ANDREY PLATONOV
Translated from the Russian by
Robert and Elizabeth Chandler,
with Katia Grigoruk, Angela
Livingstone, Olga Meerson, and
Eric Naiman
Afterword by John Berger

2008

Sheppard Lee, Written by Himself
ROBERT MONTGOMERY BIRD
Introduction by Christopher
Looby

Poems of the Late T'ang
Translated from the Chinese and
with an introduction by A. C.
Graham

Unforgiving Years*
VICTOR SERGE
Translated from the French and
with an introduction by Richard
Greeman

*Twenty Thousand Streets Under
the Sky: A London Trilogy*
PATRICK HAMILTON
Introduction by Susanna Moore

Belchamber
HOWARD STURGIS
Introduction by Edmund White
Afterword by E. M. Forster

A Journey Round My Skull
FRIGYES KARINTHY
Translated from the Hungarian by
Vernon Duckworth Barker
Introduction by Oliver Sacks

The Widow†
GEORGES SIMENON
Translated from the French by
John Petrie
Introduction by Paul Theroux

The Post-Office Girl*
STEFAN ZWEIG
Translated from the German by
Joel Rotenberg

Afloat*
GUY DE MAUPASSANT
Translated from the French and
with an introduction by Douglas
Parmée

The Summer Book
TOVE JANSSON
Translated from the Swedish by
Thomas Teal
Introduction by Kathryn Davis

The Family Mashber
DER NISTER
Translated from the Yiddish by
Leonard Wolf
Introduction by David Malouf

*Names on the Land: A Historical
Account of Place-Naming in the
United States*
GEORGE R. STEWART
Introduction by Matt Weiland

The Chrysalids
JOHN WYNDHAM
Introduction by Christopher
Priest

*The Snows of Yesteryear: Portraits
for an Autobiography*
GREGOR VON REZZORI
Translated from the German by
H. F. Broch de Rothermann
Introduction by John Banville

2009

*The Rider on the White Horse and
Selected Stories*
THEODOR STORM
Translated from the German and
with a foreword by James Wright

School for Love
OLIVIA MANNING
Introduction by Jane Smiley

Chaos and Night
HENRY DE MONTHERLANT
Translated from the French by
Terence Kilmartin
Introduction by Gary Indiana

A Meaningful Life
L. J. DAVIS
Introduction by Jonathan Lethem

Short Letter, Long Farewell
PETER HANDKE
Translated from the German by
Ralph Manheim
Introduction by Greil Marcus

Slow Homecoming
PETER HANDKE
Translated from the German by
Ralph Manheim
Introduction by Benjamin Kunkel

Season of Migration to the North
TAYEB SALIH
Translated from the Arabic by
Denys Johnson-Davies
Introduction by Laila Lalami

The Foundation Pit*
ANDREY PLATONOV
Translated from the Russian by
Robert and Elizabeth Chandler,
and Olga Meerson
With notes and an afterword by
Robert Chandler and Olga
Meerson

The Complete Fiction
FRANCIS WYNDHAM
Introduction by Alan
Hollinghurst

*The One-Straw Revolution: An
Introduction to Natural Farming*
MASANOBU FUKUOKA
Translated from the Japanese by
Larry Korn, Chris Pearce, and
Tsune Kurosawa
Edited by Larry Korn
Preface by Wendell Berry
Introduction by Frances Moore
Lappé

Summer Will Show
SYLVIA TOWNSEND WARNER
Introduction by Claire Harman

The Old Man and Me
ELAINE DUNDY
With an introduction by the
author

Niki: The Story of a Dog
TIBOR DÉRY
Translated from the Hungarian by
Edward Hyams
Introduction by George Szirtes

*Stones of Aran: Labyrinth**
TIM ROBINSON
Introduction by John Elder

Hard Rain Falling
DON CARPENTER
Introduction by George Pelecanos

*The Cost of Living: Early and
Uncollected Stories**
MAVIS GALLANT
Introduction by Jhumpa Lahiri

*Memories of the Future**
SIGIZMUND
KRZHIZHANOVSKY
Translated from the Russian by
Joanne Turnbull with Nikolai
Formozov

*Poem Strip including an
Explanation of the Afterlife**
DINO BUZZATI
Translated from the Italian by
Marina Harss

*No Tomorrow and Point de
Lendemain*
VIVANT DENON
Translated from the French by
Lydia Davis
Introduction by Peter Brooks

*The Way of the World**
NICOLAS BOUVIER
Translated from the French by
Robyn Marsack
Introduction by Patrick Leigh
Fermor
Drawings by Thierry Vernet

*The Journal, 1837–1861**
HENRY DAVID THOREAU
Edited by Damion Searls
Preface by John R. Stilgoe

*Alien Hearts**
GUY DE MAUPASSANT
Translated from the French and
with a preface by Richard Howard

*Everything Flows**
VASILY GROSSMAN
Translated from the Russian by
Robert and Elizabeth Chandler
with Anna Aslanyan
Introduction by Robert Chandler

*The True Deceiver**
TOVE JANSSON
Translated from the Swedish by
Thomas Teal
Introduction by Ali Smith

Irretrievable
THEODOR FONTANE
Translated from the German and
with an introduction by Douglas
Parmée
Introduction by Phillip Lopate

A Posthumous Confession
MARCELLUS EMANTS
Translated from the Dutch and
with an introduction by J. M.
Coetzee

Fair Play
TOVE JANSSON
Translated from the Swedish by
Thomas Teal
Introduction by Ali Smith

*Ice Trilogy**
VLADIMIR SOROKIN
Translated from the Russian by
Jamey Gambrell

*Songs of Kabir**
KABIR
Translated from the Hindi and
with an introduction by Arvind
Krishna Mehrotra
Preface by Wendy Doniger

The Three Christs of Ypsilanti
MILTON ROKEACH
Introduction by Rick Moody

*Fatale**
JEAN-PATRICK MANCHETTE
Translated from the French by
Donald Nicholson-Smith
Afterword by Jean Echenoz

The Pumpkin Eater
PENELOPE MORTIMER
Introduction by Daphne Merkin

*Dancing Lessons for the Advanced
in Age*
BOHUMIL HRABAL
Translated from the Czech by
Michael Henry Heim
Introduction by Adam Thirlwell

Love's Work
GILLIAN ROSE
Introduction by Michael Wood

Reveille in Washington: 1860–1865
MARGARET LEECH
Introduction by James M.
McPherson

The Judges of the Secret Court
DAVID STACTON
Introduction by John Crowley

*When the World Spoke French**
MARC FUMAROLI
Translated from the French and
with a preface by Richard Howard

The Mangan Inheritance
BRIAN MOORE
Introduction by Christopher Ricks

*Hav**
JAN MORRIS
Introduction by Ursula K.
Le Guin

The Mirador: Dreamed Memories of Irène Némirovsky by Her Daughter*
ÉLISABETH GILLE
Translated from the French by Marina Harss
Afterword by René de Ceccatty

Dime-Store Alchemy: The Art of Joseph Cornell
CHARLES SIMIC

Masscult and Midcult: Essays Against the American Grain*
DWIGHT MACDONALD
Introduction by Louis Menand
Edited by John Summers

Act of Passion†
GEORGES SIMENON
Translated from the French by Louise Varèse
Introduction by Roger Ebert

Red Shift
ALAN GARNER
With a new introduction by the author

Alice James
JEAN STROUSE
Preface by Colm Tóibín

The Adventures of Sindbad
GYULA KRÚDY
Translated from the Hungarian and with an introduction by George Szirtes

The Letter Killers Club*
SIGIZMUND KRZHIZHANOVSKY
Translated from the Russian by Joanne Turnbull with Nikolai Formozov
Introduction by Caryl Emerson

Proud Beggars
ALBERT COSSERY
Translated from the French by Thomas W. Cushing with revisions by Alyson Waters
Introduction by Alyson Waters

2012

An Ermine in Czernopol*
GREGOR VON REZZORI
Translated from the German by Philip Boehm
Introduction by Daniel Kehlmann

Walkabout
JAMES VANCE MARSHALL
Introduction by Lee Siegel

Berlin Stories*
ROBERT WALSER
Translated from the German and with an introduction by Susan Bernofsky
Edited by Jochen Greven

A Game of Hide and Seek
ELIZABETH TAYLOR
Introduction by Caleb Crain

The Other
THOMAS TRYON
Introduction by Dan Chaon

Voltaire in Love
NANCY MITFORD
Introduction by Adam Gopnik

The Stammering Century
GILBERT SELDES
Introduction by Greil Marcus

Going to the Dogs: The Story of a Moralist
ERICH KÄSTNER
Translated from the German by Cyrus Brooks
Introduction by Rodney Livingstone

*Happy Moscow**
ANDREY PLATONOV
Translated from the Russian by Robert and Elizabeth Chandler and others

*The Gate**
NATSUME SŌSEKI
Translated from the Japanese by William F. Sibley
Introduction by Pico Iyer

*Basti**
INTIZAR HUSAIN
Translated from the Urdu by Frances W. Pritchett
Introduction by Asif Farrukhi

2013

Testing the Current
WILLIAM MCPHERSON
Afterword by D. T. Max

Diary of a Man in Despair
FRIEDRICH RECK
Translated from the German by Paul Rubens
Afterword by Richard J. Evans

*An Armenian Sketchbook**
VASILY GROSSMAN
Translated from the Russian by Robert and Elizabeth Chandler
Introduction and notes by Robert Chandler and Yury Bit-Yunan

Speedboat
RENATA ADLER
Afterword by Guy Trebay

Pitch Dark
RENATA ADLER
Afterword by Muriel Spark

The Crisis of the European Mind, 1680–1715
PAUL HAZARD
Translated from the French by J. Lewis May
Introduction by Anthony Grafton

The Green Man
KINGSLEY AMIS
Introduction by Michael Dirda

The Alteration
KINGSLEY AMIS
Introduction by William Gibson

*Transit**
ANNA SEGHERS
Translated from the German by
Margot Bettauer Dembo
Introduction by Peter Conrad
Afterword by Heinrich Böll

*We Have Only This Life to Live**
JEAN-PAUL SARTRE
Edited by Ronald Aronson and
Adrian can den Hoven
Introduction by Ronald Aronson

Turtle Diary
RUSSELL HOBAN
Introduction by Ed Park

The Unrest-Cure and Other Stories
SAKI
Illustrated by Edward Gorey

Frederick the Great
NANCY MITFORD
Introduction by Liesl Schillinger

In Love
ALFRED HAYES
Introduction by Frederic Raphael

My Face for the World to See
ALFRED HAYES
Introduction by David Thomson

*The Hall of Uselessness: Collected
Essays**
SIMON LEYS
With a foreword by the author

The Bridge of Beyond
SIMONE SCHWARZ-BART
Translated from the French by
Barbara Bray
Introduction by Jamaica Kincaid

*A Schoolboy's Diary and Other
Stories**
ROBERT WALSER
Translated from the German by
Damion Searls
Introduction by Ben Lerner

One Fat Englishman
KINGSLEY AMIS
Introduction by David Lodge

Girl, 20
KINGSLEY AMIS
Introduction by Howard Jacobson

*Proper Doctoring: A Book for
Patients and Their Doctors**
DAVID MENDEL
Introduction by Jerome
Groopman

Fighting for Life
S. JOSEPHINE BAKER
Introduction by Helen Epstein

*The Black Spider**
JEREMIAS GOTTHELF
Translated from the German by
Susan Bernofsky

*The Skin**
CURZIO MALAPARTE
Translated from the Italian by
David Moore
Introduction by Rachel Kushner

Autobiography of a Corpse*
SIGIZMUND
KRZHIZHANOVSKY
Translated from the Russian by
Joanne Turnbull
Introduction by Adam Thirlwell

2014

*The Human Comedy: Selected
Stories**
HONORÉ DE BALZAC
Edited and with an introduction
by Peter Brooks
Translated from the French by
Linda Asher, Carol Cosman, and
Jordan Stump

On Being Blue
WILLIAM H. GASS
Introduction by Michael Gorra

The Gray Notebook*
JOSEP PLA
Translated from the Catalan by
Peter Bush
Introduction by Valentí Puig

Shakespeare's Montaigne*
MICHEL DE MONTAIGNE
Edited by Stephen Greenblatt;
Translated from the French by
John Florio
Introduction by Peter G. Platt

*During the Reign of the Queen of
Persia*
JOAN CHASE
Introduction by Meghan
O'Rourke

Fear: A Novel of World War I*
GABRIEL CHEVALLIER
Translated from the French by
Malcolm Imrie
Introduction by John Berger

Last Words from Montmartre*
QIU MIAOJIN
Translated from the Chinese and
with an afterword by Ari Larissa
Heinrich

*Fortunes of War: The Levant
Trilogy*
OLIVIA MANNING
Introduction by Anthony Sattin

The Professor and the Siren*
GIUSEPPE TOMASI DI
LAMPEDUSA
Translated from the Italian by
Stephen Twilley
Introduction by Marina Warner

Agostino*
ALBERTO MORAVIA
Translated from the Italian by
Michael F. Moore

The Mad and the Bad*
JEAN-PATRICK MANCHETTE
Translated from the French by
Donald Nicholson-Smith
Introduction by James Sallis

*The Burning of the World: A
Memoir of 1914**
BELA ZOMBORY-MOLDOVAN
Translated from the Hungarian
and with an introduction by Peter
Zombory-Moldovan

Augustus
JOHN WILLIAMS
Introduction by Daniel
Mendelsohn

The Captain's Daughter*
ALEXANDER PUSHKIN
Translated from the Russian by
Robert Chandler and Elizabeth
Chandler
Introduction by Robert Chandler

Totempole
SANFORD FRIEDMAN
Afterword by Peter Cameron

Conversations with Beethoven*
SANFORD FRIEDMAN
Introduction by Richard Howard

*You'll Enjoy It When You Get
There**
ELIZABETH TAYLOR
Stories Selected and with an
Introduction by Margaret Drabble

*On the Abolition of All Political
Parties**
SIMONE WEIL
Translated from the French and
with an introduction by Simon
Leys
Essay by Czesław Miłosz

Journey by Moonlight*
ANTAL SZERB
Translated from the Hungarian by
Len Rix
Introduction by Julie Orringer

*The Woman Who Borrowed
Memories: Selected Stories**
TOVE JANSSON
Translated from the Swedish by
Thomas Teal and Silvester
Mazzarella
Introduction by Lauren Groff

*In the Heart of the Heart of the
Country*
WILLIAM H. GASS
Introduction by Joanna Scott

The Use of Man
ALEKSANDAR TIŠMA
Translated from the Serbo-
Croatian by Bernard Johnson
Introduction by Claire Messud

The Land Breakers
JOHN EHLE
Introduction by Linda Spalding

Tristana*
BENITO PÉREZ GALDÓS
Translated from the Spanish by
Margaret Jull Costa
Introduction by Jeremy Treglown

Midnight in the Century
VICTOR SERGE
Translated from the French and
with an introduction by Richard
Greeman

2015

The Broken Road: From the Iron Gates to Mount Athos*
PATRICK LEIGH FERMOR
Edited by Colin Thubron and Artemis Cooper

Thus Were Their Faces*
SILVINA OCAMPO
Translated from the Spanish by Daniel Balderston
Preface by Jorge Luis Borges
Introduction by Helen Oyeyemi

The Door*
MAGDA SZABÓ
Translated from the Hungarian by Len Rix
Introduction by Ali Smith

A Legacy
SYBILLE BEDFORD
Introduction by Brenda Wineapple

Onward and Upward in the Garden
KATHARINE S. WHITE
Edited and with an introduction by E. B. White

Prometheus Bound*
AESCHYLUS
Translated and with an introduction by Joel Agee

Ending Up
KINGSLEY AMIS
Introduction by Craig Brown

Take a Girl Like You
KINGSLEY AMIS
Introduction by Christian Lorentzen

The Death of Napoleon
SIMON LEYS
Translated from the French by Patricia Clancy

The Prince of Minor Writers: Selected Essays*
MAX BEERBOHM
Edited and with an introduction by Phillip Lopate

A View of the Harbour
ELIZABETH TAYLOR
Introduction by Roxana Robinson

Naked Earth*
EILEEN CHANG
Introduction by Perry Link

The Little Town Where Time Stood Still
BOHUMIL HRABAL
Translated by James Naughton

Talk
LINDA ROSENKRANTZ
Introduction by Stephen Koch

The Peach Blossom Fan
K'UNG SHANG-JEN
Translated by Chen Shih-hsiang and Harold Acton with the collaboration of Cyril Birch
Introduction by Judith Zeitlin

2016

Black Wings Has My Angel
ELLIOTT CHAZE
Introduction by Barry Gifford

*My Marriage**
JAKOB WASSERMANN
Translated from the German and
with an introduction by Michael
Hofmann

The Book of Blam
ALEKSANDAR TIŠMA
Translated from the Serbo-
Croatian by Michael Henry Heim
Introduction by Charles Simic

More Was Lost
ELEANOR PERÉNYI
Introduction by J. D. McClatchy

Really the Blues
MEZZ MEZZROW and
BERNARD WOLFE
Introduction by Ben Ratliff

English Renaissance Poetry
Selected by John Williams
Introduction by Robert Pinsky

*In the Café of Lost Youth**
PATRICK MODIANO
Translated from the French by
Chris Clarke

*Young Once**
PATRICK MODIANO
Translated from the French by
Damion Searls

*Hill**
JEAN GIONO
Translated from the French by
Paul Eprile
Introduction by David Abram

Houses
BORISLAV PEKIĆ
Translated from the Serbo-
Croatian by Bernard Johnson
Introduction by Barry Schwabsky

*Paris Vagabond**
JEAN-PAUL CLÉBERT
Translated from the French by
Donald Nicholson-Smith
Foreword by Luc Sante
Photographs by Patrice Molinard

*A Fairly Good Time and Green
Water, Green Sky**
MAVIS GALLANT
Introduction by Peter Orner

*Memories: From Moscow to the
Black Sea**
TEFFI
Translated from the Russian by
Robert Chandler and Elizabeth
Chandler, Irina Steinberg, and
Anne Marie Jackson
Introduction by Edythe Haber

The Glory of the Empire
JEAN D'ORMESSON
Translated from the French by
Barbara Bray
Introduction by Daniel
Mendelsohn

*Tolstoy, Rasputin, Others, and Me**
TEFFI
Edited by Robert Chandler and
Anne Marie Jackson
Translated from the Russian by
Robert Chandler, Rose France,
and Anne Marie Jackson

*Existential Monday: Philosophical
Essays**
BENJAMIN FONDANE
Edited by Bruce Baugh
Translated from the French by
Bruce Baugh and Andrew Rubens

Grand Hotel
VICKI BAUM
Translated from the German by
Basil Creighton, revised by Margot
Bettauer Dembo
Introduction by Noah Isenberg

*A Visit to Don Otavio: A Mexican
Journey*
SYBILLE BEDFORD
Introduction by Bruce Chatwin

*The Continuous Katherine
Mortenhoe*
D. G. COMPTON
Introduction by Jeff VanderMeer

*Zama**
ANTONIO DI BENEDETTO
Translated from the Spanish and
with a preface by Esther Allen

Slow Days, Fast Company
EVE BABITZ
Introduction by Matthew Specktor

*Girlfriends, Ghosts, and Other
Stories**
ROBERT WALSER
Translated from the German by
Tom Whalen, with Nicole
Köngeter and Annette Wiesner
Afterword by Tom Whalen

*His Only Son**
LEOPOLDO ALAS
Translated from the Spanish and
with an introduction by Margaret
Jull Costa

*The Invisibility Cloak**
GE FEI
Translated from the Chinese by
Canaan Morse

Back
HENRY GREEN
Introduction by Deborah
Eisenberg

Loving
HENRY GREEN
Introduction by Roxana Robinson

*Iza's Ballad**
MAGDA SZABÓ
Translated from the Hungarian
and with an introduction by
George Szirtes

*Bright Magic: Stories**
ALFRED DÖBLIN
Translated from the German by
Damion Searls
Introduction by Günter Grass

Notes on the Cinematograph
ROBERT BRESSON
Translated from the French by
Jonathan Griffin
Introduction by J. M. G. Le Clézio

*Schlump**
HANS HERBERT GRIMM
Translated from the German by
Jamie Bulloch
Afterword by Volker Weidermann

Caught
HENRY GREEN
Introduction by James Wood

*The Sound of the One Hand:
281 Zen Koans with Answers*
Edited and translated from the
Japanese by Yoel Hoffmann
Introduction by Dror Burstein

*The Return of Munchausen**
SIGIZMUND
KRZHIZHANOVKSY
Translated from the Russian by
Joanne Turnbull with Nikolai
Formozov

2017

Samskara
U. R. ANANTHAMURTHY
Translated from the Kannada by
A. K. Ramanujan

*Proensa: An Anthology of
Troubador Poetry*
Selected and translated from the
Occitan by Paul Blackburn
Edited and with an introduction
by George Economou

Primitive Man as Philosopher
PAUL RADIN
Preface by Neni Panourgia
Foreword by John Dewey

*Like Death**
GUY DE MAUPASSANT
Translated from the French by
Richard Howard

*Ernesto**
UMBERTO SABA
Translated from the Italian
and with an introduction by
Estelle Gilson

Blindness
HENRY GREEN
Introduction by Daniel
Mendelsohn

Living
HENRY GREEN
Introduction by Adam Thirlwell

Party Going
HENRY GREEN
Introduction by Amit Chaudhuri

Making It
NORMAN PODHORETZ
Introduction by Terry Teachout

*The Word of the Speechless**
JULIO RAMÓN RIBEYRO
Edited and translated from the
Spanish by Katherine Silver
Introduction by Alejandro Zambra

*Nada**
JEAN-PATRICK MANCHETTE
Translated from the French by
Donald Nicholson-Smith
Introduction by Luc Sante

*Free Day**
INÈS CAGNATI
Translated from the French and
with an introduction by Liesl
Schillinger

APPENDIX

From "A Symposium on Editing," The Threepenny
Review, *Spring 2008**

OF THE things editors do, picking books and polishing (or should
that be nitpicking?) books, I mostly pick. The series of books that
I've overseen since its beginning some ten years ago is a mixture of
books that have fallen out of print and shouldn't have and translations
of books that have never made their way into English at all. Translations, it's true, can call for polishing, sometimes a lot of it, but for all
the theoretical problematizing of translation and promoting of pur-
portedly new and improved translations that has gone on of late,
translation is an essentially self-abnegating activity and the problem—anything but easy to resolve!—is to make the translation *good
enough.* The translator discovers what might be called a level at which
to deal with the original, and the editor helps the translator to main-
tain that level successfully. Great literature, Hegel somewhere said,
translates—which is why the strange efforts of some contemporary
translators effectively to *untranslate*, or exoticize, the text strike me
as misguided. They suggest how far we have come, in our provincial
global moment, from the nineteenth- and early twentieth-century
freedom of the empowered imagination, in which the Russian novels,
and later Eliot and Proust and Joyce, could travel swiftly across all
sorts of linguistic borders to enter, and actively constitute, a common
world.

But as I was saying, what I mostly do as an editor is worry about
what book to publish next, and here my job is rather unusual, in that
the books I have to pick from are almost always (translations again

*Here slightly revised.

aside) written and the writers I have to deal with dead. What I'm looking for, however, is not so much canonical books, classics in the classic sense, as books that may be little known but remain unexpectedly current, able to instruct and delight or, to put it less classically, puzzle and surprise. "Interesting" may be the ultimate brush-off, but these are books that I hope will be—precisely, entertainingly, seriously—interesting. They may be canonical texts from literary locations left, for one reason or another, mostly unexplored by American readers, for example the Soviet Union or modern Italy; they may be the great book that a great writer is not known for; they may be the work of writers eccentric to the major trends of their period, or works in genres whose fortunes have fallen (the historical novel) or never risen high (the adventure novel); they may be what I call accidents: an oddly right and beautiful book that comes out of nowhere by an author who may well have gone nowhere, never writing anything as good or even anything else at all. Those, I suppose, are my favorites, because so close to the uncertain sources (and ends) of all art, good and bad.

I am concerned too, in taking on a book, that it contribute to some ongoing and, I admit, elusive sense of the *seriesness* of the series; that the book build on or break away from what we have already done; that the series should function in some small way as a model of inquiry into ways of writing and imagining and knowing.

All of which is to say what is of course true of any editor: that the decision to publish is intuitive, whether arrived at impulsively or after deliberation or simple stalling. Thinking about the whole business the other day I was reminded a little of how I used to feel when I was a halfway decent chess player: attack here, develop, defend there. Push this piece. Protect that one. It is an absorbing game.

Also a melancholy one. Who is the opponent in this game? The present, which one hopes somehow to shake out of the muddled excitement and torpor of its self-preoccupation, so making it take note of what else there has been and might be. But then the present is not only the opponent but—necessarily, it would seem—the audience. This is a series of books from the past published for the present's sake, a present that in our own case has lost a sense of the past as having authority by virtue, among others, of its very pastness; a present, in other words, for which the past is of interest primarily as a novelty. So the game is played on the present's ground. And yet all the time I feel the claim of the past to be accepted precisely for what it was, the claim of lineage, and that this more than anything is the claim that needs to be impressed on our present, if only because it will, after all, soon itself be past. One knows the readers of one book, poring over their Talmuds and Korans and Bibles in the subway, uniquely devoted as great scholars also are (A. E. Housman with his Manilius), readers for whom the reader, rather than the book, exists as the afterthought. I envy them. My own work will take me to libraries where I wander along the shelves of unknown names, of authors, of books, and to pull one at random is to discover, more often than not, that it is not bad—to the contrary, more often than not it is not at all bad—but still it is done with. Could one publish for the sake of the dead? The dead, mercifully, appear to be uninterested in publishing. Still there is something bitter in the thought that literature as we now know it is condemned only to be alive.

—EDWIN FRANK

BIOGRAPHICAL NOTES

EVE BABITZ (b. 1943) is the author of several books including *Slow Days, Fast Company, Sex and Rage*, and a volume of previously uncollected journalism, *I Used To Be Charming*. She has written for publications including *Ms.* and *Esquire* and in the late 1960s designed album covers for the Byrds, Buffalo Springfield, and Linda Ronstadt.

HONORÉ DE BALZAC (1799–1850) was born in Tours, France. In his many novels and stories, collectively entitled *La Comédie humaine*, Balzac set out to offer a complete picture of the society and manners of his time.

ANTONIO DI BENEDETTO (1922–1986) was born in Mendoza, Argentina. He began his career as a journalist, writing for the Mendoza paper *Los Andes*. In 1953 he published his first book, a collection of short stories titled *Mundo animal*. His novels *Zama*, *El silenciero*, and *Los suicidas* were dubbed the "trilogy of waiting" by his fellow novelist Juan José Saer. In 1976, di Benedetto was imprisoned and tortured by Argentina's military dictatorship; after his release in 1977 he went into exile in Spain, returning to Buenos Aires shortly before his death.

RACHEL BESPALOFF (1895–1949) was raised in Geneva. She intended to pursue a musical career, but after an encounter with the thinker Lev Shestov, devoted herself to philosophy. In 1942, she left France for the United States, where she worked as a scriptwriter for the French Section of the Office of War Information before teaching French literature at Mount Holyoke.

DAVID R. BUNCH (1920–2000) was born in rural western Missouri and served as an army corporal during World War II. While working as a cartographer for the Defense Mapping Agency in St. Louis, he began publishing stories in science-fiction magazines and in 1971 he published *Moderan*, a collection of stories set on a future earth devastated by war and environmental exploitation. A poetry chapbook, *We Have a Nervous Job*, followed in 1983, and *Bunch!* (1993), a later book of short stories, was nominated for the Philip K. Dick Award.

FRANÇOIS-RENÉ DE CHATEAUBRIAND (1768–1848) was born in Saint-Malo, on the northern coast of Brittany, the youngest son of an aristocratic family. After an isolated adolescence, spent largely in his father's castle, he moved to Paris not long before the Revolution. In 1791, he sailed for America but quickly returned to Europe, where he enrolled in the counterrevolutionary army, was wounded, and emigrated to England. The novellas *Atala* and *René*, published shortly after his return to France in 1800, made him a literary celebrity. One of the first French Romantics, Chateaubriand was also a historian, a diplomat, and a staunch defender of the freedom of the press.

ALFRED DÖBLIN (1878–1957) was born in German Stettin (now the Polish city of Szczecin) to Jewish parents. He studied medicine at Friedrich Wilhelm University in Berlin, specializing in neurology and psychiatry. His novel *The Three Leaps of Wang Lun* was published in 1915 while he was serving as a military doctor. Döblin's best-known novel, *Berlin Alexanderplatz*, was published in 1929. He went into exile after Hitler's rise and was in Los Angeles during World War II, after which he returned to his native Germany.

EURIPIDES (c.480–c.406 BC) competed in twenty-two of the annual Athenian dramatic competitions and won the first prize five times; today eighteen of the ninety-some plays he is believed to have written survive. Little is known of the life of the writer whom Aristotle called "the most tragic of tragedians."

EDWIN FRANK was born in Boulder, Colorado, and educated at Harvard College and Columbia University. He is the author of *Snake Train: Poems 1984–2013*.

MAVIS GALLANT (1922–2014) was born in Montreal and worked as a journalist at the *Montreal Standard* before moving to Europe to devote herself to writing fiction. In 1950, she settled in Paris, where she would remain for the rest of her life. Over the course of her career Gallant published more than one hundred stories and dispatches in *The New Yorker*.

VASILY SEMYONOVICH GROSSMAN (1905–1964) was born in Berdichev, Ukraine. After making a name for himself as an up-and-coming writer, he worked throughout World War II as a reporter for the army newspaper *Red Star*. In 1952, Grossman published *For a Just Cause*, the first volume of a diptych about the battle of Stalingrad (his preferred title for the book was simply *Stalingrad*) that concludes with *Life and Fate*, completed by the end of the decade. The manuscript of *Life and Fate* was considered unpublishable by Soviet authorities and confiscated by the KGB. Grossman's final novel, also unpublished, was *Everything Flows*.

ELIZABETH HARDWICK (1916–2007) was born in Lexington, Kentucky, and educated at the University of Kentucky and Columbia University. She was the author of three novels, a biography of Herman Melville, and four collections of essays, as well as a co-founder of *The New York Review of Books*.

TOVE JANSSON (1914–2001) was born in Helsinki into Finland's Swedish-speaking minority. After attending art schools in Stockholm and Paris, she returned to Helsinki and won acclaim for her paintings and murals. From 1929 until 1953, Jansson drew humorous illustrations and political cartoons for the anti-Fascist Finnish-Swedish magazine *Garm*, where her most famous creation, Moomintroll, a hippopotamus-like character with a dreamy disposition, made his first appearance. Jansson went on to write about the adventures of Moomintroll in a long-running comic strip and in a series of books for children that have been translated throughout the world. She also wrote eleven novels and short-story collections for adults. In 1994 she was awarded the Prize of the Swedish Academy.

KABIR (c. 1440–1518), the North Indian devotional, or *bhakti*, poet, was born in Benares (now Varanasi). Next to nothing is known of his life, though many legends surround him. He is said to have been a weaver, and in his resolutely undogmatic and often riddling work he debunks both Hinduism and Islam. The songs of this extraordinary poet, philosopher, and satirist have been sung and recited by millions throughout North India for half a millennium.

GYULA KRÚDY (1878–1933) was born in Nyíregyháza in northeastern Hungary. He began writing short stories and publishing brief newspaper pieces while still in his teens, and worked as a newspaper editor for several years before moving to Budapest, where he found success as a novelist with *Sindbad's Youth*. Forgotten in the years after his death, Krúdy was rediscovered in 1940, when Sándor Márai published *Sindbad Comes Home*, a fictionalized account of Krúdy's last day.

SIGIZMUND KRZHIZHANOVSKY (1887–1950) studied law and classical philology at Kiev University and, after becoming well-known in literary circles, moved to Moscow in 1922. Lodged in a cell-like room on the Arbat, Krzhizhanovsky wrote steadily for close to two decades, paying no heed to the political demands of the Soviet state. Unpublished during his lifetime, his books only began to come out after the fall of the Soviet Union.

PATRICK LEIGH FERMOR (1915–2011) was born in London, the son of a zoologist. Expelled from school, he decided to become a writer and, in 1933, set off to walk from the Hook of Holland to Constantinople, a journey he described in *A Time of Gifts* (1977), *Between the Woods and the Water* (1986), and *The Broken Road* (published posthumously in 2013). In the Second World War, he joined the Irish Guards, served as a liaison officer in Albania, and fought in Greece and Crete. He was awarded the DSO and OBE. Leigh Fermor lived partly in Greece and partly in Worcestershire for much of his life. In 2004 he was knighted for his services to literature and to British–Greek relations.

SIMON LEYS (1935–2014) was the pen name of Pierre Ryckmans, who was born in Belgium and settled in Australia in 1970. He taught Chinese literature at the Australian National University and was a professor of Chinese Studies at the University of Sydney from 1987 to 1993. *The Chairman's New Clothes* (1971) was among the first books to expose the abuses of the Chinese Cultural Revolution of the 1960s.

JESSICA MITFORD (1917–1996), the daughter of Lord and Lady Redesdale, grew up with five sisters and one brother on an isolated Cotswold estate. Rebelling against her family's hidebound conservatism, Mitford became an outspoken socialist and, with her second cousin and husband-to-be Esmond Romilly, ran away to fight against Franco in the Spanish Civil War. Romilly was killed in World War II, and Mitford moved to California, where she married the lawyer and political activist Robert Treuhaft and made a career as a brilliant muckraking journalist.

KENJI MIYAZAWA (1896–1933) was born in Iwate, one of the northernmost prefectures in Japan. In high school, he studied Zen Buddhism and developed a lifelong devotion to the Lotus Sutra. After graduating from an agricultural college, he moved to Tokyo to begin his writing career but had to return home to Iwate to care for a sick sister. He remained there for the rest of his life.

ANDREY PLATONOVICH PLATONOV (1899–1951) was born in central Russia, the son of a railway worker and the eldest of eleven children. He studied engineering and began publishing poems and articles in 1918. Between 1927 and 1946 he wrote dozens of short stories, plays, and novels, many of which remained unpublished during his lifetime.

QIU MIAOJIN (1969–1995) was born in Chuanghua County in western Taiwan. She graduated with a degree in psychology from National Taiwan University and studied clinical psychology at the University of Paris VIII. While in Paris, she directed a thirty-minute film called *Ghost Carnival*, and not long after, at the age of twenty-six, she committed suicide. Her two novels, *Last Words from Montmartre* and *Notes of a Crocodile*, were published posthumously.

GILLIAN ROSE (1947–1995) was a British philosopher and writer. For many years she taught at Sussex University, before accepting a chair in social and political thought at Warwick University. Along with *Love's Work*, her major works include *The Melancholy Science*, *Hegel Contra Sociology*, *Dialectic of Nihilism*, *The Broken Middle*, *Judaism and Modernity*, *Mourning Becomes the Law*, and *Paradiso*.

LEONARDO SCIASCIA (1921–1989) was born in Racalmuto, Sicily. Starting in the 1950s, he established himself in Italy as a novelist and essayist, and also as a controversial commentator on political affairs.

VICTOR SERGE (1890–1947) was born Victor Lvovich Kibalchich to Russian anti-czarist exiles in Brussels. A precocious anarchist firebrand, young Victor was sentenced to five years in a French penitentiary in 1912. Expelled to Spain in 1917, he set out for St. Petersburg early in 1919 and joined the Bolsheviks. An outspoken critic of Stalin, Serge was expelled from the Party and briefly arrested in 1928. Deported to Central Asia in 1933, Serge was allowed to leave the USSR in 1936 after international protests by militants and prominent writers. He lived in precarious exile in Brussels, Paris, Vichy France, and Mexico City, where he died in 1947.

HENRY DAVID THOREAU (1817–1862) was born and lived the greater part of his life in Concord, Massachusetts. He studied at Harvard, where he became a disciple of Ralph Waldo Emerson, for whom he later worked as a handyman. On July 4, 1845, he moved into a hut he had constructed on Walden Pond, where he remained until September 6, 1847—a sojourn that inspired his great work *Walden*, published in 1854. In his later life, Thoreau was active in the abolitionist cause.

CREDITS

TITLES IN SERIES

A list of the titles in the series is also available at www.nyrb.com or write to us at:
Catalog Requests, NYRB, 435 Hudson Street, New York, NY 10014

LIONEL TRILLING The Middle of the Journey
THOMAS TRYON The Other
MARINA TSVETAEVA Earthly Signs: Moscow Diaries, 1917–1922
KURT TUCHOLSKY Castle Gripsholm
IVAN TURGENEV Virgin Soil
JULES VALLÈS The Child
RAMÓN DEL VALLE-INCLÁN Tyrant Banderas
MARK VAN DOREN Shakespeare
CARL VAN VECHTEN The Tiger in the House
SALKA VIERTEL The Kindness of Strangers
ELIZABETH VON ARNIM The Enchanted April
EDWARD LEWIS WALLANT The Tenants of Moonbloom
ROBERT WALSER Berlin Stories
ROBERT WALSER Girlfriends, Ghosts, and Other Stories
ROBERT WALSER Jakob von Gunten
ROBERT WALSER A Schoolboy's Diary and Other Stories
MICHAEL WALZER Political Action: A Practical Guide to Movement Politics
REX WARNER Men and Gods
SYLVIA TOWNSEND WARNER The Corner That Held Them
SYLVIA TOWNSEND WARNER Lolly Willowes
SYLVIA TOWNSEND WARNER Mr. Fortune
SYLVIA TOWNSEND WARNER Summer Will Show
JAKOB WASSERMANN My Marriage
ALEKSANDER WAT My Century
LYALL WATSON Heaven's Breath: A Natural History of the Wind
C.V. WEDGWOOD The Thirty Years War
SIMONE WEIL On the Abolition of All Political Parties
SIMONE WEIL AND RACHEL BESPALOFF War and the Iliad
HELEN WEINZWEIG Basic Black with Pearls
GLENWAY WESCOTT Apartment in Athens
GLENWAY WESCOTT The Pilgrim Hawk
REBECCA WEST The Fountain Overflows
EDITH WHARTON The New York Stories of Edith Wharton
KATHARINE S. WHITE Onward and Upward in the Garden
PATRICK WHITE Riders in the Chariot
T. H. WHITE The Goshawk
JOHN WILLIAMS Augustus
JOHN WILLIAMS Butcher's Crossing
JOHN WILLIAMS (EDITOR) English Renaissance Poetry: A Collection of Shorter Poems
JOHN WILLIAMS Nothing but the Night
JOHN WILLIAMS Stoner
ANGUS WILSON Anglo-Saxon Attitudes
EDMUND WILSON Memoirs of Hecate County
RUDOLF AND MARGARET WITTKOWER Born Under Saturn
GEOFFREY WOLFF Black Sun
FRANCIS WYNDHAM The Complete Fiction
JOHN WYNDHAM Chocky
JOHN WYNDHAM The Chrysalids
BÉLA ZOMBORY-MOLDOVÁN The Burning of the World: A Memoir of 1914
STEFAN ZWEIG Beware of Pity
STEFAN ZWEIG Chess Story
STEFAN ZWEIG Confusion
STEFAN ZWEIG Journey Into the Past
STEFAN ZWEIG The Post-Office Girl